SWEET DEPRAVITY

A DARK MAFIA ROMANCE

RUTHLESS OBSESSION SERIES
BOOK TWO

ZOE BLAKE

Published by Stormy Night Publications and Design, LLC.
Blake, Zoe
Sweet Cruelty

Cover Design by Dark City Designs
Photographer Wander Aguiar
Model Jonny James

This book is intended for *adults only*. Spanking and other sexual activities represented in this book are fantasies only, intended for adults.

CONTENTS

CHAPTER 1

MARY

I had every intention of murdering whoever was on the other side of that door.

Coldblooded, heartless murder.

I would get away with it too.

Anyone who pounded on someone's door at seven o'clock in the morning deserved to get murdered in the worst way possible.

After flicking open the pathetic excuse for a lock, I snatched at the brass chain secured across the door, further loosening the already wobbly screws.

Putting the chain across each night really was a useless endeavor.

Basically only good for a false sense of security.

An asthmatic eighty-year-old man could cough on this ancient door and it would fall open.

Such was the life of a penniless graduate student

living in a first-floor apartment in a slightly dodgy neighborhood.

With a huff, I threw the door open. "Who the hell do you think you—?"

My mouth fell open.

In a rather ironic twist, there wasn't a doubt in my mind.

The man standing on my threshold had come to murder *me* instead of the other way around.

There really was no other reasonable conclusion.

The fact that I had done nothing, at least to my knowledge, to warrant someone wanting to murder me was immaterial.

I couldn't imagine this man being anything other than a murderer or at the very least a violent criminal.

This was all incredibly confusing considering he was also the most devastatingly handsome man I'd ever laid eyes on.

He was insanely tall.

I mean, really?

Was it absolutely necessary to be that much over six feet tall?

All those extra inches did was make a girl feel small and vulnerable, and make her wonder what it would feel like if he crowded her against a wall and did that super sexy lean in move.

The darkly inked tattoos on his hands and neck

were in stark contrast to the obviously expensive tailored suit he was wearing.

His jet-black hair was wet and slicked back as if he had just showered. I could pick up the hints of musk and jasmine from his aftershave.

Scariest of all were his eyes; they were dark blue and hooded, almost like the demon eyes from *Buffy the Vampire Slayer*.

His head was slightly down as he stared at me, giving him an even more sinister appearance.

My hands shook as I tightened the belt on my leopard print silk robe with the pink trim.

Those same demon eyes flashed down to my waist, then slowly rose to my chest, then back to my face to pierce me with a glare.

Thankfully, I'd been so tired last night I fell asleep in my bra and panties instead of naked as I usually did. It wasn't much but at least they were some protection beyond just my flimsy robe.

He twisted his jaw as he gestured to me with his left hand, which seemed weighed down by a heavy silver signet ring. "Is this how you answer the door? Dressed like a woman begging to be fucked?"

It took a moment for my mind to register what he said because of the heavy Russian accent.

My eyes widened the moment it did.

With an outraged cry, I tried to slam the door in his face.

His flattened palm prevented it.

I had no choice but to take a step back as he entered the apartment and closed the door.

He reached behind him and twisted the lock just above the doorknob. It slid into place with an ominous click.

The air seized in my lungs.

Since they'd painted half the windows shut and the other half were rusted shut, there really was no other way out of the apartment.

I could scream but I doubted even my next-door neighbor, old Mrs. York, would hear me. The only good thing about the dilapidated brick building my apartment was in was its crazy-thick walls. Well, usually it was a good thing for when you wanted to play your music loud or have a party.

When you were being threatened by a possible homicidal criminal, not so much.

My phone!

My phone was in my purse on the sofa.

Keeping my gaze trained on him, I took a few steps back.

The sofa was in my peripheral vision. I needed to get to the other end to my Loungefly-embossed skulls and Hello Kitty black and pink purse.

The man surveyed my apartment with a mixture of disgust and shock on his face. As he turned his attention to the locks on the door behind him, I made my move.

I lunged over the back of the sofa and stretched

out my arms to grab my purse. My hand slipped inside and grasped the rounded edge of my cellphone.

Dragging it out of my purse, I swiped the screen with my finger and moved to tap the emergency button on the lower left-hand corner when a pair of warm hands wrapped around my hips.

His legs pressed against the backs of mine, making me painfully aware of the short length of my robe.

With me bent over like this, it barely covered my ass.

His entire body leaned over mine as his right hand slid up my outstretched arm and pulled at the phone in my grasp.

I clung to it tightly, as if it were my only lifeline.

His other hand tightened on my hip, an unmistakable warning.

His breath teased the skin on my neck as he breathed near my ear, "You won't be needing this."

With his accent, the *you* sounded like a low purr, and the *won't* sounded more like the scary villain *von't*. Instead of putting the inflection at the end of the sentence, he put it in the middle, which strangely emphasized the force of his command.

He pulled the phone free and tossed it out of my reach.

Not willing to give up so easily, I started screaming, "Hey, Siri! Call the police!"

'Don't Stand So Close to Me' by The Police played.

Oh, great. Hey, Siri, please play my *Perfect Songs to Get Murdered To* playlist.

Shifting my hips, I placed my weight on my left foot and tried to break free of his grasp. I was spun around and pulled flush against his body by a powerful arm wrapped around my waist.

My head tilted back to stare up at his uncompromising face.

Caught between him and the back of the sofa, my hips ground against his.

Something hard and long, really long, pressed against my abdomen.

Oh. My. God.

The handsome criminal quirked an eyebrow, the right corner of his upper lip rising with a satisfied smirk.

He had the audacity to not show the least bit of chagrin. Meanwhile, my cheeks flamed scarlet.

Grasping at the open neckline of my robe, I scrunched the fabric near my collarbone in my fist as I lowered my head to avoid his arrogant scrutiny.

Raising my chin with a finger, he asked, "Is this the apartment of Emma Doyle?"

Once again, his Russian accent was so thick, I had to focus on the words as he rolled his R's and made my roommate and best friend's name sound more like Eeema than Emma.

It finally clicked.

He was a big fucking scary Russian dude and my roommate was dating a big fucking scary Russian dude.

This could be bad.

Either this man was a friend of Dimitri's—or an enemy.

Until I knew which, I couldn't possibly endanger my best friend.

Twisting my head to break his grasp on my chin, I dug my fingernails into my palms to keep myself from shaking.

Inhaling a hesitant breath, I said, "I don't know who that is."

The tip of his finger traced over my cheekbone, down the side of my face and under my jaw to stop at the base of my throat. "Your beautiful throat flutters, right here, when you lie."

I licked my lips and watched as his dark gaze zeroed in on my mouth. "I'm … I'm not lying. I've never heard of anyone named Emma Doyle."

His hand moved quickly to grasp me around the throat just under my jaw.

Dropping my grip on my robe, I wrapped my fingers around his wrists and tried to claw at him, but my short red nails did nothing to force him to relent.

He leaned in low, the scent of coffee and peppermint on his breath. "Tsk. Tsk. Tsk. Don't you know it is dangerous to lie to a man like me … Mary?"

My body jerked as if someone had slapped me.

He knew my name.

I swallowed. "What do you want?" I rasped.

He shifted back slightly and looked down. With his free hand, he slipped two fingers inside the neckline of my robe and pulled it open.

I whimpered, but his grip on my throat held me in place.

His hooded gaze flicked up to mine. *"Shhh, krasotka. Ne dvigaysya. Ya prosto khochu prikosnut'sya."*

I had absolutely no idea what he was saying, but it sounded both scary and sexy as hell, which was so beyond twisted and wrong that it would take half a bottle of tequila for me to even start analyzing what I was thinking right now.

There was just something about his heavy Russian accent. It was so deep and low, a somber purr that was hypnotic.

His fingertip traced the red ribbon that ran in and out of the lace outline of my black bra. "It was wrong for you to open the door dressed like this, *krasotka*. There are many dangerous men out there who would take advantage of a beautiful woman such as yourself … who's all alone."

"Dangerous men, like you?"

He rubbed the pad of his thumb over my lower lip. "Exactly like me."

I rose on my toes to try to loosen his grip. "I'm not alone. My boyfriend will be back any second now."

He smiled—and it was terrifying.

"I hope for his sake you are lying to me again. I hadn't planned on killing anyone today, but if a man were to walk through that door and try to claim you as his own, I would shoot him between the eyes."

Claim me? What was I, a piece of luggage on an airport baggage carousel?

Who talks like that?

Had he really just said he hadn't planned on killing anyone—*today*?

Meaning on other days that option was up for grabs?

He released his grip and took a step back.

He flicked open the button on his suit jacket and opened the flaps to reveal a shoulder holster with a gun in it.

Wrapping his fingers around its handle, he pulled the weapon free. It was gold-plated and massive, like something out of an action movie.

He leveled the gun at the door and pulled back the hammer. "So which is it, *krasotka*? Are you lying or do I shoot the next person who walks through that door?"

My shocked gaze raced between the gun, his thin-lipped, determined expression, and the closed door.

This couldn't be happening.

Of course there was no boyfriend.

There hadn't been a boyfriend in ages, but there was my best friend, and she could return home at any moment.

Raising my arms, I waved my palms. "Stop! Stop! There is no boyfriend. Please put the gun down."

He un-cocked the hammer and set the weapon down on the side table.

Curling his hands into fists, he leaned in and rested them on the top of the sofa on either side of my hips, caging me in with his body. "So you were lying to me … again."

What the hell was I supposed to say? My mind went blank. "I … I …"

He shifted and pressed his lower body against mine.

I stilled at the threatening press of his hard shaft, afraid to even breathe.

Everything about this man screamed *danger, run away,* from his demeanor to his intimidating height, from his arm and chest muscles to his tattoos.

He wasn't tall with lean muscle like someone who worked out at the gym or played sports. He had that bulky, brute strength kind of build. The kind that said gyms were for posers; I'd rather just get into bar fights and flip cars to keep in shape.

With his dark looks and arrogant smile, he also screamed bad boy trouble.

Which is of course why my nipples were hard and

pressing against the scratchy cheap lace of my bra, and my thighs were clenched.

My brain was shrieking *homicidal criminal psychopath, run*!

While my body was ready to lie back and scream *take me now, make it hurt*!

With a single finger he started to circle one erect nipple through the silk of my robe.

His voice was deceptively soft and low. "What kind of punishment do you think you deserve for lying to me?"

My cheeks flamed as he continued to caress the curve of my breast.

Humiliated he had even noticed my involuntary response to him, I swallowed past the dry fear in my throat. "I know what you are trying to do and you don't scare me. I'm not telling you anything."

He ran the back of his knuckles over my stomach. "Your bravado is admirable but unnecessary. Dimitri Kosgov sent me. We are business partners. He is concerned about the lack of security in your apartment. He wants to make sure you and Emma are safe."

There was absolutely no reason why I should, but I believed him.

It sounded like precisely the type of thing Emma's new overbearing and overprotective boyfriend would do.

Slipping that single finger into the knot at my waist, he tugged, loosening the belt.

As my robe fell open completely, exposing my bra and bare midriff, he continued, "And trust me, *krasotka, scaring you* is the last thing I want to do to you right now."

My knees buckled.

I reached back to grasp the sofa behind me to stay upright.

I had to force myself to breathe, feeling every shaky breath that entered and left my lungs as I tried to focus on his intense gaze. "Who are you?"

"My name is Vasili Lukovich Rostov, but you may call me Vaska."

"Why are you doing this?" I was no longer referring to why he was in my apartment asking about Emma.

He shrugged. "Because I can. In my world, nothing is off limits. If I see something I want," he paused and ran his heated gaze over me, "I take it."

I blinked. I wasn't expecting such raw honesty. "In my world, a man asks permission first."

He chuckled and responded in his heavy Russian accent, "Then I guess it is a good thing we are not in your world."

"We are in my apartment," I boldly fired back with more moxie than I felt.

"True, but it is still my world, and in my world, I make the rules and decide the punishments for those who break them." His fingertip traced the top of my panties.

This had gone way, *way* too far.

There was allowing myself to get lost in a dangerous bad boy fantasy for a moment and then there was the reality of a dangerous man with a gun standing in the middle of my living room threatening to punish me.

My shrieking brain finally won out.

I ducked under his arm and desperately ran across the living room.

Crossing the threshold to my bedroom, I turned and slammed the door shut, locking it.

I backed away and frantically scanned the room looking for something to prop against the door.

The room was too small for anything more than a double bed and a rickety vanity with two loose table legs.

I could hear his measured footsteps on the other side of the door.

I backed away as I tightened the dangling robe belt around my waist and braced for his angry shouts or pounding fist.

Vaska did neither.

Without warning, he kicked the door open and stalked into my bedroom.

CHAPTER 2

VASKA

"If we are going to be friends, you really should try not to anger me, *krasotka*."

My God, she really was a *beautiful girl*. Absolutely stunning.

When my good friend and business partner, Dimitri, asked me as a favor to swing by his new girl's apartment to supervise our crew installing a security system, I hadn't looked forward to the task.

From Dimitri's description, I assumed his Emma was a sweet little thing who didn't favor makeup, jewels, or all the other things that made a woman desirable.

In other words, she may be his type, but she was far from mine.

So naturally I assumed her roommate, Mary, would be the same.

That she'd probably be a nondescript graduate

student who wore jeans and one of those dreadful hoodies that hid a woman's body from a man's view.

I was not expecting … her.

When the door had flown open, a pair of gorgeous indigo blue eyes struck me.

Almond-shaped and perhaps a little too big for her delicate features, thick black lashes framed them and they flashed with anger.

Her hair brought the slight hints of purple in her irises out. It reminded me of a raven's wing. Sleek and so inky black, I could see flashes of cobalt and amethyst in the sheen. It fell past her shoulders to curl on the ends and made me want to wrap the glossy lengths in my fist and pull her to me so I could kiss those full lips.

They were stained a bitable cherry red from the remnants of her lipstick, which created a slightly smudged outline around her lower lip that only made me want to kiss her more.

All of these flashes of color were highlighted by her porcelain skin. I wanted to lick her neck to see if she tasted like sweet cream.

Then my gaze moved lower, and I barely contained a possessive growl.

This woman was built for a man's hands—my hands.

She barely reached my shoulder, but damn if she wasn't all tucked-in waist and dangerous curves.

Her breasts practically spilled out of the skimpy

leopard print robe she was wearing. The neckline gave the tiniest glimpse of a red ribbon and black lace bra. From the tight pink belt around her waist, I could make out the generous swell of her hips.

Damn if I didn't love a woman with a pair of sexy hips.

Overly skinny women held no appeal for me.

I wanted a woman who could fill my hands.

Then she'd had the moxie to try to slam the door in my face, and that sealed the deal.

As my cock hardened, I realized I needed to fuck her like I needed my next breath.

There was no way I was letting a morsel this delectable fall into my lap and just walk away.

Now she stood defiantly staring me down with those amazing eyes, her back literally against the wall.

Her chin rose as she gripped the belt of her robe. "I have no intention of being *friends* with you. Now get out!"

She had spirit.

Good. I loved a woman with fight in her.

They were a rare gem.

And this was one diamond I had every intention of making mine.

I hadn't amassed the wealth I had without knowing when to snatch up treasure when I found it.

With a chuckle, I shrugged out of my suit jacket and slung it over the padded red and black stool positioned in front of a vanity painted the same shade of black with red roses.

Her eyes shifted from my jacket to the open door behind me.

Escape was not an option.

The only way she was leaving this room was with a sore pussy after I fucked her raw.

I loosened the knot of my tie and pulled it free from the collar, tossing it on the bed in case I wanted to tie her up.

If I used it to bind her wrists it would ruin the silk of the expensive Armani tie, of course, but it would be worth it.

I unlatched a cufflink. "No."

"I'll scream."

I smiled as I tossed the cufflink onto her vanity and reached for the other one. "Please do. I'd be offended if the woman I was fucking didn't scream."

Her beautiful mouth fell open.

Fuck, I couldn't wait to have her on her knees with those same red lips stretched wide around my cock.

Her beautiful gaze pleading with me to let her breathe as I shoved every inch deeper and deeper down her throat.

She crossed her arms over her chest. "You're insane if you think I'm having sex with you."

While it was supposed to be a gesture of defiance, all it did was push her glorious breasts up and closer together. I couldn't wait to sweep my tongue between them and taste her skin.

I rolled up one sleeve as I kicked off my shoes. "Who said anything about sex?"

She blinked as her head tilted to the side.

Her heavy curtain of hair fell over her shoulder, exposing one cute little ear.

I'd buy her diamond earrings first, I decided as I rolled up the other sleeve. I wanted to see the rainbow flash, from when the light caught the stones, reflected in her hair and eyes.

I stepped further into the room.

She bent to the left and picked up a crystal vase filled with the stems of six dead red roses.

Not even a full dozen, I scoffed.

An unreasonable, sharp stab of jealousy hit my gut.

A woman usually only received red roses from a man. She had said earlier there was no boyfriend, but there was no reason to believe her. I had been holding a cocked gun at the time. Although I knew that if there was a boyfriend, they were done as of this moment.

The man obviously did not know how to take care of a woman, judging by this tiny apartment with its disgraceful lack of security.

If he were a real man, he'd see his woman in a proper condo in a high-rise with proper security and a doorman.

He would also see that she always had fresh flowers to perfume the air and make her smile, not make her hold on to a handful of dead petals.

And as much as I admired her black lace bra from the glimpses I had gotten of it, it was apparent to me it was not high quality. When I'd touched it, the lace felt stiff and scratchy.

A woman like her should have only the finest silk lingerie against her skin.

As her new man, I would make sure of all of it.

It was extraordinary.

I hadn't even fucked her yet, and already I wanted to set her up as mine.

I had never experienced that with a woman before.

Hell, I'd never wanted to buy one a condo and jewels before either.

There was just something so fiery and vivacious about her.

The simple and pure name of Mary did not do her justice.

I knew before even holding her it was going to be like holding the sun.

Closing the distance between us, I snatched the vase out of her hand and tossed it away, uncaring as the crystal smashed the moment it hit the thinly carpeted floor.

"Don't even think about it."

She raised her other hand to slap me, but I caught her around her wrist.

She defiantly repeated, "I'm not having sex with you."

"I'm not having sex with you either. I'm going to *fuck* you."

Her eyes flashed as her lip curled. "It's the same thing and no matter what you call it, it will not happen."

I lifted her arm high, pinning it against the wall.

I clasped her throat with my other hand and tilted her head to the side so I could place my mouth on her neck.

I could feel and hear her gasp as my tongue flicked out to tease the space just below her ear.

I wedged my leg between hers, knowing with my superior height she would be forced onto her toes as she practically rode my upper thigh.

Biting her earlobe, I rasped in her ear, "You're wrong. Sex is functional, no different from eating or breathing. It serves a purpose, to scratch an itch, and nothing more. It is unnecessary to have a connection or even genuine passion. When it is over, you go on with your life, unchanged."

I reached down to undo the belt at her waist.

I pulled it free from its loops and tossed it onto the bed. Her robe fell open. I cupped one perfect breast and lowered my head. I ran the tip of my tongue over the lace edge of her bra.

"Fucking is different. Fucking is primal. A raw, untamed response to the body in front of you. A deep gnawing need to claim and possess."

Her breath came in quick gasps as I moved my hand over her belly to dip my fingers into her panties.

I traced the lush fullness of her lower lip with my tongue before whispering against her mouth, "Fucking leaves you sweaty and sore, with marks on both your skin and soul. Fucking leaves a limp, satiated body unable to think clearly beyond the delicious euphoria that continues to rush over you in waves, long after your bodies are no longer connected. Fucking is an all-consuming lust that will not be denied. It's feeling used and cherished all at the same time, and desperately craving the feeling again before the warmth of your partner's touch has left your skin."

I slipped my finger along the folds of her pussy, relishing her slick heat. "Deny it if you like, but I know you want this. Those big beautiful indigo eyes of yours are telling me. So is this pretty flush on your cheeks. Your open lips and shallow breathing. Your rapid pulse."

I tightened my hold on her wrist and said harshly, "So tell me again you don't want to fuck."

Mary bit her lip and swallowed a groan as the tip of my finger teased her clit with soft circles.

I licked the corner of her mouth. "Tell me," I commanded.

Her brow furrowed.

Her beautiful gaze captured mine. "I don't want to fu—I don't want you," she inhaled as she turned her head, breaking our connection. "You need to leave, please." The final word was uttered as a whispered plea.

"You're not just lying to me—again—you're lying to yourself, and your body has betrayed you."

I released her wrist and drove my fingers into her hair as I spun her away from the wall.

Pulling my fingers free of her panties, I held the first two up so she could see them glistening from her arousal.

Her pretty cheeks turned pink as she tried to look away.

My grip on her hair prevented it. "Eyes on me," I growled.

When I had her attention again, I sucked my fingers between my lips. My tongue flicked out over my lower lip. "So sweet."

Mary groaned as she raised her arms to press her hands against my chest.

Ignoring her feeble protest, I pulled her to me, claiming her mouth.

I wanted to taste her, and I needed her to taste her own arousal, proof of my effect on her.

Her fists beat against my chest.

I captured her wrists and pulled her arms behind her back.

The movement pushed her ample breasts against my front.

The anticipation of tearing that bra off her body, and finally feasting my eyes on her naked breasts, lengthened my cock to a painful degree.

Our tongues dueled, swirling and tasting each other.

I could feel the moment her resistance faded as her mouth opened and her body leaned into mine.

I released her wrists and yanked the robe off her body.

"Wait," she protested.

I unclasped her bra and gripped the shoulder straps.

Her crossed arms over her breasts prevented me from ripping the offensive garment off her body.

She tried to take a step back, but the bed prevented it. "Stop! This is madness. I don't even know you!"

Wrapping my hand around her neck, I pulled her in for another kiss. "You know all you need to know right here."

I then brought her hand down to my hard shaft, letting her feel its girth and length through my suit trousers.

It pleased me when her eyes widened.

I wrenched her arms away and pulled her bra free.

Her breasts were beautiful, soft and full with blush-pink nipples.

My large hands wrapped around her waist.

I lifted her high until her toes no longer touched the floor. Her hands fisted into the fabric of my shirt as I latched onto one nipple and sucked hard, dragging the edge of my teeth against the soft flesh.

"Oh, God!" she exclaimed.

Laving the nipple with my tongue, I turned my attention to her other breast before tossing her backward to land in the center of the bed.

Her body bounced twice before she sprang up to rest on her knees and palms. Her dark hair hung in wild disarray over her bare shoulders and breasts.

With my gaze trained on her, I reached for my red silk tie. Holding the length between my hands, I watched as recognition of my intent washed over her face.

She shook her head and shimmied backwards. "You're not tying me up."

I raised an eyebrow. "Yes, my *krasotka,* I am."

Her eyes narrowed. "You keep calling me that, what does it even mean?"

Putting a hand under her chin, I lifted her face higher. "It means you are my beautiful girl."

Her eyes flashed with defiance. "But I'm not yours."

I released her chin and twisted the tie in my hand into two loops. I overlapped them, then threaded the left loop through the right, creating a handcuff knot.

Snatching her wrists, I expertly forced a hand through each loop and pulled the silk tie tight.

After pulling her backwards, I secured the ends into a tight knot around a spindle in her headboard.

She twisted this way and that as she desperately pulled against her binds, succeeding only in tightening them further.

I planted a hand on either side of her head and stared down at her struggling form.

"Yes, you are. You're under my control now, Mary Fraser, and I have no intention of letting you go."

CHAPTER 3

MARY

This was beyond wrong.

A catastrophic mistake.

I knew with my matte red lipstick and leopard print fuck-me pumps I gave off the vibe that I did this sort of thing all the time, but that was definitely not the case.

I hadn't had a boyfriend since freshman year in college, and it had been ages since I had even had sex.

Truth be told, the men in my life were boring.

Predictable.

And worse, they were mediocre, at best, in bed.

I wasn't all that different from my roommate, Emma.

She dreamed of book boyfriends.

I dreamed of actor boyfriends.

I didn't want Mr. Darcy from *Pride and Prejudice.*

I wanted Spike from *Buffy the Vampire Slayer,* Jax

from *Sons of Anarchy,* Dean from *Supernatural,* Sebastian from *Cruel Intentions.*

That was my curse.

I lusted after the arrogant alpha asshole who confidently sauntered into a room and owned the women in it.

The man who knew precisely what a woman wanted and gave it to her—over and over again until she screamed for mercy or in ecstasy.

Fortunately, I was intelligent enough to know that those types of men made the worst kinds of boyfriends.

They would bring only heartbreak.

Maybe that was part of their appeal, the dancing with danger, buying your pleasure now with the pain that would come later.

That was probably why I didn't date all that much.

Well, that and the fact that this type of man didn't exist beyond the glowing screen of a television.

Or at least I thought they didn't.

Sure, Emma seemed to find a man like that in Dimitri, but I figured he was a unicorn.

A big, sexy, masculine unicorn, but still a unicorn.

Men like that weren't supposed to exist in the actual world.

So who the fuck would have guessed there'd be *two* badass, arrogant, hot-as-hell Russian men running around Chicago?

Vaska stared down at me and slowly unbuttoned his shirt.

I forgot to breathe.

Dear God.

The man's chest was sculpted rock covered in ink.

As he shrugged out of his shirt, I saw two eight-pointed stars in vivid blood red, gold, and black on the front of each shoulder.

I remembered from that book Emma got to investigate Dimitri's tattoos that two eight-pointed stars denoted a high-ranking thief or master criminal.

Damn.

Was it wrong that he'd just gotten even sexier?

Of course, it was wrong.

It was crazy, psychotic wrong.

This wasn't a movie, for fuck's sake.

There was no guarantee of a happy ending.

For all I knew, I was about to either have the best sex of my life or get murdered literally tied to my bed.

He turned his back and crossed the room. His whole back was covered in ink as well.

As I focused in to decipher the mosaic of bright images, he did something unforgivable.

He unzipped his pants, letting them and the rest of his clothing fall to the floor. The man had the greatest, tightest ass I'd ever seen.

He reached into the suit jacket that was slung over

my vanity stool and pulled out some small gold foil packets.

Vaska turned and walked back to the bed.

And that was when my late panic set in.

I shook my head violently from side to side as I kicked with my legs, trying to get to a seated position so I could work on the binds around my wrists. "No! No! Stop! We can't do this."

The man was enormous.

There was no way he was putting that *thing* into my body. Nope.

Vaska tossed the Magnum condoms onto the bed and reached down to stroke his shaft. "Don't worry, *malyshka,* I'll make sure you're wet enough to take every inch."

He placed a knee on the bed and reached for me.

I kicked at his hand.

My fight only amused him.

Climbing fully onto the bed, he easily captured my flailing legs and tore my panties off. Pressing his cock near my entrance, he forced my legs over his shoulders.

I stilled.

He grinned. "That's more like it."

I squeezed my eyes shut and braced for the lethal pounding I was sure I was about to endure.

The bed squeaked slightly as he shifted.

Instead of the hard, painful thrust of his cock, I felt the warmth of his mouth.

My eyes flew open to see his head nestled between my thighs, his arms wrapped securely around the base of my legs, holding me open.

He met my gaze and winked.

Opening his mouth, his tongue stretched out to flick at my clit.

Without volition, a throaty groan left my body.

His tongue continued to swirl and tease every nerve. Each time I tried to buck my hips, Vaska held me still with his firm grip.

My hands balled into fists as I gripped the sheets and threw my head back, giving in to the delicious torment of his mouth.

The man wasn't just going through the motions, like most men. He was a wizard. It was like he knew what I wanted, what I needed, before I did. He read every sigh, every shimmy, every held breath and used it against me. Not once did I have to say higher, or softer, or a little to the left, or not so fast.

He was perfectly in tune.

And damn, the man didn't just lick; he feasted.

My back arched as the pressure built.

Just then he pushed a single finger inside of me as he increased the speed of his tongue.

I came so hard, I forgot to breathe.

Stars burst behind my eyelids as the sound of rushing waves filled my ears. My body hung limp from the silk tie binds.

He rubbed my cunt in soothing circles with four

fingers and whispered to me in Russian, *"Ne volnuysya, detka. Ya tol'ko nachinayu."*

I slowly opened my eyes and stared at him in wonder, as I tried to catch my breath. "What?" I gasped.

This time he pushed two fingers inside of me, before saying, "I said, do not worry, baby. I'm just getting started."

Without warning, he flipped me over.

I had to push up onto my knees to ease the increased pressure of the twisted tie around my wrists. I had expected him to position himself on his knees behind me, but instead, he lay on his back and his head went between my thighs.

I cried out in alarm. "No. You can't. It's too sensitive now."

I had never even tried to come twice in a row because my clit was always too sensitive after the first orgasm. I honestly didn't think it would even be possible.

His warm breath tickled the inside of my thigh as he chuckled. *"Ty zakonchila kogda ya skazal chto ty zakonchila. Ya khochu bol'she chem etu sladkuyu pizdu."*

I did not know what he was saying, but I was certain it was dirty.

Before I could ask, his mouth was back on me and I had to bite my pillow to keep from screaming. I didn't want to give him the satisfaction of knowing he was right.

As I recovered from my second mind-blowing orgasm, his warm skin brushed the backs of my thighs.

I tensed.

His left hand caressed my back as his right rubbed my pussy. He pushed two fingers inside, then a third.

"Ow! Wait!"

"Shhh. This is happening, *krasotka*. Let me prepare you."

His fingers shifted in and out of my body, opening me as his other hand continued to rub my back.

Still, I couldn't stop the rising panic.

He was too big. I pulled at my binds. "Untie me."

"No."

The distinctive sound of a foil wrapper being torn open sounded out like an alarm.

"Please, I don't want to be tied up anymore."

"No," came his same unrelenting reply.

My voice became high-pitched and strained. "You can't say no when I'm saying no."

"Yes, I can."

With a cry of frustration, I yanked on the silk tie, which only tightened it further around my wrists, causing angry red marks.

Before I could argue again, my body rocked forward as a sharp sting of pain radiated from my right ass cheek.

He had spanked me!

The bastard had actually spanked me.

Casting an outraged look over my shoulder, I raged, "How dare you?"

He spanked me again.

"Stop that!"

He raised his arm. My eyes widened. "Don't you dar—"

I wasn't even able to finish my threat.

He spanked me a third time.

By now, my skin was on fire. Hot needle pricks ran over my ass and down my thighs. The worst part was it seemed to heighten the pleasurable soreness I was already feeling between my legs.

"Are you going to be a good girl and obey me, or do I keep spanking you?"

Under normal circumstances, the sexual threat of that sentence would be scary, but when it was uttered in a heavy Russian accent by a huge Russian criminal who currently had me tied to a bed, it was terrifying.

"Please," I begged, although I wasn't sure what for.

He leaned down to whisper in my ear, "Tell me you're going to be my good girl." His free hand reached under my body to caress my breast before pinching my nipple.

The sharp stab of pain was another warning.

"Yes," I breathed. "I'll be your good girl."

His knuckles brushed my inner thigh as he fisted his cock and rubbed the heavy bulbous head through my slit. I couldn't contain a whimper.

Vaska kissed my shoulder. "Shhh, *krasotka*. This first time will hurt, but I promise it will be worth it."

He pushed the head into my tight entrance.

I fisted my hands, driving my nails into my palms. "Oh, God!"

His arm wrapped around my waist, holding me in place as he pushed inside. His thick cock stretched and strained my inner muscles. With his free hand, he caressed my breast as he whispered soothing words in Russian I couldn't understand.

He pushed in another few inches.

A fine sheen of sweat broke out on my back as I strained to accept him. "Please. You're too big. It hurts."

He ignored my pleas and pushed in another few inches.

My body would have buckled forward if not for the binds around my wrists and his grip on my hip.

After an eternity of him slowly thrusting forward inch by inch, I felt the pressure of his hips against my ass.

He was fully seated inside of me.

I tried to concentrate on my breathing, taking deep breaths in and out to control the overwhelming feeling of pressure and fullness. It felt like someone had shoved one of those novelty dildos you know couldn't possibly fit inside a woman's body ... inside of me.

He stopped moving, letting me adjust to the feel

of him. I could hear his harsh breathing and the flexing and tightening of his fingers on my hip, as if he was trying to keep control.

Gradually, my body opened and relaxed around his length.

After another moment, I could feel the return of a delicious sensation between my legs. I pulled my hips slightly forward, feeling him slide out a few inches, and then pressed back into his hips. I rocked slowly back and forth like this several times, each time only letting him slide out an inch or two.

Finally, I felt confident enough to shift my hips forward enough to allow several inches of his shaft to slide out, then I pushed back with more force than before.

Vaska groaned but stayed perfectly still.

Then I crossed a line.

I repeated the motion, but this time I boldly shimmied my ass against his abdomen.

The moment I did so, I knew I was in trouble.

All the air left the room in a rush.

The atmosphere crackled with renewed sexual tension.

He fisted his hand into my hair and wrenched my head back.

Biting my earlobe, he growled, "That was just what I was waiting for."

Oh, God.

Vaska took complete control.

He pulled out and thrust in deep, pounding into my body again and again, every thrust more powerful than the last.

His painful grip on my hair held me in place as he rocked his hips into me. Several times he added to the pleasurable pain by spanking my ass with each rhythmic push of his shaft.

He consumed me.

There wasn't an inch of my body that didn't feel his touch, his brand, in some way.

He was right; this wasn't sex, not even close.

This was fucking.

My willpower was gone.

As I climaxed for the third time, I screamed.

I didn't have to turn to know he was smirking. I had submitted and given him precisely what he wanted, right down to my orgasmic scream.

Releasing my hair, he drove into me several more times before reaching his own completion.

I collapsed forward onto the pillows, my arms stretched above my head.

The heat of his skin scorched my back as he reached over me to untie my wrists. The bed shifted as he rose. He draped a soft blanket over me.

I kept my eyes closed as I listened to him dress.

Outside there was a clamor of raised voices and slamming of car doors.

He peeked through the curtains and nodded. "My crew is here to install the security system."

For a moment, I was confused, until I remembered his real purpose for even being here this morning. It was funny how three unbelievable orgasms from a completely hot-as-fuck stranger could really scramble a girl's brain.

I guessed now he would leave.

At least I wouldn't be surprised if he did. That was how these things always ended in the movies. The guy got what he wanted and then he'd split.

I was sure I should be feeling some kind of Catholic guilt bullshit or regret, and maybe I would once I felt human again.

For now, I was a satisfied puddle of melted bones.

Dressed again in his trousers and shirt, he held his suit jacket as he leaned over and brushed the hair from my face.

He gave me a kiss on the forehead.

Here it comes. The promise to call. A promise he would have no intention of fulfilling.

Without saying a word, he left.

That bastard!

The least he could have done was lie to me.

I waited to hear the closing of the front door, but it never came. A moment later he returned to the bedroom holding my phone. "Unlock it."

"What?"

"Your phone, unlock it."

"Why?"

He sighed. "Mary, you are going to need to work

on this nasty habit you have of questioning my orders. I'm being patient and forgiving now, but that will not last."

This is him being patient?

What would him being impatient look like?

With him staring down at me with those dark, inscrutable eyes, I didn't have a choice. I typed in zero, one, one, nine, Buffy's birthday, and unlocked the phone.

He took it from me and typed something.

The phone in his pocket pinged.

He handed my phone back to me and shrugged into his suit jacket. As he buttoned it, he said, "Whatever plans you have this evening, cancel them. I'll be here at eight."

My mouth fell open.

So it was like that? "Just because I let you … *fuck me* … doesn't mean I'll let you do it again. This was a one-time thing."

Vaska ran his knuckles down my cheek. "You didn't *let me* do anything. I took what I wanted and yes, it will happen again … and again."

My cheeks burned at the truth of his implication.

Before I could object, he turned to leave the room but not before calling over his shoulder, "Be ready at eight and put some clothes on. If I find out you were half naked in front of my men, there will be hell to pay tonight."

Springing up onto my knees, uncaring for my

naked state, I threw the bed pillows at his retreating back.

I heard his laughter until the front door closed.

Bastard.

Well, he was in for a rude surprise if he thought I was going to be here dutifully waiting for him later tonight with my legs open.

CHAPTER 4

MARY

After wrapping the blanket around myself, I scrambled off the bed and crept over to the window.

Careful to stay to the side, out of view, I peeked through the curtains.

I watched as Vaska walk toward his crew of five men unloading a ladder and equipment out of an unmarked black van.

The moment he approached, they all stopped what they were doing and gave him their full attention. This was even more astounding given the rough appearance of the crew.

They all screamed *recently paroled*.

It was obvious Vaska demanded respect.

It was even a little sexy watching him in command.

I mean, it had to take a real badass to get the respect of a dangerous-looking crew like that.

Well, a badass or a fellow criminal who was even more dangerous than them. Yikes.

I shifted my stance as I felt a twinge of pleasure between my legs as the scene sparked memories of how he had been in command in this bedroom not an hour earlier, ordering me about, expecting and getting my immediate obedience.

As Vaska walked away, climbed into an impossibly expensive-looking car, and drove off, I flopped back onto my bed.

Staring at the ceiling, I replayed the events of the morning over and over in my head.

I needed to understand how that man, a complete stranger, had voodooed me straight into bed like that. There had to have been some kind of dark magic involved.

The problem was no matter how I tossed it about in my head, the sequence always seemed the same.

Open door to crazy hot, sexy, dangerous-looking bad boy stranger.

He flashes a gun.

Scream his name while tied to my bed.

The end.

I rubbed my eyes.

I really needed to stop drinking cheap tequila.

Obviously, the tequila shots I had done with

Dimitri last night before he left with Emma had scrambled my brain.

Thank God I had no intention of ever seeing Vaska again.

The idea was ludicrous.

A man like that would swallow me whole and spit out my tiny bones when he was done with me.

If this was how I acted within minutes of meeting him, I wouldn't stand a chance if I was actually dating him.

Not that he was even offering to date me.

It was far more likely he now expected me to be a fun piece on the side.

The type of girl he could just fuck whenever and wherever he wanted at the snap of his fingers.

What angered me … I mean … what really, really pissed me off?

He would be right.

With orgasms like that, I would become his little devoted puppy, following him around begging for a treat and, worse, forgiving him when he kicked me. And trust me, the kicks were coming. I had seen enough movies and television shows to know the kicks always came with a man like Vasili Lukovich Rostov.

My phone buzzed as the screen lit up.

Grabbing it off the bed, I read the text. It was from Vaska.

My men are coming inside.

There was a pause, then another text.

You better be dressed.

I looked down at the blanket only loosely wrapped around my body.

Fuck.

I had on a pair of black capris and my favorite black cardigan with the two clusters of embroidered cherries on the shoulders before I realized that the man had snapped his fingers and I had jumped to obey his command.

Damn him.

At the loud knock on the door, I slipped on a pair of red velvet pumps and raced to open it.

After that it was just pure chaos.

As far as I could tell, they all spoke only Russian and knew just a few English catchphrases and words.

No matter what I said or asked, they nodded their heads and said yes and then kept doing whatever they were going to do.

One of the men dropped a heavy pile of iron rods onto the living room carpet as another one tore down our delicate lace curtains. I guess we were getting bars on our windows now. I couldn't help but think our apartment would be like a birdcage.

Was that how Emma's boyfriend Dimitri and men like Vaska liked to keep their women?

Locking them up in pretty cages where they'd feel safe and protected but not free?

I shook my head. That was unfair.

The truth was a security system would be a blessing.

This building was the best we could afford as graduate students, but it was far from safe and Lord knows the landlord didn't give a shit about our well-being.

A third man was adjusting a ladder near the door and had already begun drilling holes into the wall. For what reason, I did not know, but there were lots of electric cords and what looked like a security motherboard resting on a toolbox near his feet.

The fourth was drilling a hole high in the wall on the outside of the door and the last man was checking the fuse box, probably double-checking that all of this twenty-second century super-techy security equipment would not blow out our anti-quated apartment's 1950s fuses.

The man with the iron rods picked one up and came dangerously close to smashing the glass in my framed copy of a signed *Buffy the Vampire Slayer* script. It was the 'Restless' episode from season four where Buffy was stalked by a primal animal force.

I tripped over an end table in my race to pull it off the wall and save it.

Amid this chaos, Emma walked in.

Grabbing her by the hand, I dragged her into my bedroom where the noise was down to a muted roar.

"What is going on?" she asked.

Shoving the perfume bottles on the top of my vanity aside, I propped up my Buffy frame.

It was then I saw Vaska's cufflinks.

He had forgotten them. They were silver with two large blood-red rubies that looked like two demon eyes staring back at me, damning me.

I snatched them up and shoved them into my pocket.

And then I did something I never thought I'd ever do.

I lied to her.

Straight to her face.

I lied to my best friend.

Actually, technically, I didn't lie as much as omit some pertinent facts.

I couldn't even explain why I did it.

It's not like Emma wouldn't understand.

She'd had a similar experience with her own Russian man.

I knew she wouldn't judge me, just like I hadn't judged her and really there was nothing to be judged about.

I was a grown woman who'd had some amazing sex, end of story.

For some insane reason, I decided to gloss over the more pertinent events and make light of the entire encounter.

I told myself it was because I didn't want to get into the salacious details while there were five

Russian men on the other side of the door, and that was partially true, but not the whole truth. I didn't know how I felt about my encounter with Vaska and, at least for now, didn't want to talk about it until I processed my feelings.

Plus, I could tell Emma really liked Dimitri, and I knew he was going to be great for her.

She needed someone to shake up her world a little bit. Someone to challenge her to be more adventurous and outgoing. He was just the man to do it and I didn't want my impulsive mistake with his business partner to in any way jeopardize or screw that up for her.

I rambled the entire half-truth. "It's the craziest thing. At the ungodly hour of seven o'clock, there's a knock on our door. I open it to find this *drop-dead gorgeous* man dressed in the most expensive suit I've ever seen. Iz zees the aparrrtment of Eeema Doyle, he says. I said yes. Then he says, my name iz Vaska."

Fortunately for me, we were both late for class so she didn't quiz me further.

As I took a seat in the back of the room at my *Reading and Writing in Linguistically Diverse Classrooms,* a requirement for the focus I wanted to have with my education graduate degree, I reached into my pocket and pulled out the pair of cufflinks.

There was no way these weren't real rubies, which meant these cufflinks were probably worth a small fortune. I could pawn them and cover a portion of my and Emma's rent for this month with them.

The thought had merit.

It smacked a little of payment for services rendered, but I could get over that part as I imagined Vaska's face when I cheekily told him I'd pawned his cufflinks.

Not that I had any plans to see him ever again.

I had every intention of being nowhere near my apartment at eight p.m. tonight, just in case he showed up expecting a repeat performance of this morning.

After that, he'd probably lose interest, especially if I ignored his texts.

I was quite proud of myself for not responding to his text from earlier.

The fact that I had reread it a hundred times didn't count.

I refused to become intrigued by this man. He was trouble with a capital stay-the-fuck-away T.

I rolled the cufflinks around on my palm.

Even under the awful fluorescent lighting of this classroom, they still sparkled with crimson fire.

Did I dare pawn them?

What would happen if Vaska tracked me down and learned the truth?

I bit my lower lip.

Maybe he would spank me for being a bad girl.

I shifted in my seat.

Maybe he would tie me up to the bed and take off his belt and whip my ass as he made me beg for forgiveness.

Or maybe he would make me crawl across the room in penance like that scene from *Nine and 1/2 Weeks*.

Would he take out his cock and force me to suck it?

The idea made my cheeks flame as I imagined the terrifyingly long length of his shaft being thrust down my throat.

I shifted again and felt a slight twinge of pain. My pussy was still sore from the pounding he had given me earlier.

I reached for my water bottle and cast my gaze around the classroom, nervous someone was watching me and guessing my illicit thoughts.

I had no idea where these thoughts were even coming from. I had never really been the kinky sex type of girl. This morning was the first time a man had ever dared spank me in bed. I still couldn't believe how much it had turned me on.

How much it still turned me on.

Was I actually considering pawning this man's property just to piss him off to see what he would do to me in bed as a punishment?

The idea was crazy, especially since I had no intention of ever seeing him again.

On the way back to my apartment after class, I

passed a pawnshop on Devon Avenue. Without giving it further thought, I walked through the door. The man behind the counter gave me an odd look when I laid the cufflinks on the small black velvet square.

Picking up a jeweler's loupe, he examined one then the other. "Nice quality. Five carats each. Untreated. Probably an R6/5, maybe even an R7/5." Lowering the loupe, he narrowed his eyes as he asked, "Where did you get these?"

I shrugged. "My grandfather passed away. It's my inheritance."

"If it's your inheritance, then why are you pawning them?"

"I'm a graduate student. Tuition trumps sentimentality."

He rubbed his chin. "It's still early in the day, all I have on hand in cash is about eleven thousand. Take it or leave it."

Eleven thousand?

Thousand? Eleven of them?

Oh. My. God.

How much money do you have to have to casually forget cufflinks worth eleven thousand dollars?

Stunned, I found myself nodding.

He snatched up the cufflinks. "Wait here."

When he returned, I watched him count out the cash, swallowing as the stack got higher and higher.

It would have taken me half a year to earn this much in tips at my crappy bar job.

In a daze, I filled out the necessary paperwork before shoving the money and pawn slip into my Hello Kitty purse.

Silly me, thinking an expensive pair of cufflinks would be worth about seven hundred and fifty bucks and wouldn't be missed.

I wonder what kind of punishment you got for stealing eleven thousand dollars from a man like Vaska Rostov?

CHAPTER 5

VASKA

I reached for the leather-wrapped steering wheel and noticed my loose cuff.

I patted my palm over the inner pocket of my suit jacket and found nothing; I must have left my cuff-links on Mary's vanity.

If Dimitri hadn't been waiting for me at the ware-house to take care of a pressing issue with the Petrov brothers, I would have turned around.

I could definitely think of worse ways to spend a morning than in Mary's bed. I shifted in my seat. Damn, just the thought of that woman and I was already getting hard.

Something about this morning was—different, unusual.

There was this clawing feeling in my chest that something in my life had just changed, shifted unex-pectedly.

It wasn't a sense of doom, but rather a sense of … something.

I couldn't put my finger on it, but it was like that crackle of energy you feel in the air just before a thunderstorm.

You have this primal sense that something is about to happen.

That pressure was building and about to be released in a ball of energy and chaos.

I chuckled.

A ball of energy and chaos.

What a perfect way to describe Mary.

She practically hummed with sensual energy kept barely in check by a chaotic contradiction of innocence and sin.

It wasn't surprising that I'd fucked a beautiful woman within moments of meeting her.

Most men were bumbling idiots who didn't know how to talk to—or handle—a woman.

I wasn't most men. I knew what they wanted to hear, what they craved. I could read them like a book and give them precisely what they desired. Yet, this time was different.

Mary was different.

For the first time in my life, I wanted to stay in bed with a woman after I'd satisfied us both.

And it wasn't just so that I could fuck her again once my cock recovered, although I certainly would have.

It was something more dangerous.

I wanted to hold her.

Cuddle her close and watch her sleep.

I wanted to press my hand to her heart and feel it beat while I listened to the soft sounds of her breathing.

Never in my life had I craved intimacy with a woman like I did with Mary.

It made little sense. I had literally never laid eyes on the woman before this morning, and suddenly I was fighting the urge to ditch the condom and ride her bareback, something I'd never done in my life since I'd lost my virginity at fourteen to a very willing teacher.

I hated having even a thin piece of rubber between us.

I drove up to the window at the drive-thru Starbucks.

The woman at the counter giggled as she handed me the two large black coffees.

I winked back, which only made her giggle more as her cheeks reddened. She was pretty in that suburban American blonde sort of way.

As I drove off, I reached for one of the coffee cups and noticed a phone number and the name Alice with a heart over the 'i.'

I shook my head.

The only thing women loved more than a bad boy was a bad boy with money.

Between my expensive car, suits, and tattoos, I fit the fantasy better than most. Any other time, I would have turned the car around and coaxed her out of that green apron and into my car for a quick blowjob, but not today.

My brow furrowed as I realized I wasn't interested. You'd think it was because I'd just fucked my brains out not an hour earlier, but that had never stopped me before.

It wasn't thoughts of a cute skinny blonde that played across my mind, but rather a feisty brunette with full pink lips, indigo blue eyes, and curves that could bring a man to his knees.

I parked behind Dimitri's Mercedes, which was still a few blocks away from the warehouse, and reached for the brown coffee tray before stepping out.

As I walked to our meeting location, I thought again of Mary.

Fuck.

This could get complicated.

From what I could see, Dimitri had more than a passing interest in her roommate, Emma.

I'd known him since our school days, and the man had never before installed a security system in a woman's apartment as a gift. Jewelry, flowers, even a car once, all yes, but a security system?

No. Jewelry said I want to fuck you.

A security system said I care about you … and I want to fuck you.

It would probably be for the best if I kept my encounter with Mary under wraps for now.

Strolling into the warehouse, I extended my arm, offering him a coffee.

He snatched it up with what I could only describe as a snarl. "What has you in such a foul mood?" I asked before taking a sip of the hot, bitter brew.

He lifted the lid of his coffee before responding. "I left a warm bed to deal with these two morons."

Setting my coffee to the side, I put my car keys in my pocket and rubbed my hands together. It was cold as balls in this empty warehouse, but it couldn't be avoided. This wasn't exactly the corporate office conference room type of meeting this morning, not with our business.

When you dealt in illegal arms, desolate warehouses and empty airport hangars were usually your office.

Today we had a meeting with the idiot Petrov brothers.

The morons were trying to palm off some counterfeit guns on us. Not only were they pissing in our backyard, but they were flooding the market with poorly made knockoffs, which was bad for business.

Casting a glance in Dimitri's direction, I flat-out lied to my best friend. "At least yours wasn't empty," I complained, which wasn't entirely untrue, since technically I had slept alone in my cold bed last night.

It was this morning in Mary's bed that had warmed me up.

Dimitri laughed. "Karina mad at you again?"

Karina was a rather problematic high-end escort I often hired. I wasn't exactly the boyfriend type, so escorts made life easy, usually, but Karina was nothing but bullshit drama.

She had a habit of getting shitfaced drunk and throwing things like knives.

I sighed. "I'm getting too old for this shit. At first it was fun but now … hell, I don't know."

That part was at least true.

I used to think women like Karina added some fun and excitement to my life, but after this morning I realized it was all just negative energy drama.

The genuine excitement was the kind that came from being with a firebrand like Mary. A woman with spirit and intelligence.

Dimitri clasped me around the neck. "If we are to get old, we will get old together, my friend, and thanks for overseeing that task this morning."

I turned slightly away so my intuitive friend could not read my expression. "Actually, I should be thanking you. That roommate of hers is something else."

"You and she would probably get along. She shares your taste in cheap liquor."

Oh, we definitely got along.

And she certainly shared my taste in something—kinky-as-fuck, mind-blowing sex.

Changing the subject, I said, "Let's get this over with. There's a rare steak and a bottle of Chianti with our name on it at Gibson's."

He checked his watch. "They're late."

Defying all the logic of an off-the-radar, private meeting place, the idiot Petrov brothers roared into the loading dock driving a ridiculous metallic gold Ferrari.

"Jesus Christ," I cursed under my breath, shaking my head before sharing a sympathetic, annoyed glance with Dimitri.

The Petrov brothers emerged from the vehicle, wearing matching white and red Adidas tracksuits.

Dimitri shifted closer and asked, "You still carry that .30-caliber Tokarev with you?"

"Of course."

"Good. Shoot me."

"I'd rather shoot them, but this is a new suit."

"Vaska Lukovitch! Dimitri Antonovich!" the brothers called out in unison.

Ignoring them, I paid closer attention to the three thugs they brought with them.

"My friends! You are looking good," said one brother.

Dimitri and I both stayed silent.

It was a useful tactic; most people talked too

much. You could be significantly more intimidating for what you didn't say as opposed to what you did.

The only thing more ludicrous than their car was their appearance and the fact they had deliberately purchased the same luxury watch as Dimitri.

Christ, save me from moronic posers.

Seriously, I left Mary's bed for this?

It stretched the imagination how these two had managed to get their hands on two crates of ORSIS-CT20s, the latest and best Russian sniper rifles, even counterfeit ones.

One of the brothers, I didn't know which—they both looked and acted the same to me—said, "Do you like our ride?"

Dimitri smirked. "It's a great way to spend twice as much as for a Mercedes SL550."

I snorted. "With none of that annoying good engineering or sleek style."

"As much as I'd love to chat about cars and watches in a freezing warehouse all morning, I really do have other matters to attend to today," Dimitri said, sipping his coffee.

I nodded. "Anatoly, Andrei, if you would be so kind as to show us the merchandise? We do have other matters to attend to this morning."

With thinly veiled patience, we watched the struggle to unload and then open the crates.

I drew out my silver flask and unscrewed the cap, taking a swig before handing it to Dimitri. It was a little early, even for me, but there was no way I was going to survive this encounter with the Petrov brothers completely sober.

Dimitri took a swig and hid a rough cough behind the back of his hand. "Damn you and that rotgut Moskovskaya vodka you like!"

I smiled.

No one appreciated good vodka. I kept things real by drinking the vodka of the people, not that elitist crap Dimitri and our friends, Gregor and Mikhail, preferred.

It drew our attention back to the brothers who had each pulled out gold-plated Desert Eagle handguns and were pointing them at each other.

I sighed. "I'm getting too old for this shit."

Dimitri stepped forward. "Gentlemen, if I may?"

He picked up the crowbar and made quick work of the case lid. As we both pushed aside the straw packing, Dimitri snatched up the first exposed rifle. After flipping it over, he handed it to me.

I looked to the left of the receiver but didn't see the expected Izhevsk factory stamp of an arrow in a triangle. Instead, there was a bunch of Latin numbers. They were fakes from Afghanistan.

The Petrov brothers had truly reached an epic level of stupid to try to sell men as dangerous as Dimitri and I fake guns.

"So do we have a deal for both crates?" asked Andrei. "I need to know now. We have many interested buyers, but as a courtesy to the Motherland we are coming to you first."

I raised an eyebrow and repeated, "A courtesy. Did you hear that, Dimitri, the Petrov brothers were giving us a courtesy."

I pulled my .30-caliber Tokarev and pressed it against Andrei's head. Both started shouting and crying.

"Shut the fuck up," Dimitri yelled.

The hired henchmen shifted their feet but didn't step in, clearly unwilling to die for whatever the Petrov brothers were paying them.

"Tell your girlfriends to leave," Dimitri snarled.

"Get back! Now!" called Anatoly.

The henchmen scattered like rats.

"Looks like you weren't a very good fuck in bed," I taunted.

Dimitri spoke. His voice was calm and controlled, something I knew would freak out the brothers. "Gentlemen, you have jeopardized a lucrative business deal of ours."

Andrei tried to speak.

I cocked my gun. "Did we give you permission to talk?"

His lips turned down as his eyes widened in a comical expression. Then I heard piss. I jumped out of the way. "Goddamn it! These are Italian!"

"As of today, you are no longer in the gunrunning

business, have I made myself clear?" Dimitri threatened.

"But there's enough business for everyone," whined Anatoly.

I shrugged. "I guess you weren't clear."

Dimitri shot him in the knee. Over the brother's screams of agony, he said, "Have I made my point, or do I need to repeat myself?"

I shook my head. "He really hates repeating himself."

The other brother conceded. "Okay! Okay! No more guns."

"And you'll leave the city tonight."

"Yes! Yes!"

Dimitri nodded as he returned his gun to his shoulder holster. "Good. Since I know you are sorry for the trouble and inconvenience you've caused, we'll accept these crates as an apology."

I thought about it for a second. "And the Ferrari."

Dimitri gave me an odd look, but I brushed it off.

While it was a stupid car for two grown men, Mary would look incredibly sexy behind the wheel. A beautiful woman deserved to drive a flashy, if impractical, sports car. I would give it to her tonight when I picked her up for dinner.

"And the Ferrari," repeated Dimitri.

After arranging for a cleanup crew, Dimitri and I tied up loose ends at Midway Airport where the brothers had taken possession of the counterfeit guns before parting ways. I was busy arranging to have one of my crew pick up the Ferrari and drop it off at Mary's when I got a call from a pawnshop owner.

Dropping everything else, I battled traffic for forty minutes to arrive at the rundown Cash for Gold pawnshop. Pushing open the filthy glass door, I surveyed the cluttered space filled with instruments, old computers, and a dingy glass case displaying black velvet trays overflowing with jewelry, mostly abandoned engagement rings and cross necklaces.

The man behind the counter mopped his brow with a crumpled paper towel the moment I entered.

He was pale, with a large face propped up by several folds of flesh under his jaw. I didn't recognize him, but judging by the fear in his shifty, rat-like eyes, he certainly recognized me. That wasn't surprising. Pawnshops were just on this side of the law and Dimitri and I were very well known in the criminal underworld.

"Mr. Rostov, I hope I did the right thing."

"Let me see them."

He nodded vigorously. "I have them in the back in the safe."

As he disappeared through a doorway that seemed almost too narrow for his bulk, he continued to talk to me from the other room. "I hope I did the right thing. I recognized your crest from the engraving on the back of one of the cufflinks. I hope I did the right thing."

He returned to the main shop area.

I held out my hand, and he dropped the cufflinks into my open palm.

The engraving he recognized was the same as on my distinctive silver signet ring. It was a double-headed eagle with an intertwined VR. It was extremely small on the back of the cufflinks, but noticeable through a jeweler's loupe.

Without a word, I raised my left arm and pulled on the cuff, latching the first link through the buttonholes. I did the same for the right cuff.

The pawnshop owner smiled. "I knew it," he nodded, causing the flesh rolls under his chin to jiggle. "I knew it. Don't you worry, Mr. Rostov, I got the thieving bitch's information."

Reaching across the counter, I grabbed him by the shirt and dragged his considerable bulk closer. "What the fuck did you just say about my girl?"

His eyes bulged. "I'm sorry, Mr. Rostov. I didn't know! I didn't know! I'm sorry!"

I released him and wiped my hand on my trousers, then reached for my money clip. "How much?"

The man's eyes shifted. "Fifteen thousand."

I raised an eyebrow and said nothing.

He shook. "Did I say fifteen thousand? I meant twelve thousand ... no, eleven! Eleven."

The corner of my mouth quirked. The man obviously didn't realize he'd had ten carats of authentic

Burmese pigeon blood rubies, easily worth half a million dollars, in his brief possession.

I counted off fifty hundred-dollar bills and tossed them on the counter. I then snatched up a pen and pulled his receipt pad toward me. I wrote a location and six thousand dollars on the paper and signed it. "Here's five. Take this piece of paper to that location and you'll get the rest."

The man nodded.

I waited until I was in my car to smile.

I had to admit I wouldn't have thought my feisty *krasotka* would have had the stones to pawn my cufflinks.

Damn, this woman just became even more irresistible to me.

My cock hardened as I thought about all the creative ways I planned to punish my beautiful little thief.

CHAPTER 6

MARY

I raced home to my apartment, or should I say Fort Knox.

The Russian recently paroled prison crew was long gone and everything had been left neat as a pin, but completely changed.

All the windows now had black wrought-iron bars on them.

Adhered to the security motherboard next to the door was a Post-it with a stupefying eight-digit code to activate it.

There was another note in broken English saying to enter the code in backwards if we were ever in danger.

Yeah, sure.

No problem.

Turning to drop my purse on the end of the kitchen counter, I had to shove aside a small dictionary that passed for the new manual to our security motherboard.

Saving learning the second language of our new security system for later, I ran down the hall to my bedroom and stashed the money from the pawnshop in the best place I could think of, my underwear drawer.

I then hopped in the shower.

The entire time, I could hear the money calling out to me like *The Tell-Tale Heart*.

What had started out as a silly impulse now had me completely freaked out.

First thing tomorrow before class, I would head back to that pawnshop, turn in the slip, and get those cufflinks back.

With a towel wrapped around my torso, I swiped my palm across the steamed mirror before checking my phone.

It was seven p.m.

I had to hurry.

Vaska would be here in an hour and there was something about the man that told me he was the punctual sort.

Brushing out my wet hair, I wrapped it in Velcro rollers and quickly dried it.

After taking the rollers out, I grabbed a section and rolled it into a perfect victory roll off my forehead and inserted a few strategic bobby pins. I did the same for the other side, framing my face before using a red silk scarf as a headband. I knotted it below and to the side of my ear, letting the ends trail over my shoulder.

Applying a liquid black eyeliner for a quick cat eye and some crimson red matte lipstick, I raced into my bedroom to get dressed.

It was seven-forty p.m.

I had to hurry.

He would be here at any moment.

Inside my walk-in closet, I snatched the first outfit that caught my eye.

One of my favorite dresses.

It was an off-the-shoulder sailor print that had navy blue bands with white buttons across the upper arms, a bright red and white striped print across the torso, and an A-line navy blue skirt. I paired it with a pair of red ballet flats. Dumping the contents of my Hello Kitty purse onto my bed, I picked up my wallet, keys, and lipstick and tossed them into a smaller novelty purse shaped like a cherry.

As I headed down the narrow hallway, I leaned into the bathroom and grabbed my phone.

The screen lit up.

It was seven fifty-five.

Fuck.

I was almost late.

He would be here any minute.

Peeking through the curtains, I saw the same elegant black sports car Vaska was driving earlier pull up behind a rather ridiculously out of place gold Ferrari.

A car that ostentatious stuck out like a sore thumb in our slightly rundown neighborhood.

I couldn't even imagine the loser who probably drove it.

Hurriedly I headed to the front door and quickly locked it, then ran down the hallway.

Instead of turning right, which would have led to the front entrance walkway that Vaska was probably strolling up this very moment, I turned left.

Thankfully, the emergency exit in the building had been broken for years, so no alarm sounded when I hit the crash bar, crept out the back, and made my escape.

I crossed the lawn and slipped between two brick buildings before hailing a cab on the other side of the street.

Settling into the backseat, we were several blocks away before my heart stopped racing. It started up again when my phone pinged.

I pulled it out of my purse to see a text from Vaska.

Bad girl.

I stared at my phone for the rest of the ride, anxiously waiting to see if he would text me again.

Perhaps asking where I was, or why I broke our supposed date, or even if I had his cufflinks, but there was nothing.

My stomach clenched.

Usually when a man didn't text you it was because he was just being a pain in the ass, selfish boy.

This felt different.

Vaska not texting me again after that felt more … ominous.

Shaking off the feeling, I paid the cab driver and stepped onto the sidewalk in front of my favorite bookstore.

I thought about hiding from Vaska in the library since I had a paper on the use of voiceless alveolar lateral fricatives in language due for one of my English courses, but thought better of it.

There was no way I'd be able to concentrate.

Emma was working tonight at her job at the Newberry Library, so that would have been an option, if Dimitri hadn't texted me looking for her.

I warned Emma he was going all Angel from *Buffy* season two episode fourteen.

He was totally showing up there, and the chance that Vaska could be with him was too great to risk it.

I swung open the glass door and stepped inside the hushed atmosphere, leaving behind the bustle, car horns, and generous chaos of the Chicago city streets.

This was definitely a better plan.

I would spend the evening killing time, hiding amongst the stacks, sipping a café latte with an extra shot of vanilla.

After getting my drink, I wandered among the narrow stacks to the back right-hand corner of the shop.

Selecting Nick Groom's *The Vampire: A New History,* I settled into a cozy, slightly worn upholstered bucket chair and started flipping through the pages. The book was brand new and only available in hardcover.

As a poor graduate student, I didn't plunk down twenty-five bucks unless I was certain I'd enjoy the book.

I tried to engross myself in the chapter pertaining to Stoker's *Dracula* while thinking of the time when I would have my own classroom of English students to teach, but it was no use.

I couldn't stop thinking about another dangerously elegant man with a hypnotic gaze and seemingly supernatural influence over me.

I had literally known the man for barely twelve hours, and yet he consumed my thoughts.

There was just something so intense about him, an irresistible sexual pull. That I couldn't stop thinking about him or this morning was proof positive I needed to stay far away from him.

I would retrieve his cufflinks from the pawnshop and find a way to return them to him without actually seeing him.

I knew in my heart … and lower … I couldn't trust myself in the same room with the man.

I nodded.

It was settled.

I would return the cufflinks and walk—no, run—the other way.

I was so caught up in my thoughts I failed to notice the change in the store's atmosphere until it was too late.

There is a certain lullaby of sounds to any bookstore.

The soft tones of conversations in hushed whispers.

The *whoosh* of the steamer on the espresso machine.

The muted *ching* of the cash register when the drawer opens.

The sound of flapping bird wings a book makes when it's dropped with its pages open.

One by one those sounds disappeared, as if snuffed out like a candle.

I checked my phone.

It was only eight forty-five p.m.

Granted, it was a cold Tuesday night so there hadn't been many people in the store or the café part when I entered, but still they had at least another hour and a half before they closed.

Leaning forward in my chair, I strained to listen.

There was only silence.

The chimes sounding over the entrance doorway gave me a moment of ease until the silence resumed.

Then there came the unmistakable harsh metal clack of a lock being flipped into place.

Careful not to make a sound, I slid the book I had been reading onto the top of some books on a nearby shelf and stood.

My heart was pounding so loudly in my chest it was hard to listen for any other sounds. I opened my mouth to call out, but it was too dry to speak.

I licked my lips and tried again, calling out a hesitant, "Hello?"

No one answered.

No. One. Answered.

Then I heard it.

A heavy footfall.

Then another.

The measured step of someone wearing shoes … not sneakers like pretty much a hundred percent of the college students who liked to come to this bookshop.

One step.

Then another.

Closer and closer.

I shifted backwards, bumping into the bookshelf behind me. It rattled slightly.

The steps stopped.

I held my breath.

Then the footsteps started again.

Oh, God.

What was happening?

Were people still here in the store and just forced to keep quiet because someone was holding a gun?

That was the only scenario that made sense.

I needed to figure out what my options were. I could call nine-one-one, but if I spoke that would give away my location within the store. I was fairly certain what I'd heard was the front door being locked, so I couldn't risk making a run for it in that direction.

I could try to get to the unisex bathroom, but the door was really flimsy and the lock usually broken.

On the rare occasions I used it, I would always lean over and hold the knob, ready and eager to call out an 'occupied' at a second's notice.

There was probably another way out through the kitchen.

If I crept alongside the bookcase, maybe I could circle around.

Leaving my purse where it was, in case I needed my hands free, I put my phone in my pocket and crept along the edge of the aisle, straining to hear any more footsteps.

Then a low, measured voice broke the silence. "I know you're in here, Mary."

My hand flew over my mouth to stifle my cry.

It was Vaska.

A thousand questions flooded my brain.

How had he found me?

Why would he make everyone leave the store?

Did he know I'd pawned his cufflinks?

Was he now here to murder me because of it?

It sounded trivial, but there wasn't a doubt in my mind that Vaska was a dangerous man.

Dimitri, Emma's boyfriend, was dangerous too, but somehow he seemed like a different kind of dangerous.

The kind that was dangerous to other people, but not to her.

It was obvious he was enamored of Emma and would never hurt her.

I could not say the same for Vaska and me.

I was simply the girl he'd fucked this morning who'd then stolen his super-expensive eleven-thousand-dollar cufflinks on a lark and ditched him later.

Oh. My. God.

He's totally going to kill me.

I didn't have to date a lot of men to know that men like Vaska didn't enjoy having their egos bruised. Hell, that was the theme of half the action-adventure movies out there.

I was nothing to him, a nobody.

He would probably shoot me dead and not think twice about it.

Before I could decide what to do, he spoke again. "You've been a very bad girl, *krasotka*. Come out now and face your punishment before you make me any angrier than I already am."

Face my punishment?

My punishment?

Like my murder?

No, thanks.

Forcing my legs to move, I crept further down the aisle as I peeked over the tops of the books on the shelves, hoping for a glimpse that would tell me his position within the store.

As I got to the end, I bent my body in half and poked my head out.

He was several aisles over on the other side of the now empty store. Small café tables and the espresso counter lay between us.

If I bolted out of my hiding place fast enough, I could make it to the kitchen and out the back door.

Thank God I wasn't wearing heels right now.

I closed my eyes and said a quick prayer.

Then sprinted across the store.

I heard Vaska's shout through the loud rushing in my ears, but it only spurred me on faster.

I raced around the scarred wooden counter into the bright lights of the small kitchen.

Daring a glance over my shoulder, I saw Vaska, dressed in a button-down white shirt and a pair of jeans, vault over the counter as if it were nothing.

I ran past the stainless-steel tables and launched myself at the back emergency door.

I slammed my body weight against it.

It didn't budge.

I shouldered it a second time.

Nothing.

I scanned the door, but it was one of those industrial metal doors.

There was no obvious lock.

I was trapped.

"It looks like I have cornered a cute little rabbit."

I turned to see Vaska standing a few feet away, arms crossed over his chest. He'd rolled his sleeves up to expose all sorts of tattoos, both gray and black and colorful. I knew enough from Emma's book on the subject to know the gray and black ones were probably prison tattoos.

He is going to murder me, and they'll never find my body.

My frenzied gaze swept over the kitchen.

In desperation, I snatched up a knife from a nearby cutting board filled with lemon slices.

I held it out in front of me with both hands, pointing it directly at his chest.

Vaska's eyes narrowed as he slowly shook his head. "You shouldn't have done that, baby."

CHAPTER 7

MARY

"I'll give the money back! I didn't mean it! It was just a stupid prank."

Vaska's gaze shifted to the weapon in my hand. "Put down the knife."

I shook my head as I backed away. "No."

He uncrossed his arms and fisted his hands at his sides. "Mary, I will not ask again, put down the goddamn knife."

I tightened my grasp on the handle as my palms sweated. "I have the money. I'll give it back, I wasn't going to keep it. I'll get your cufflinks back, I promise."

"I don't give a fuck about the money and I already have my cufflinks back."

"You don't? Wait, you do? How?"

"Keep the money. I don't want it."

This made no sense.

He wasn't here about the money?

He wasn't here to murder me?

"If you don't want the money and you have your cufflinks, then what do you want?"

Vaska's lips lifted in a slow smile. "You."

The one word hit my gut like a lightning bolt, sending blistering heat from my core to my toes.

I had to force myself to remember he was not the type of man to be trusted. I was nothing but a conquest.

He'd have his fill before the week was over, leaving me feeling used and brokenhearted.

My chin jutted out. "I'd rather just give you back the money."

He raised an eyebrow. "Then I guess it is a good thing I don't plan on asking your permission."

My eyes widened.

He took a step forward, and I stumbled back, lifting the knife higher. "Stay away from me."

His dark gaze hardened. "No."

"This is crazy. You could have any woman you want. They probably fall into your bed. Go choose one of them. Why do you have to chase after me when I clearly don't want to be with you?"

He raised his arm to rub his lower jaw with his right hand as his gaze slipped from my face down my body and back up, leaving a trail of warmth on my skin as if he had physically touched me.

Keeping his gaze trained on me, he unbuttoned

the top buttons of his shirt, exposing tanned skin with thin swirls of dark hair.

"What ... what are you doing? Stop that!" I ordered.

He pulled his shirt from his jeans and finished unbuttoning it.

Helpless to resist, my gaze traveled over his heavily muscled and tattooed chest to his flat abdomen. His jeans rode low, showing off the sharp edges of his hipbones.

I swallowed.

He took a step forward.

I jerked my head up as I lifted the knife high again, having lowered my arms while distracted by the arrogant display of raw sexuality in front of me.

Vaska chuckled as he lowered his head to flick open the button over his jeans zipper, before once again piercing me with his dark hooded gaze. The swollen outline of his hard shaft was evident against his inner thigh.

My mouth fell open.

"We can do this the easy way or the hard way, baby girl, but either way that sweet pussy of yours is getting fucked tonight."

I gasped.

He stepped forward.

I tried to step back, but the cold rounded edge of a stainless-steel countertop prevented me. I waved the knife at him. "I mean it, Vaska. Stay back."

"No."

He stepped forward again. He was now only a few inches from the sharp tip of the knife.

"This is insane. The owner or staff could be back at any minute."

He smirked. "No, they won't, not with what I just paid them to convince them to stay away."

I inhaled a shaky breath. "Fine. A customer then."

"The door's locked."

My hands shook. "Stop having an answer for everything!"

He shifted forward. The knife point rested against his skin. "The only thing that will stop me from claiming you is if you kill me. Drive it in deep, *krasotka*. You'll need to use enough force to thrust past the bone and sinew to hit my heart."

I hesitated.

With a growl, he knocked the knife out of my hand and snatched me to him. Driving his hand into my hair at the nape of my neck, he forced my head back to claim my mouth.

His tongue thrust past my lips, giving no quarter as his other hand palmed my breast. His embrace was warm and strong as he lifted me high, placing me on the counter.

His hands cupped my knees and pushed my legs open so he could step between my thighs. His mouth ruthlessly fell on mine again as his hands pulled on the off-the-shoulder top of my dress.

I wasn't wearing a bra, so the movement exposed my breasts.

He latched on to my right nipple, pulling and sucking hard, sending shockwaves up my spine. With a hand in the center of my chest, he pushed me to lie back along the counter.

He then grabbed my hips and pulled me forward until my ass was on the edge of the counter and my legs were draped over his shoulders.

Flipping up my dress skirt, he stroked my pussy through the thin cotton of my panties.

"I'm flying you to Paris and buying you an entire wardrobe of lingerie. From now on, I only want to see the finest silk covering this pussy."

He slipped his fingers into the hem and tore the cheap cotton off me.

I cried out as I fisted the fabric of my dress skirt.

He lowered his head and slowly ran his tongue up along the seam of my pussy.

I closed my eyes and groaned.

"Eyes on me, beautiful," he commanded, and I obeyed.

I watched the erotic sight of his head once more lowering between my thighs to lick and taunt each sensitive nerve.

Swiping two fingers from my clit to my entrance, he used my arousal to push inside of me.

I groaned as my hips lifted off the counter. I was

still sore from this morning, but that didn't stop the wave of pleasure at his touch.

He pushed a third finger inside of me as his tongue flicked and swirled around my clit, until I was screaming his name as I climaxed.

His firm hand reached under my now pliant body and pulled me up to a sitting position. Leaving his hand on my lower back, he reached above us to a small shelf where there was a silver canister with a white nozzle and handle.

I had been a server enough times to know it dispensed whipped cream.

Holding the canister up, he ordered, "Open your mouth."

As my lips opened, he pressed the handle, sending a swirl of sweet, fluffy whipped cream onto my tongue.

I started to close my mouth, but he stopped me. "No, leave your mouth open. I want to watch the cream melt onto your tongue while I fuck you."

He unzipped his jeans and pulled out his cock.

Once more, I was struck with a shiver of trepidation over its size and girth.

Fisting its length, he stepped forward to position himself near my entrance.

I swallowed the whipped cream and placed restraining hands on his shoulders. "Wait. A condom."

His eyes narrowed. "I don't have one. I left them at your place."

I remembered the small pile he had tossed onto my bed, obviously planning ahead for later tonight.

I shook my head. "You can't."

He leaned in to kiss the side of my neck before whispering in my ear, "Not an option, baby. Don't worry, I'm clean and I know you are too. I also know you're on birth control."

I shifted back. It was true, but how would he know?

At my questioning look, he smiled. "Money buys a lot of things."

Apparently access to my college medical center records was one of them.

"But …."

He lifted the canister and sprayed more whipped cream into my mouth, preventing further objections. At the same moment, he grasped my hip with his free hand and thrust in deep, straight to the base of his cock.

My eyes widened. *Oh, God.*

He thrust as I clung to his shoulders. "Keep that mouth open, baby. I want to see the cream on your tongue."

The sweet cream dripped down the back of my throat as he thrust harder and harder, rocking my hips back and forth. My body stretched to accept him.

I had never felt so filled or overwhelmed in my life.

He sprayed more whipped cream into my mouth, then leaned over to lick a small dollop from the corner of my mouth.

His hips moved faster, driving hard into me. My stomach clenched as my legs tightened around his middle.

Throwing my head back, I clawed at his bare shoulders with my nails as I came for a second time that evening.

He wrapped his hands around my waist and lowered me to my knees.

"Keep that mouth open," he commanded.

He stroked his hard shaft several times before thick streams of come hit my tongue, mixing with the melted cream.

I let it slide down my throat before licking my lips.

Vaska groaned as he lifted me to my feet. "Jesus Christ, you're going to be the death of me."

We both glanced at the knife on the floor a few feet away. Taking me by the chin, he turned my face back to him. He winked as he pulled my dress back up into place. He then reached for his shirt and buttoned it as I smoothed down my skirt, grateful to feel my phone still lodged in the deep pocket.

It could have fallen out and smashed on the floor for all I would have noticed.

"Where are the rest of your things?"

Not trusting myself to speak just yet, I nodded toward the front of the store.

We left the kitchen, and I led him to the corner where I'd been sitting.

I picked up my cherry-shaped purse and retrieved the book I had been reading from where I had placed it on the shelf. "I just need to put this back."

He took it from my hands and read the title. He then smiled.

Walking down the aisle, he stopped before the vampire section and selected two more books--an anthology of classic Victorian vampire stories called *Dracula's Guest* and *The Lost Journal of Bram Stoker*. "You'll like these as well."

He read vampire stories?

Could this man get any sexier?

Reluctantly, I tried to hand them back to him. "I can't afford all of them. I'll just get the one."

He took all three books from me, wrapped an arm around my waist and marched me to the front of the store. "I have it on pretty good authority you just scored eleven grand of free money today. Besides, I'm buying."

I blushed. "Why do you not even seem mad about that?"

He shrugged. "You're not the first woman to steal from me. In all honesty, you're not even the first woman to pull a knife on me."

I certainly could believe that. Still, I fired back, "And here I thought I was special."

He ran the back of his knuckles down my cheek. "Oh, believe me, *krasotka,* you are definitely special. For starters, while you may not be the first woman to steal from me, you are the first to steal a half a million dollars from me."

My brow furrowed. "What are you talking about? I swear I only pawned the cufflinks you left behind."

He tapped me on the nose. "I know."

A half million dollars? For a pair of freaking cufflinks?

My chest tightened. "So you did come after me because of the money."

He shook his head. "No. I didn't lie. This has nothing to do with the money and, not to sound like an asshole, but it's a fairly inconsequential amount for me."

I huffed. "Must be nice. How did you find me, anyway?"

Turning away, he tossed a few twenties on the bookstore counter and gathered up my books. "Come on, I'm taking you home."

I let him change the subject—for now. "You can't come in. Emma might be there."

Leading me outside, he opened the passenger door to his car, which was parked right out front. "I'm not taking you back to your apartment. I'm taking you home."

He shut the door.

I had to wait as he circled around the back of the car and then got in on the driver's side. "Vaska, I'm not going home with you. This can't keep happening. Seriously. We have to stop. Plus, I have class tomorrow and a paper due."

As I rambled, he pulled away from the curb and went in the opposite direction of my apartment.

At the first stoplight, I let my hand drift toward the door handle.

The locks clicked loudly into place.

I swiveled my head to the left to see Vaska giving me a knowing look. Crossing my arms over my chest, I sighed. "Anyone ever tell you, you're an arrogant bastard?"

Vaska laughed. "All the time, but never from lips as sweet as yours."

My cheeks flamed. "We've already had sex. I don't know why you're dragging me back to your home."

"Because you owe me."

"I owe you? What?"

He had already said repeatedly he didn't care about the money and he had his super insanely expensive cufflinks back.

"A punishment."

My eyes widened. I licked my lips. "What do you mean, a … punishment?"

We stopped at another traffic light.

He reached over and hooked his hand around my neck, drawing me close. "Just because I forgive you for pawning my cufflinks, doesn't mean I will not punish you for it."

He kissed me hard on the lips before returning his attention to the road.

Just in case I was mistaken, I pulled on the door handle.

Locked.

The car roared forward into the dark night.

CHAPTER 8

VASKA

I finally would have her all to myself, and there would be no escape for her.

Turning off Michigan Avenue, I pulled onto Huron Street and after only two blocks, I steered the car into the underground garage of my building.

After parking, I hurried around the car to Mary's side, not entirely certain she wouldn't make a run for it.

It's not like we were in the middle of nowhere and I was her only option.

My home was in the center of downtown Chicago.

If she wanted to make a run for it, she could be out of the garage and into a taxi in seconds flat.

I opened the door, but Mary stayed seated.

"Mary."

She didn't respond.

"Mary, get out of the car."

Without turning her head, she said in a prim tone, "I would once more like to renew my objection and to request formally that you take me home."

Suppressing a smile, I responded, "Your formal request has been taken under consideration and is denied. Now get out of the car before I drag you out, flip up your skirts, and fuck you on the hood of this car."

She gasped and turned to me. "You wouldn't dare."

I gave her a stone-faced stare.

She got the message and got out of the car.

Placing a hand on her lower back, I guided her to the private elevators reserved for those tenants who had homes on the upper floors.

As the polished brass elevator doors closed, she cast a sidelong glance in my direction. "You wouldn't have really done that, would you?"

I shrugged. "There are several video cameras throughout the garage, which means I would have had to track down any security guard who had seen you naked and kill them, but yes."

She shook her head. "I can't tell if you're kidding or not."

I looked down at her.

Damn, she looked adorable.

Her red lipstick was smudged, giving her a thoroughly kissed appearance, especially with her still pink cheeks.

But it was her eyes that especially drew me in. They were the most fascinating color. Mostly a deep blue, but if you caught her in the right light, or the right mood, they turned a startling indigo. They were so expressive, giving away her every emotion. In this moment, they glowed with an exciting mix of fear and desire.

I winked at her but said nothing.

As we entered my home, I was strangely nervous.

This wasn't the first time I'd had a woman here, but this was the first time I gave a damn whether they liked it. I tossed my keys and wallet into the marble bowl on the entranceway table and strolled further inside, expecting Mary to follow.

She gasped as we entered the primary space. It was a mostly open floor plan taking up an entire floor of the building. She walked straight to the wall of windows and stared out at the glittering lights of the city below.

Turning her head to the left then right, she asked, "Is the entire place literally just a wall of windows?"

I nodded.

"Even in the bedroom and bathroom?"

I nodded again.

She smiled and turned back to the stunning view.

Although it was dark, you could make out some

whitecaps from the waves on Lake Michigan as the water hit Navy Pier.

"That is so cool! Can people see inside?"

"No, they tint the windows," I responded, incredibly pleased she seemed to like my home.

She turned her attention to the living room then strolled into the kitchen and the gaming room and the library beyond before returning.

While she explored, I selected a bottle of Château Margaux from the wine bar and poured us two glasses.

She joined me at the marble top kitchen island. "Why is everything so white?"

I glanced around. "What do you mean? There's color."

She laughed. "Black and white photographs, strictly speaking, don't count as," she held her hands up and did air quotes, "color. You have a white sofa, chairs, throw rugs, all the candles and decor. The library is even white with white bookshelves. Never in my life have I seen a *white* library. I'm surprised you didn't rebind the books in white leather."

I took a sip of wine as I thought about what she was saying.

No one had ever bothered to ask, so I'd never had to explain myself, but for some reason I wanted to tell Mary. "It sounds absurd to say it out loud, but when I was a child living in Russia things were very difficult. There was no money. It wasn't until the fall of the regime that my family regained their wealth. Until then, everything we owned was threadbare, used, or dirty. Now that I have money, I want things to always feel new and clean."

She lowered her gaze and stared at her hands.

I leaned over and lifted her chin. "What's the matter, *krasotka*?"

She sighed. "I wasn't expecting a sadly endearing reason from your childhood. I was half expecting you to say it was easier to see the blood splatter that way, and now I'm feeling guilty for thinking it."

I laughed and pushed the crystal wineglass toward her. "Drink."

Her eyes widened, and she stared at me as if I had just handed her a cup of poison. "No way! This is red wine."

"So?"

"I'm not drinking red wine in here! What if it spills on something?"

"Then I buy another one."

She shook her head and pushed the glass back toward me.

Without saying a word, I walked over to my white sofa, which was positioned to have a spectacular view of the lake and cityscape, and held my glass high over it.

Mary cried out, "No!"

Ignoring her, I poured the contents directly onto the fabric, permanently staining it. "Feel better now?"

She covered her mouth as she laughed. She was beautiful when she laughed. I would have to remember to make her do it more often. "I can't believe you just did that."

"Now will you have a drink with me?"

She took the glass and held it up in a silent toast before taking a sip. "You know, we could have just switched to vodka."

I tapped my forehead. "Now you tell me. I'm hungry. Did you eat?"

"Does a bag of Ruffles Sour Cream and Cheddar potato chips between classes count?"

"No."

"Then, no."

Taking her glass, I put both wineglasses down on the counter and took her hand, leading her past the ruined sofa and down the hallway that led to the bedrooms.

When I opened the first door, she pulled back. "Listen, I …."

"Calm down. Stay here."

I left and returned with my Russian National hockey team long-sleeved jersey. With its bold red color and the gold double-headed eagle emblazoned on the chest, it would match her coloring perfectly.

She was such a little thing it would fall almost to her knees.

"Change into this. You'll be more comfortable."

Before she could object, I left the room and

returned to the master suite, where I changed into a pair of gray sweatpants and a white t-shirt.

Padding in my bare feet back down the hallway to the kitchen, I pulled the ingredients I would need out of the refrigerator as I set a pan on the stove and melted the butter.

I was whipping the flour, sugar, salt, and whole milk in a bowl when she finally emerged. My hand stilled as I stopped and stared.

She lowered her head and tugged on the hem of the jersey as she tucked a lock of hair behind her ear. "Does this look okay?"

She was gorgeous.

There was no other word for it.

She had washed the rest of the makeup off her face. Her ivory skin glowed.

It was the first time I was seeing her lips without either red lipstick or the stain from it.

Her lips were actually a soft, pale pink. The same color as her nipples.

She had taken the rockabilly curls and scarf out of her hair, leaving it to fall in waves over her shoulders.

And the sight of this stunning creature in my favorite worn hockey jersey made my chest tighten with possessive need. I had never had this kind of intimacy with a woman before, and I was finally seeing the draw.

Placing the bowl on the counter, I crossed to her.

I slipped my hands to either side of her neck and

tilted her head back. Without saying a word, I claimed her mouth, needing to taste her more than I needed my next breath.

Swirling my tongue around hers, I lifted her high, wrapping her naked legs around my waist. I turned and placed her on the counter without breaking the kiss.

With a hand on her lower back I pulled her forward, rubbing my cock against her core.

The feel of her hands in my hair nearly drove me mad.

Showing enormous restraint, I broke free.

I still had plans for her, and they didn't include fucking her on a counter for a second time this evening. I wanted her in my bed, but first I had to feed her. Handing her a glass of wine, I returned to whipping up my ingredients.

Instead of trying to jump down, she crossed her legs and stayed on the countertop.

I tried to get a peek between her legs knowing she wasn't wearing any panties because I had torn them off her earlier, but she noticed and with a chastising glare, pushed the jersey fabric down to cover herself.

"What are you making?" she asked, as I slowly added the melted butter to my batter.

"Crepes."

"Seriously?"

"Yes, why?"

"I don't know. I figured you were going to say

something more down-to-earth, common, and less froufrou like pancakes."

"For starters," I glanced down at my hard cock that dangled between my legs, the outline visible through the sweatpants material, "there is nothing common about me."

She raised an eyebrow and smirked as her gaze went to my crotch. Her cheeks pinkened as she grabbed her wineglass and swallowed the rest of the contents.

I poured her another glass as I waited for the crepe pan to heat.

"Second, there is nothing froufrou about a crepe."

When the pan was hot and smeared with melted butter, I ladled out a small amount of the batter and spread it in a thin layer over the pan's surface. When it was ready, I flipped it, exposing its warm golden-brown side. I did this several times until we had a stack of about fifteen. I pulled the rest of the ingredients from the refrigerator.

Selecting a large glass platter from a nearby cabinet, I had to rinse off a layer of dust before using it. I rarely ate at home and had never cooked for a woman before, let alone gone to such an effort to entertain one.

Placing the fluffy folded crepes in one corner, I dolloped sour cream in the center and added some chopped hard-boiled egg, salmon caviar, and diced scallions.

This was one of my favorite dishes, so I always had the ingredients on hand.

Without bothering to move into the dining room, we stayed where we were with her cross-legged on the kitchen island and me leaning against it.

I prepared the first bite for her and held it just shy of her cute mouth. "Now, I cannot promise this will be the best crepe you've ever had, usually the batter is supposed to rest for at least an hour."

"Since I've never actually eaten a crepe in my life, I think you're good."

I forked the bite into her mouth.

She groaned as she chewed, catching a small drop of sour cream at the corner of her mouth with her fingertip before I could lick it with my tongue.

"Oh, my God! These are so good! They're so buttery and salty and delicious!"

I shrugged as I took my own bite. "What can I say? I'm a man of many hidden talents."

She tilted her head and looked at me as if she were seeing me differently. "You certainly are, Vasili Lukovich Rostov. How do you say this is delicious in Russian?"

I forked another piece past her lips. "*Eto vkusno.*"

She repeated, "Eetav … vos … co."

"Watch my mouth. Et … af … koos …na."

"*Eto vkusno,*" she said, getting it perfect the second time.

I fed her another bite. "You are a natural. I will have to teach you more Russian."

"Like what?" she asked, a teasing light in her eyes.

I leaned in closer and gently kissed her lips before rasping against her mouth, "Like, *potseluy menya*."

Pulling back and staring at my mouth, she was slightly breathless when she asked, "What does that mean?"

"I'd rather show you."

I then claimed her mouth with a growl. Shoving my hands into her silky hair, holding her head steady as I plundered her mouth.

I lifted her off the counter and carried her to my bedroom.

Placing her in the center of the bed, I stepped away and crossed to a nearby bureau. I opened the top drawer and withdrew a folded black leather belt. It was thick and heavy, but soft from repeated use. I tested the weight in the palm of my hand.

This bit of domestic intimacy had proven to me that Mary was different and very special.

For the first time in my life, I wanted a genuine relationship with a woman, but if this was going to work, she would have to learn to obey my rules.

Pulling stunts like selling my cufflinks at a seedy pawnshop or ditching our evening plans would not be tolerated.

Being with me would make her vulnerable to attacks from my enemies.

I wasn't too worried; I was powerful and feared enough to protect her, but only if she respected my rules.

Knowing her whereabouts wasn't about me being possessive or controlling, although in all honesty that was part of it, but mainly it was about keeping her safe.

I also grabbed several silk ties and turned back toward the bed.

Mary saw the belt in my hand and sat up.

She shifted her knees under her and shimmied back on the bed, her wary gaze shifting from my hands to my face. "What is going on, Vaska?"

I took a deep breath. "I told you I was bringing you here to punish you."

Her mouth fell open.

After a moment of stunned silence, she spoke. "I'm leaving."

"No, you're not."

"You can't keep me here against my will."

"Yes, I can, but we both know you're not here against your will."

"If you think I'm going to let you punish me like a naughty child, you're out of your mind."

"You openly defied me tonight, Mary. That cannot go unpunished."

She waved her arms in front of her. "Do you hear yourself? Do you hear how over-the-top insane that sounds?"

"You're in my world now. My world operates differently from yours. There are rules. Rules that need to be obeyed, or else."

"This is bullshit. I never wanted or asked to be dragged into your world. I was home minding my own business. *You* forced yourself into *my* world."

"Regardless, you're here now and here you'll stay."

She tried climbing off the bed.

Standing in her way, I wrapped my hand around her neck.

She stilled.

"Don't make this harder than it needs to be, *krasotka*. I'm not letting you leave this bedroom. Submit to me."

A single tear rolled down her cheek.

CHAPTER 9

MARY

I couldn't stop shaking.

Why was I doing this?

I could tell myself it was because he was forcing me, but I knew that wasn't entirely true.

Although I had no reason other than my gut, something told me Vaska wasn't a heartless monster.

I couldn't imagine he'd truly force me.

Of course, there were many types of force beyond just the physical.

There was his mesmerizing psychological hold on me.

There was something about this man that brought me to my knees.

I now found myself lying naked face down in the center of his bed. I cried out as he tightened the silk strap around my right wrist and secured it to the bedpost. My left was already secured.

I squeezed my eyes shut as more silent tears fell.

I startled at his touch on my back. It wasn't his hand. It was soft and warm, but firm.

Oh, God.

It was the belt.

My body trembled.

"Why are you being punished, Mary?" he asked in soft, yet carefully controlled tones.

I shook my head as I buried my head in his pillow. The spicy scent of his cologne that clung to the fabric was oddly soothing.

The belt caressed the curve of my ass.

"I asked you a question, Mary."

"I don't know," I choked out.

There was no noise, not even a whisper of leather against skin. No warning.

The leather belt came down across my ass.

My mouth opened, but no scream came out as my skin erupted into fiery needles.

I pulled on my wrists.

The belt struck me a second time.

"Don't lie to me, Mary. Now, why are you being punished?"

"Because I pawned your cufflinks."

The belt slapped against my upper thighs. "Wrong."

I let out a low keening wail and desperately tried to give him the answer he wanted. "Because I wasn't at my apartment when you came."

I tried to twist my hips away but his hand wrapped around my left ankle, holding my body in place.

He ruthlessly snapped the leather tongue of the belt against my ass cheeks again and again.

I screamed and cried. "I don't know what you want! Stop! Stop!"

He rubbed the palm of his hand against my punished skin.

His touch was more threatening than soothing. "You're being punished because you disobeyed me."

My body shook as I pulled on my binds. My ass and thighs were on fire. Even making the slightest move seemed to make the pain worse.

The bed dipped. Risking a glance over my shoulder, I saw him kneeling between my thighs.

He had taken off his clothes.

All I could see was thick muscle, scary tattoos, and the beast coming to life between his legs.

I shut my eyes.

How could he possibly think to fuck me like this? There was no way I would be wet. It would hurt like hell. Would he stop if I begged him?

Something touched my pussy, but it wasn't his fingers.

Holding himself up on one arm, he leaned over my body and held the belt up for my inspection. The black leather had a dark, wet stain on it. My arousal.

"It looks like my baby likes the pain," he rasped in my ear.

His pillow muffled my reply as I buried my head in shame. "No. No, I don't."

"You're lying to me again, and I can prove it."

He rose on his haunches and teased my pussy with his fingers, then I felt something hard press against my asshole.

I jerked. "No! Don't!"

Despite my pleas, he pushed his thumb in deep.

I was in agony.

The humiliation hurt as much as the unwanted intrusion.

He thrust his thumb in and out.

I kicked my legs as I drove my fingernails into my palms.

"Admit you were a bad girl."

With no hesitation, I did what he wanted, hoping it would end my torment. "I was a bad girl."

"And what happens to bad girls?"

I sniffed. "They get punished."

He pushed his thumb in deep as he thrust two fingers into my still-sore pussy.

How could something so painful feel so good at the same time?

I felt filled and dominated and overwhelmed. I just wanted to collapse at his feet and submit to whatever he wanted.

The idea terrified me.

He pumped his fingers in and out of my pussy as he kept his thumb buried in my ass. His hard thighs kept me from twisting my hips or closing my legs. He then spanked me with his free hand.

"Are you going to disobey me again?"

"No," I cried. I would have admitted to anything and told him anything in that moment.

"Tell me you're mine."

"Please, Vaska. I can't. This is … it's too much."

He pulled on my hair, sending a sharp sting over my scalp and down my spine. "Tell me," he ground out.

"I'm yours! I'm yours."

What was beyond sick and twisted, I wasn't even lying.

I was his completely in that moment.

He owned me, body and soul.

My back bowed as he pulled his fingers free and pinched my clit.

Against my will, an orgasm was torn from my body like a scream.

It was the most intense, most extreme emotional and physical release of my life.

And in that moment, I hated Vaska with a vengeance for forcing it on me.

I didn't want to feel anything this deeply, this completely.

It was too much.

A pane of glass shattered in my mind, the pieces never to be whole again.

This. This right here is what I'd been worried about, what I feared about getting involved with a man like him.

I knew, instinctively I knew, I would not survive intact.

Even if I left this bedroom never to set eyes on him again, I would never be the same.

No woman survived a man like this.

He would devour me whole, leaving only a shell behind when he was finished with me.

And I had just given him the power to destroy me by submitting to him.

In the aftermath, I shook violently; even my teeth rattled. I barely felt it when he released my wrists.

He pulled a blanket over both of us and tried to pull me close to his body from behind.

I turned on him with nails bared. "Get off me! I hate you! I hate you!"

I clawed at his chest, drawing blood.

He captured my wrists and pulled my arms over my head before pinning my body beneath the weight of his own. His mouth crashed down on mine, swallowing my protests.

I tore my lips away, burying my face in his neck as I cried.

He let go of my wrists and cradled my head as he

rolled to the side, holding me close. He whispered to me in Russian as he kissed my head and stroked my hair. *"Ya tak vinovat, krasotka. A nikogda ne khotel, chtoby eto proizoshlo. Ya ne mogu eto ob"yasnit', no ya znayu, chto shchas ne mogu otpustit' tebya."*

Then remembering I didn't speak his language, he repeated, "I'm so sorry. I never meant for this to happen. I don't know how to explain it, but I know I can't let you go now."

I tried to push back, but his arms tightened around me.

He reached up and cupped my face, brushing away my tears with his thumb.

My lips trembled. "Yes, you can. You can let me go. We only just met. You know nothing about me."

"I know enough to know I want to know more."

"But why? Why me?"

He shook his head slowly. "I can't explain it. There is an energy, a spark, about you that calls to me. I felt it the moment I first laid eyes on you."

My eyes teared up again. "You're going to break my heart, aren't you?"

His lips thinned as his eyes hardened. Still, he answered with a raw honesty that shocked me. "Yes."

I lifted my hands to touch his face as I pleaded, "Then why are you doing this to me? Why chase me down? Just let me walk away before this goes too far, before it's too late for both of us."

His warm palm settled over my hand and he looked deeply into my eyes. "*Net.*"

I didn't have to speak Russian to know that was a no.

It was too late. I was already his.

CHAPTER 10

MARY

My phone rattled on the counter.

I ignored it.

I pulled the security system's instruction manual closer. "It says here you need to press star and pound at the same time, then enter the number twenty, then enter the installer four-digit code, then press star ninety-nine."

I looked over my shoulder at Emma who was standing in front of what we were now officially calling the motherboard.

She threw her hands up in frustration. "You can't be serious. Is that what it really says?"

I picked up the book and walked over to her. "Swear to God, see for yourself."

We were both home trying to figure out our new security system.

Emma told me how Dimitri had gotten a call

early this morning and had to leave town suddenly on business.

I didn't mention to her I'd been in the car with Vaska when her boyfriend received that call.

Vaska had been taking me home after I spent the night with him.

After my emotional outburst, he'd held me tight for the rest of the night.

It was strange. I had spent the night with a man before of course, but with Vaska it was different. It was hard to explain. The few and far between times in the past, it had been just sleeping next to someone.

With Vaska, it was sleeping within his protective embrace.

There wasn't a single moment the entire night that I hadn't been aware of his arm around my waist or his body next to mine. It was so warm and cozy it was hard not to feel safe and loved.

And that was the most dangerous thing of all.

I wasn't safe with him and I sure as fuck wasn't loved.

Allowing myself to fall in love with Vaska was like Buffy falling for Spike.

It was all kinds of fucked up wrong and everyone knew it wouldn't end well. So why do it? Why does anyone fall for the bad boy?

For the excitement of the fast ride, certainly not for the inevitable crash.

Vaska wasn't just a romantic bad boy—he was a *bad man*.

His phone conversation with some unknown man and then Dimitri this morning proved it.

There was something about a delayed shipment of surface-to-air missiles and over five hundred cases of Winchester Magnum sniper rifles to Morocco.

I didn't know what was worse. The fact that Vaska felt comfortable enough to openly chat about whatever super illegal arms deal he was putting together right in front of me, or the fact that I didn't seem to care.

It was probably the casual business vibe to the entire conversation. There was no cloak and dagger, or threats of violence, or *Godfather* quotes about *the heat* being on them and owing favors. It was actually a pretty boring conversation about contract payments and shipping containers and papers for the port authority.

As Emma was reading, my phone rattled again.

I had turned the ringer off and put it on vibrate.

I wasn't brave enough to turn it completely off.

Emma shot me a look and nodded in the direction of my phone. "Is that another text?"

I pretended to study the security manual. "Yep."

"You're not even going to look at it?"

"Nope."

The phone rattled again.

This time it kept rattling.

Emma spoke up again. "That sounds like a phone call."

I nodded. "Probably."

"And you're not going to answer it either?"

"Nope."

"You want to tell me what's going on?"

I put the manual down. "I have to start getting ready for work. You're coming to help tonight, right?" I asked, trying to change the subject.

I had a shift at the Last Call Bar tonight as a bartender and Emma had agreed to help me out since my boss said we were going to be short-handed and there was a big party of pharma assholes who would be there drinking and being generally obnoxious.

Emma's eyes narrowed. "What aren't you telling me?"

I hesitated.

Her head tilted to the side as her hands went to her hips. "Come on! I told you about how Dimitri …." she lowered her voice and continued in a conspiratorial tone, "*spanked* me last night. And you're not going to share with me? That is so unfair!"

She was right.

There was no reason why I couldn't tell her.

There was just something holding me back.

Like how Buffy didn't tell her friends about Spike at first. Maybe I was afraid of being judged for entering into a relationship with a man I was certain was wrong for me and going to break my heart.

I returned to the kitchen and pulled out two shot glasses and the bottle of Jose Cuervo. Emma grabbed the Doritos from the pantry cabinet.

I poured us both a shot. We raised our glasses high and then shot the cheap tequila down.

I took a deep breath. "I had a one-night stand last night."

Emma poured us a second shot. "You slut!" she laughed.

I knew she was teasing because that was what I'd teasingly called her when she confessed her initial one-night stand with Dimitri.

She continued, "I want all the dirty details."

I smirked. "Let's just say you weren't the only one who got," I leaned in and, using her same conspiratorial whisper from earlier, confessed, "*spanked* last night," before biting into a nacho chip.

Emma cried out in delight as she slapped her palm on the counter. "I knew I couldn't be the only book nerd with a kinky side."

I shrugged. She leaned over the counter and asked, "Who was it?"

"No way. I'm not saying."

"You have to tell me!"

"Nope."

It wasn't time to tell her.

It was obvious that what she had with Dimitri was real and could turn into a legitimate relationship.

There was no point in muddying that up by

announcing I was fucking her boyfriend's business partner. That would only complicate things, especially when the inevitable crash came.

"I know it can't possibly be a graduate student. I can't imagine any of those geeks having the balls to pull off the whole *are you my bad girl* kinky spanking in bed," she said, mimicking Dimitri's deep voice and Russian accent.

My cheeks flamed as I ducked my head and turned my attention to selecting the perfect Dorito chip.

She wasn't fooled. Her hand covered her mouth as she laughed out loud again. "Oh, my God, you slut! That's what the mystery man said in bed, wasn't it? Wasn't it? Fess up!"

I shoved a chip in her mouth to stop her from talking. "Fine. Yes, that is what he said, among other … dirty things."

Emma's eyes lit up. "It's sexy as hell, isn't it? Especially when he growls it like he's mad, but you know he isn't really all that mad, but you kind of want to make him even madder to see if he'll growl again."

I buried my head in my hands and groaned. Without looking up, I said, "That is exactly what it's like. What is wrong with us?"

Emma shrugged as she selected another chip. "Nothing. You said yourself only a few hours ago there is nothing wrong with enjoying a little kink."

I looked up. "Yes, but that was when it was *you*."

"What is that supposed to mean? It only applies to me? Are you saying you don't believe that?"

I sighed and reached for the shot Emma had poured.

I really could only have one more after this. I had to work in less than an hour, but there was no getting through this conversation completely sober.

"No, I was just saying what I thought you needed to hear, but I'm just not sure I'm the kinky type."

Emma tilted her head and stared at me. "You wear red high heels with jeans and have every animal print dress imaginable, but don't think you're the kinky type?"

"It was a lot more intense than I thought it would be. It was almost cathartic in a strange fucked-up way."

She nodded sagely. "I totally get that."

"It's not how it looks in the movies, though. It's just supposed to be a little slap and tickle, all in fun. What this guy did to me last night … let's just say it was a helluva lot more than an innocent slap and tickle."

"Did you like it?"

"What?"

"Did you like it? Nothing else really matters if you liked it."

"That's just it, I'm not sure how I felt about it. It was sexy but overwhelming and more than a little scary at times and then when it was over I wasn't sure if I wanted to run away, claw his eyes out, or kiss him."

I drank the shot and relished the burn of the tequila, hoping the sting would bring clarity.

Emma thought about what I said for a minute. "Maybe he did it wrong?"

The idea of her thinking Vaska was inept in the bedroom had me choking on my shot.

Emma had to pat me on the back to get me to stop. Wiping away tears, I responded, "No. Trust me, he did it right."

My phone rattled again.

We both stared at it.

It then rattled again.

Seeing the intent in her gaze, I dove for it the same time she did.

"Don't you dare!"

"Just let me peek!" she cried out as we wrestled for control of the phone.

I snatched it out of her grasp and shoved it in my cleavage.

She pouted. "Spoilsport."

She reached for the bottle and poured us a final shot. "There is only one thing left to ask … WWBD?" She held the shot glass out to me.

What would Buffy do?

It really was amazing how many of life's dilemmas could be solved by that show.

I laughed and answered, "She'd fuck Spike's

brains out and to hell with the rest."

"To Buffy and Spike!" Emma shouted before we drank together.

I headed down the hallway to my bedroom to get ready for work.

Digging the phone out from inside my bra, I looked at the missed phone calls and texts.

They were all from Vaska.

8:10a.m. Call me.

8:12a.m. Missed call from Vaska

8:17a.m. Baby, talk to me.

11:03a.m. Lunch?

11:15a.m. Missed call from Vaska

11:17a.m. Heading into a meeting. Will call when done. Pick up.

3:23p.m. Missed call from Vaska

3:34p.m. Missed call from Vaska

3:35p.m. Baby, do I need to remind you about the rules? Pick up your phone.

4:07p.m. Mary, you're starting to anger me.

4:28p.m. Missed call from Vaska

4:29p.m. Ty moya. Pomni ob etom.

The last text was in Russian.

I'm not sure if that meant he'd just slipped into his native tongue accidentally, or that's what happened when he was really pissed off.

I copied the phrase and pasted it into Google translate.

You are mine. Remember that.

Damn.

I had to give it to him.

That was sexy as hell.

I still wasn't going to answer.

Whether it was self-preservation or just sheer stupidity, I had no intention of ever seeing Vaska again.

Call me a coward. Call me a fool for passing on the best sex of my life, but I had no choice. Buffy had freaking superpowers, I didn't.

After getting ready, it took us fifteen minutes to leave the apartment. Fourteen and a half of them were trying to figure out how to arm the security system. Eventually we gave up since we were going to be late.

As we left, Emma pointed out the gold Ferrari parked on the street out front.

"Whose car do you think that is?"

Mine, I almost answered.

That had been another fun little surprise from Vaska.

Before getting out of his car this morning, he'd pointed to that incredibly over-the-top sports car and told me it was now mine and tried to hand me the keys. I'd thought he was kidding at first. When I learned he was serious, I adamantly refused.

That's when he grabbed me to him, kissed me senseless, and told me as his baby girl I would have to get used to being spoiled.

His baby girl.

Swoon.

Damn him.

I'd stashed the car keys in my underwear drawer with my ill-gotten cash from pawning his cufflinks. I had no intention of ever getting behind the wheel. Imagine me, a poor graduate student and future teacher, rolling up to class in that gold monstrosity?

When the timing was right, I would give them both to Dimitri and have him return them to Vaska. Hopefully, Dimitri wouldn't ask too many questions.

Answering Emma, I said, "Probably some dumb chick who should know a car like that is out of her league and she is way too inexperienced to handle it."

Emma gave me an odd look. "Or that douchebag who just moved into 4B. The one who practically screams *I'm a drug dealer.*"

"Yeah, or him," I agreed lamely. "Let's grab a cab at the curb."

Just then my phone vibrated inside my purse like a literal tell-tale heart.

I didn't look. I still felt the fiery brand in my chest from his last text message.

You are mine. Remember that.

CHAPTER 11

MARY

He'd pulled out a gun.

A gun.

A fucking gun.

I couldn't smother my shocked gasp.

Dimitri turned on me, eyes narrowed.

I froze.

He then looked over my shoulder to Mike, my bar back. "You there. Make some fucking noise."

Mike jumped to do his bidding, shouting at the kitchen staff to bang pots together.

Dimitri turned his gaze back on me. "Step back and cover your ears."

I obeyed as I cringed against the dingy white subway tile wall of the kitchen.

He aimed at the door handle and fired.

The sound reverberated around my brain,

crashing through my emotions, forcing an undeniable truth on my reluctant mind.

This was what it was truly like to date a man in the mafia.

The evening had started out boringly normal.

Emma and I had shown up at the Last Call Bar, where I worked as a bartender some weekday evenings when needed and most weekends.

Since we were short-staffed and had a big group of businesspeople slumming it there for an off-the-books pharma party, David, my boss, was grateful I'd brought Emma to help out. She often picked up a random shift or two.

She didn't know how to bartend, so she usually just helped me behind the bar by clearing glasses, cutting lemons and limes, and fetching liquor from the back.

Everything had been going fine.

I mean the customers were rowdy assholes who thought tipping a dollar on a nine-dollar craft beer made them some kind of high tipper and entitled them to a free round of grab ass, but that wasn't anything I couldn't handle.

Then Dimitri showed up looking like Thor after someone stole his favorite hammer.

"Where is she?" he demanded.

After scanning the bar and asking Mike, we realized she had gone in the back to fetch some rum from the liquor cage but hadn't returned in some time.

I'd been so busy making slippery nipple shots for a bunch of snickering idiots I hadn't even noticed.

Rule number one in bartending is never abandon your bar.

Fuck that rule. If I got fired, I got fired.

I hated this job anyway.

If Emma was in trouble, it was my fault for asking her to work a shift and not paying closer attention.

Motioning for Mike to follow me, we left the bar and raced after a charging Dimitri as he barreled through the crowd, making his way to the small square of fluorescent light from the staff door leading into the kitchen that shone like a beacon through the dense fog of music, vape smoke, and drunken bodies in the dimly lit bar.

We caught up to him just as he was rattling the handle of the liquor cage door.

It was locked.

Why was it locked?

That door was never locked during service.

Oh, God, Emma!

After I confirmed that Emma could be locked in there, Dimitri pounded on the door, demanding it be opened.

Turning, I raced down the narrow hallway back into the main kitchen and cried out to get the attention of our grill cook. "Phil! Phil! Find David. Tell him it's an emergency. We need the key to the liquor storage."

David was probably holed up in the storage room that passed for a manager's office on the other side of the building.

He was the only one with the key we needed. It wasn't that unusual for someone to lock the liquor room innocently. Usually it was a new employee who thought they were being extra conscientious by securing the booze.

The problem was we didn't have any new staff and Emma still hadn't reappeared, which meant odds were she was in there. Someone could easily unlock the door from the inside.

The fact that she wasn't opening it must have meant that someone was *preventing* her from opening it.

We used the word emergency pretty frequently in the hospitality industry.

Running out of fries was an emergency.

No paper in the credit card machine was an emergency.

Having to pee and no one to watch your bar was an emergency.

Fortunately, David knew that in the hierarchy of emergencies, running out of liquor when the bar was packed ranked pretty high, so I was certain he would drop everything and haul ass down here to reopen it for us, no questions asked.

I ran back down the hall to tell Dimitri that help was on the way, when I saw him pull out his gun.

Before I could do more than gasp, he had fired the handle off the door and kicked it open.

Some piece of shit had Emma pinned against the cage wall.

The look of sheer terror on her face brought tears to my eyes.

Before any of us could react, Dimitri pulled the man off Emma and shoved the end of his gun into the guy's mouth.

Oh, my God!

He was going to blow the man's head off, right here and now.

Right in front of all these witnesses.

Without even looking over his shoulder, he barked a command. "Get her out of here."

The whole violent scene had me so stunned I didn't react at first.

Dimitri called out again, "I said get her out of here!"

This time I snapped out of it and sprang forward, wrapping my arms around a struggling Emma and dragging her out of the small room as she cried and reached for Dimitri. "Come on, Emma. You don't need to see this."

"No! Dimitri! Don't, please!" She continued to struggle in my grasp.

I called out to Mike, "Mike! Help me."

With his help, we dragged her out of the liquor room and down the hallway.

Emma kept pleading and calling out to Dimitri. "You have to stop him! He can't do this! Please! Dimitri! Please!"

The sight of her torn shirt and tearstained eyes made my stomach heave with revulsion.

This was my fault.

My best friend had been attacked because of me.

I should have kept her closer.

I should have protected her.

I knew the assholes tonight had the potential to get out of hand, I should have been more cautious.

Why hadn't I thought to make Mike do the liquor runs and keep Emma behind the bar?

I swiped at the tears streaming down my face and blurring my vision.

Emma broke free and ran back down the hallway.

I caught her before she reached the threshold of the liquor room.

I didn't know what Dimitri was doing to that man in there, but I did know two things. One, the fucking predator deserved it and two, Emma shouldn't see it.

As I placed my body in front of her and latched onto her upper arms, holding her back, she cried out, "Dimitri, I need you! Please, don't do this!"

Her plea broke my heart.

Finally, David arrived with two bouncers in tow.

Phil must have alerted him that the situation was way beyond just a locked door.

I motioned behind me with my head as I held a crying Emma close. I shuffled us both closer to the wall as they passed. Just as they neared, the asshole who'd attacked Emma ran straight into their arms. They dragged him off.

I couldn't believe he wasn't covered in blood … or dead.

Even more, I couldn't believe Dimitri was just letting him leave.

Then cold, hard reality hit me.

He wasn't letting that man *live*.

He was just letting that man *leave*.

He recognized there were too many witnesses here. That man would be dead before morning.

I tried to summon up some moral outrage but couldn't.

He had attacked my friend.

And judging by how arrogant and bold he'd been to do it in a crowded bar, she probably wasn't the first woman he'd attacked.

Nope. No matter how I thought about it, I couldn't conjure up one hot give a damn for that dead-man-walking asshole.

Dimitri emerged from the room, tucking his gun behind him in the waistband of his jeans. Emma broke free of my grasp and ran to him. He enfolded her in his embrace.

A minute ago he'd been this larger-than-life raging beast about to tear the head off the man who'd hurt Emma, and now he looked like a big teddy bear as he held her close and whispered soothing words against the top of her head.

She looked so tiny in his embrace, like a little living doll, and yet instead of being crushed by his paws, she was held gently, almost reverently.

I was watching a live version of that scene from *Beauty and the Beast* after the Beast saved Belle from the wolves.

This was love.

This man loved her and would move heaven and hell for her, of that I was certain.

It was a remarkable moment to watch. It made little sense. They were nothing alike. They came from two completely different worlds and they barely knew one another, but this was love.

If it were a romance novel, it'd be called *The Bad Man and the Librarian*. There was a pang of slightly jealous longing in my chest.

I thought of Vaska and all that I was walking away from with him.

No, I wasn't just walking away; I was full tilt running away.

Was I making a mistake in not giving him a chance?

Dimitri and Emma approached me.

Guilt practically bringing me to my knees, I

touched her arm. "I'm so sorry, Emma. I didn't know."

We hugged each other. "It wasn't your fault. I should have realized he followed me back here."

"I'm going to clock out. We'll go home. I'll run you a bath and—"

Dimitri interrupted me. "She's coming home with me."

I swiped at my tears, careful to wipe under, not over, my lashes so I didn't hopelessly smear my mascara. "Of course. Yes, that would probably be best."

Emma tried to object. "But—"

Dimitri wasn't having any of it. "You are in enough trouble as it is, *moya kroshka*. Don't push me on this. You are coming home with me."

I patted her arm. "It's fine, Emma. You should go with Dimitri."

It was only right. After a terrible experience like that, she'd want to feel safe and protected, and it was obvious she felt that way with Dimitri.

Still Emma objected. "Dimitri, Mary has had a scare too. I don't want her to be alone right now."

I shook my head and tried to reassure Emma I was perfectly fine and capable of taking care of myself when Dimitri interrupted after typing a quick text to someone. "Mary, you remember my friend, Vaska Lukovich?"

Fuck.

Fuck.

Fuck.

Please don't say what I think you're about to say, I silently prayed.

My throat closed. I couldn't speak, so I just nodded, afraid even that was giving away too much.

"Good. He is on his way over here to escort you home. He will also stay as long as you need."

I shook my head violently as a hot flush crept up my chest and cheeks.

This couldn't be happening.

I had been avoiding Vaska's calls and texts all day.

Visions of last night and his hand on that folded leather belt and my aroused reaction to being punished started pummeling my already bruised mind.

"That isn't necessary. I'm fine getting home on my own. Really."

Desperation made my voice high-pitched and strained-sounding.

Dimitri stared at me with one eyebrow raised.

He knew.

It was all over my face.

I might as well have it scrawled across my forehead in Sharpie marker: *I fucked your friend and now I'm avoiding him.*

Dimitri placed his arm more securely around Emma before responding in that commanding tone that allowed no argument. "It's done. I recommend you be here when he arrives."

He leaned down to meet my gaze even more directly. "He doesn't have my *sweet* demeanor and will be upset if he has to … track you down."

My eyes widened. "Yes, sir," I squeaked out past my stiff lips.

The moment Dimitri and Emma left I raced behind the bar and grabbed my purse and turned to leave.

David called out to me, "Where are you going? You still have a shift to finish!"

I stopped and turned pleading eyes to Mike, who was standing nearby.

He nodded in understanding. "Don't listen to him. I've got this covered. Go."

Not wanting to risk leaving by the front entrance, I ran through the kitchen and swung open the back exit door—and ran straight into a brick wall.

CHAPTER 12

VASKA

I wrapped my arms around Mary.

Thank God she was safe.

When I'd gotten the call from Dimitri about someone attacking Emma, I was already on my way here.

I had given Mary space all day, but my thin patience was at an end.

I used the tracking software I'd installed on her phone when she unlocked it for me yesterday to find her location.

I flexed my hand, wincing at the sting from my cut and bloody knuckles. That's what I got for punching the back window of my Mercedes. I was so furious she had put herself in danger by coming to this dive bar I'd punched the first thing I'd seen. It hadn't helped. I was still pissed.

Fortunately, I would take out my rage on the man

who attacked Emma later. One of my men was tracking him down and bringing him to the warehouse at this moment.

But for now, my primary concern was Mary.

I set her away from me and looked her up and down, wanting to be certain she wasn't injured in any way.

What I saw had me clenching my jaw so tight I thought I'd cracked a tooth.

"What the fuck are you wearing?"

She blinked. "What?"

"Are you telling me you wore this in a room full of drunk men?"

She looked down at her clothes, then back up at me. "There is nothing wrong with my outfit."

"The hell there isn't," I raged.

My girl loved that distinctive rockabilly style, which fit her personality perfectly.

The problem was it also fit her curves, creamy skin, and red lips.

Tonight she was wearing skintight black pants with an off-the-shoulder black top with obviously no bra underneath and a suggestive sequined heart over each breast. Around her throat was a silk red scarf, which drew attention to her lush cleavage and brought to mind tying her to a bed and fucking her senseless.

And if I was thinking it, then you know every

goddamn piece of shit in that bar had been thinking it too.

I couldn't contain my rage. "You're damn lucky you weren't attacked like Emma. You are never to set foot in this bar again, do you hear me?"

She pulled away from me. "That's going to be pretty hard since I work here."

She worked here?

How had I not known?

I should have known that and prevented her from coming in tonight.

This is what I got for trying to play the gentleman and give her space to get accustomed to the idea that she now belonged to me.

From this point forward, there were going to be some new rules for my baby, and rule number one was she no longer worked here or anywhere.

If she needed money, I would give it to her and she sure as hell wouldn't be going to any more bars alone without me by her side.

I grabbed her by the chin and tilted her head back. "You *used* to work here. I forbid you to come here again."

She turned her head, breaking my grasp. "You forbid it? You *forbid* it?"

I crossed my arms over my chest. "That's right. *I forbid it.*"

She mimicked my stance and crossed her arms over her chest.

The movement pushed her breasts up and had my cock lengthening.

This was ridiculous; I would not stand in the middle of a fucking parking lot arguing with her.

I would get her home and we could finish this conversation with her over my knee with a red ass, until she pleaded for me to forgive her for putting herself and her friend at risk.

She visibly bristled. "Well, you can take that forbid and shove it up your—"

The metal exit door swung open, interrupting her.

A man in a wrinkled t-shirt and pair of jeans burst over the threshold, his arm raised, pointing a finger at Mary. "Mary, if you don't get your pretty ass back behind that bar, you're fired."

Mary rounded on him. "David, you can't expect me to—"

I grabbed him by the throat and lifted him off the ground as I walked forward the two steps necessary to shove him against the grimy brick wall. "What the fuck did you just say to my girl?"

He clawed at my hand as his feet kicked out in vain. "Nothing," he choked out. "Nothing."

I tilted my head to the side. "Really, because I could have sworn you said something disrespectful about her pretty ass?"

David shook his head as much as my grip would allow.

I opened my hand, allowing him to crumple to the ground among the refuse the rats had scattered after digging in the dumpster.

His shoulders heaved as he choked, trying to catch his breath. Finally, he rasped, "I'm sorry, Mary. Take all the time you want."

I rested my hands on my hips as I stared down at him in disgust. "And she's not fired?"

David waved his hand, palm up. "No. No, of course not."

I grabbed Mary's hand. "Good, because she quits."

I dragged her toward my car.

She pulled on my grasp. "No, I don't! I don't quit! You can't tell him I quit."

"I just did."

"You have no right to order me about like this."

I released my grip on her hand and took a step forward, caging her between me and my car. I planted my palms on the hood and leaned down, my mouth a few inches from hers.

"How many times do I have to tell you that you're mine now? And I have every right to say that no woman of mine works anywhere, let alone shows off her tits at some sleazy bar for tips," I ground out.

Her eyes widened as her mouth dropped open, right before she raised her leg to knee me in the balls.

Fortunately for me … and my balls … I knew her well.

Just like I'd known to go to the back entrance and

not the front, anticipating she would try to sneak out that way. I shifted back as my right hand reached down to grab her under that knee. I swung her leg out and stepped forward.

Pushing my hard cock against her core.

I wrapped my hand around her throat and tilted her head back.

I whispered harshly against her lips, "Go ahead, *krasotka,* keep testing my patience. Don't think I won't drag these tight jeans off your body and fuck that pretty ass of yours raw before putting a bullet in David's head, solving both of my problems."

I ground my hard cock against her pussy to emphasize my intent.

I then claimed her mouth.

She tried to resist, but I pressed my fingers against her soft cheeks, forcing her lips open.

This wasn't a kiss, it was an ultimatum.

She either stopped fighting me or faced the consequences.

To my surprise, after her initial resistance, she kissed me back. Her fingers delved into my hair as I wrapped my arms tight around her.

Every nerve in my body screamed for release but I broke the kiss.

Resting my forehead against hers, I inhaled several deep breaths and tried to cool my blood. I badly needed to sink my cock deep into her sweet pussy but not here, not in some filthy parking lot where anyone could be watching.

Picking her up, I carried her around to the passenger side of my car. Placing her on her feet, I opened the door and helped her in. Not waiting for her to do it on her own, I reached over and buckled her seat belt for her.

As I got in on the driver's side, she gestured to the pieces of shattered glass covering the back seat and the broken window. "Should I ask?"

I shook my head. "No, you shouldn't."

I started the car and pulled out of the lot.

"Where are you taking me?" she asked.

"Home."

There was a long pause.

When she finally spoke, her voice was so soft and beaten down I almost pulled the car over to the curb and pulled her into my arms again. "Can you please just take me to my apartment?"

I gripped the steering wheel until my knuckles showed white, making the bloody scratches stand out even more starkly against the skin of my right hand. I didn't have all the details, but I knew enough about what had happened in that bar to know she was probably more than a little traumatized.

She'd basically walked in on her best friend almost getting raped by some drunk asshole. As angry as I was that she'd put herself in that situation, I wasn't a monster.

I was sympathetic but that didn't mean I didn't want her under my roof and in my bed. I wanted her safe, fully under my protection, and if she thought I was just going to casually drop her off at the curb in front of her apartment, she had another—

Her next words interrupted my thoughts. "You can stay if you want, but I want to go home … my home."

The tightness in my chest eased.

I wasn't known as a man who liked to compromise, but for her I would make an exception. I reached over and cupped her jaw, caressing her cheek with my thumb. "Okay, baby. We'll go to your place … for tonight."

I knew Dimitri had plans to move Emma out of that apartment as soon as possible, which meant I definitely would not be allowing Mary to stay there on her own.

The security system we had installed was a Band-Aid, but the truth was as much as they may love it, that apartment was not fit for the girlfriends of two powerful men like us.

They deserved the best and their tiny first-floor place was not it. For starters, being with us meant they were targets, so even a top-of-the-line home security system would not cut it. They both needed to be in a building we owned with twenty-four/seven security cameras at all entrances and our men patrolling the property.

Starting tomorrow, I would move her things to my place.

It was strange how I wasn't even questioning that decision.

It had never even crossed my mind to move in with any of the women I had casually dated in the past, and yet I'd known this spitfire for less than forty-eight hours and already I was practically picking out china patterns for our wedding. It didn't bother me in the least.

I wasn't a stupid man.

When you found a woman as amazing, as spirited and beautiful and intelligent as Mary, you held on to her with both hands and that was precisely what I intended to do.

We pulled up behind the Ferrari. After seeing her expression earlier today, I'd realized my mistake in giving it to her.

While I thought she would look sexy as hell behind the wheel of it, it clearly didn't truly match her style. It was too trashy for a classic beauty like her and having it parked here would only draw unwanted attention to the building.

I texted two of my men to grab the spare keys from my place and swing by and retrieve it. I also told them to bring the Range Rover and take the Mercedes home.

I couldn't have it on the street with a broken

window, and I had no intention of leaving Mary alone to switch it out on my own.

I then walked around the car and opened her door.

I could see the exhaustion on her face.

The night's events were finally settling on her shoulders. Ignoring her feeble protest, I lifted her into my arms and carried her into the building. I held her close as she rooted around in her cherry-shaped purse for the apartment key.

As we entered, I deposited her on the sofa and turned to plug in the security code to disarm the system, only to see it wasn't armed.

"You know we didn't install this for wall decor. It only works if you actually arm it."

Mary slumped back on the sofa. "We tried, but the motherboard beat us."

I pinched the bridge of my nose.

I did not know what that was supposed to mean, but it only reinforced my decision to move her out of here and into my place as soon as possible.

Shrugging out of my coat, I rolled up my shirt-sleeves and headed into the kitchen. "Have you eaten?"

"Does three shots of tequila and half a bag of Doritos count?"

"No."

"Then, no."

Shaking my head, I looked in the refrigerator.

There was a container of Chinese food that I was afraid to open and half a packet of processed cheese. "How the hell do you girls survive?"

She peeked up at me from over the back of the sofa. "We have the essentials."

"What essentials? There are no eggs, no vegetables. There isn't even butter or milk or bread," I responded as I rummaged through her cabinets.

"There's tequila, coffee, and chips. That covers the primary food groups of any graduate student."

With a resigned sigh, I reached for my phone. "Do you like Italian?"

She nodded.

I called La Scarola, the best Italian restaurant in the city in my opinion. When they answered I told them to put the owner on the phone. I then ordered a small feast of calamari, bistecca alla Zorich, capellini fra diavolo, antipasto, bruschetta, and some tiramisu.

When I hung up, Mary protested. "Are you inviting a small army over to dine with us?"

Tossing my phone on the counter, I walked over to the sofa and took both of her hands to raise her up. Without saying a word, I walked her down the hallway.

"What are you doing? We just ordered food."

"It won't be here for at least an hour. Besides, they can leave it at the door," I responded as I led her into the bathroom and leaned over to start the shower.

After adjusting the water, I turned back to her. “Arms up.”

She of course did not do as I asked; instead she objected, “What are you doing?”

I grasped her wrists and raised her arms for her. “Taking care of you.” I pulled her shirt over her head.

She lowered her arms and covered her bare breasts.

Her beautiful blue eyes narrowed with suspicion. “Men like you don’t do stuff like this.”

I raised an eyebrow as I reached to unbutton her pants. “What do you know about men like me?”

She nodded. “Good point, but I’m perfectly capable of showering by myself.”

The small room filled with steam.

I wrapped my arm around her waist and pulled her close. “Maybe, but you’re not capable of doing what I have planned by yourself.”

CHAPTER 13

MARY

"Technically, a dildo could—"

Vaska pulled me against his chest by the waistband of my pants. "Don't even finish that sentence unless you want me to blister your backside with my belt."

He finished unbuttoning my pants and gruffly ordered me to step out of them.

I slipped out of my heels, panties, and my black Capri pants.

Of course, without my heels, my head barely reached his shoulder.

It made me feel small and vulnerable but in that sexy, who's-your-daddy, dominate-me kind of way. That was what was so mesmerizing about Vaska. Other men were just posers acting a part when they tried to be all tough in the bedroom.

Vaska was the real deal.

He untied the red silk scarf from around my throat. He set it aside and said with a wink, "I'll keep this on hand for later."

I reached up and peeled off the thick fringe of fake eyelashes and put them on the small plastic dish by the sink.

He gave me a sweet look and stroked my cheek before saying, "Beautiful. So beautiful."

I scoffed. "You don't have to do that, you know."

His brow furrowed. "Do what?"

I shrugged as I stepped past him to pull back the bright pink curtain with white daisies before stepping over the tub edge into the shower.

I gasped at the heat of the water hitting my chilled skin before continuing, calling out over the rush of the shower, "You know. Acting like I'm beautiful without makeup. I'm on to that player trick." I lathered my hands with soap and scrubbed the rest of my makeup off.

"I wasn't going to say that at all. I prefer you with makeup on."

I was so shocked I accidentally got soap in my mouth.

Spitting and coughing, I tilted my head back to fill my mouth with water, swished it about and spat it out. I couldn't believe he had just said that.

Didn't that violate some cardinal rule in the male-female relationship book?

Of course, we weren't in a relationship; I was just

the one-night stand that wouldn't end, so I guess it didn't matter.

"Good to know," I chirped, trying not to show any annoyance at his answer.

I reached for my loofa poof and dumped way too much liquid soap into its center as I took my frustration out on the bottle.

In a peevish mood now, I said, "Are you sure you still want to shower with me? Perhaps you'd rather shower with some *natural* beauty or a chick with her makeup tattooed on?"

Vaska spoke from the other side of the curtain. "You are a stunning woman with or without makeup, but with makeup you show your personality. Those gorgeous red lips that make me just want to smear your lipstick with my cock. And the way the thick fake eyelashes and black cat-eye eyeliner make your eyes look big and bold. I swear, I can see your indigo eyes from across a crowded room. I really love how you don't wear a lot of blush on your cheeks. It challenges me to say things to bring a little pink there."

My hand had stilled on my belly, the suds sliding down my thighs then the drain as I stood there frozen in shock.

That was possibly one of the most genuinely honest compliments I had ever received.

While every woman wanted to think they looked beautiful without makeup, we used makeup for a reason. For me especially, it was almost an art form, a form of self-expression. And the fact that this man had picked up on that floored me.

The curtain was abruptly pulled aside.

There was a momentary blast of cold air before Vaska stepped naked into the shower with me. Reaching around to my front, he pulled me into his embrace, his hard cock pressing against my lower back. His hands caressed my belly then moved up to cup my breasts.

He kissed my neck before whispering into my ear, *"U tebya derzkiy rot. Ne dozhdus' zaglushit' tvoy rot moim chlenom."*

I had to grab on to the metal wire shelf around the showerhead to keep my knees from buckling.

There should be a law against a man this handsome speaking in Russian.

It was such a deep, rough-sounding language filled with growling R's and rolling L's.

Fuck French.

Russian was the language of love.

No wait, not love, it was too raw-sounding to be the language of love—it was the language of fucking.

"What did you just say?" I breathed as my head lolled to the side, giving him more access to my neck and earlobe.

He pinched both of my nipples before shifting his hand over my throat to caress my bottom lip with his fingertips. "I said you have a sassy mouth."

He then pushed his thumb between my lips.

Without thinking, I swirled my tongue around it, tasting his skin. He then continued in a low, seductive purr, "I cannot wait to silence it with my cock."

Oh. My. God.

He turned me around and fisted my wet hair, pulling my head back. His mouth crashed down on mine. My fingers splayed over his wet chest, feeling every sculpted muscle as he took complete possession of my mouth.

He bit my lower lip, then asked, "Tell me now, *krasotka*. Do you want me to be gentle or rough?"

Damn him.

No. He couldn't do this to me.

I needed him to stay in the role of insensitive, arrogant player.

I needed that to remind me I was nothing more than a current fuck for him.

I couldn't have him asking sensitive questions like this. I knew he was only asking because of what had happened at the bar, but that he was sensitive enough to wonder would drive me over the edge.

It would have me foolishly thinking he gave a damn about me and that was a one-way road to certain heartbreak.

I answered the only way I could, with the only thing I wanted, or at the very least should want, from him. "Rough."

His cock twitched between our bodies. "Are you sure, baby? Once I start, I won't stop."

It was all kinds of wrong that that statement sent a bolt of arousal straight between my legs.

I tried to nod, but his grip on my hair prevented it. "I'm sure."

He ran his open mouth over the edge of my jaw. "Remember, you asked for this."

My abdomen muscles clenched in sick anticipation.

He painfully pulled on my hair before commanding, "*Stanovis' na koleni.* On your knees."

He gripped my upper arm as I slowly lowered to my knees.

The scalding water pounded against my back as I braced my hands on the tops of his heavily muscled thighs.

From any angle his cock was enormous, but from this angle it was *terrifyingly* enormous.

It was just so long and thick … and long.

As I stared at its length, I saw a tattoo at its base.

It looked to be a few words in Cyrillic, but they were faded and his dark curly hair covered them.

Before I could ask, he tugged on my hair again. "Open your mouth."

I licked my lips. "You're not going to shove it in too hard, are you?"

He looked down at me from his towering height. He raised one eyebrow. "What do you think, *krasotka?*"

Fuck.

I opened my mouth and tipped my head forward, taking the bulbous head between my lips.

It filled my whole mouth, and I panicked. I tried to pull back, but his fist in my hair prevented it. Breathing heavily through my nose, I swirled my tongue around the head as he pushed in another inch. Then yet another inch.

My nails dug into his thighs as I struggled to accept his thick girth. My lips felt stretched thin around the shaft.

"That's it, baby, swallow my cock," he coaxed as he stared down at me with those dark intense eyes.

He pulled back slightly, then pressed in again.

I reached between my legs with my right hand and rubbed my clit as I took him in deeper, the idea of him choking me with his cock arousing me to the point of pain.

He pushed in again, this time hitting the back of my throat.

I gagged.

He pulled free for a second, but then used his grip on my hair to force my mouth back onto his shaft.

With the pressure of his hand, I bobbed my head up and down, each time taking his shaft a little further down my throat.

"Fuck, baby. Yes. God, yes," he growled.

My throat was slowly relaxing, allowing him deeper.

Soon, he was full-on fucking my mouth.

No matter how hard I tried, I couldn't take him all the way to the base, but I was close. Something I was strangely proud of. As he increased his pace, I pushed two fingers into my pussy, matching his punishing rhythm. It wasn't long before I came. I smashed my thighs together as I rode out wave after wave of pleasure as he continued to abuse my throat.

His cock twitched and seemed to get even harder. He let out a guttural roar before thick streams of come shot into my mouth.

Taken by surprise, I choked at first then pulled free.

"Eyes on me," he ordered, slightly out of breath. "Open your mouth. I want to see my come on your tongue."

I obeyed, tilting my head back and pushing my tongue past my lips so he could see the thick semen coating it.

His gaze glistened with desire. "Good girl. Now swallow it."

I swallowed.

"Lick your lips."

I licked my lips.

He leaned down and wrapped his hands around my upper arms. He drew me to my feet. Without saying a word, he retrieved the loofa poof from its hook and added more liquid soap.

Seeing his tanned and scarred hands covered in soft white soap bubbles as he clutched a pink poof was incredibly erotic. In slow sweeping circles, he ran the loofa over my skin.

The slight scratch of the poof followed by the silky bubbles fired up all my senses. With his bare hand he collected some bubbles and rubbed between my legs.

A groan escaped my lips.

He turned me around to face the tiled wall. His hands ran up my arms to wrap around my wrists. He stretched my arms high over my head.

"Keep your arms right there. If you move them, you'll be punished."

Yes, please.

Wrapping his arm around my waist, he pulled me back, forcing my ass out. Cool liquid pooled onto it, slipping into the crack.

I looked over my shoulder to see him dribbling liquid soap onto my body. He caught my gaze and winked. Placing the bottle back on the wire rack, he ran his index finger between my ass cheeks, teasing the dark entrance there.

I squirmed. "Wait!"

"Shhh, baby. Don't worry. You'll like the pain."

Before I could object further, his finger pushed into my ass—deep.

He worked the liquid soap inside of me, swirling first one finger then two, around and around, opening me.

"But … I … I've never … please."

I couldn't even formulate a coherent sentence.

My body was screaming yes, bring it on, while my brain was freaking out over the coming pain.

He leaned in to kiss my neck. "Trust me, beautiful."

As he said the words, the thick head of his cock pushed against my puckered hole.

I clenched.

He smacked my ass, the sound bouncing off the tiles.

I gasped and opened for him. He slid in.

"Oh, God! It hurts!"

He pushed in a few inches.

My mouth opened on a silent scream.

As my body bucked, his hands wrapped around my wrists, anchoring me in place.

His feet kicked at mine, opening my legs as wide as possible and forcing my hips further back onto his cock.

"Is my baby going to be a good girl and take my cock up her ass?"

Fuck, I loved when he talked dirty like this. It made me want to promise him anything, which was why I moaned *yes*.

"Good girl."

He pushed in deeper.

I rose up on my toes but couldn't escape the unbearable pressure as he thrust inside me, breaking through my body's resistance. I cried out.

"Hold on, baby. Almost there," he breathed as he pushed in the final two inches.

His hips cradled my ass as his chest met flush with my back. I couldn't believe he'd fit his entire cock inside of me.

The pressure and full feeling was overwhelming. It was as if my body was no longer my own but fused with his.

He stayed still, allowing my body to relax and adjust to his thick shaft piercing my flesh. He kissed my shoulder then scraped his teeth along the delicate skin of my throat.

"Say it, *krasotka*. Say it for me. I want to hear you beg for it."

There was just something so deliciously filthy about him making me ask for my own punishing pleasure. "Fuck my ass, Vaska."

He shifted slightly but stopped. "What do you say?" he teased.

"Please! Please, fuck my ass!"

He chuckled. "Whatever my baby wants."

He pulled out almost to the head, then thrust back in. My body rocked forward until my cheek rested against the tile. If it weren't for his hands around my wrists, I would have fallen into a puddle onto the floor of the tub. He pounded into me, not even breaking rhythm when I cried out from a sharp stab of pain from him going too fast or too deep.

One of his hands released my wrist and cupped

my breast. He pinched my nipple before moving between my legs to tease and taunt my clit. “Come for me. I want you to come as I make your ass mine.”

As with everything else, I did as he commanded. Stars burst behind my eyelids as I forgot to breathe. Hot waves of pleasure crested over every inch of my body until my bones melted.

He pumped into my ass a few more times before pulling out and coming onto my back. The rest of the shower was a blur as he washed us both off then wrapped me in a warm fluffy towel. As he dried me off, our apartment buzzer rang.

He smiled. “Good, the food is here. I really need to feed you before I fuck you again.”

Again? Seriously?

He wasn’t human.

He really was Spike, an immortal arrogant vampire male with an insatiable sexual appetite.

I was living inside my own fucked-up episode of *Buffy the Vampire Slayer* … complete with a Buffy and Spike romance … and that was the problem.

CHAPTER 14

MARY

"I don't understand. Where did the body go?" asked Vaska.

I laughed.

We were sitting on the sofa.

I was in my favorite Buffy t-shirt and leopard tights.

Vaska had tossed his jeans back on but kept his shirt off. So of course he looked sexier than any man had a right to.

We were eating the Italian to-go food straight out of the containers.

"The bodies just kind of disappear in this haze of black sand and smoke," I explained. I was introducing Vaska to the best show ever made.

He smirked. "Must be nice. Killing is easy. It's disposing of the body that's a pain in the ass."

I paused halfway to my mouth with a piece of

fried calamari suspended from a fork. "Can we just pretend you said that from an observational point of view and not from a real-life one?"

"I'm just saying maybe this vampire slayer little girl would not be so effective if she had to cart all these heavy vampire bodies away to the middle of the desert at the end of every episode. Or worse if she had to cut them up and—"

"Stop!" I pleaded.

Shaking my head, I poured myself another tequila shot. I was not ready to have the guess-what-I'm-a-big-badass-criminal conversation with him just yet.

He poured himself a vodka shot from his flask. "Are you sure you don't want to try it again?"

"I don't care what you say. That gasoline swill you call vodka is an abomination to mankind."

"Blasphemy! Moskovskaya is the best vodka in Russia. And better than that cheap shit you are drinking," he objected.

I pretended to hug the Jose Cuervo bottle to my chest. "Don't you talk like that about Jose. I'll have you know we've been in a very long-term, committed relationship and I love him."

Vaska gave me a smoldering look. "I didn't know it was possible to be jealous of a bottle."

Swoon.

"It's not fair that you can practically recite a grocery list and it would still sound sexy," I pouted.

His brow furrowed. "What?"

I rolled my eyes. "Oh, please." Then in a deep, fake-Russian accent, I said, "Oi deent know eet vus posseeble to be jeelous of a bootle."

Vaska playfully snatched me up around the middle and pulled me onto his lap. "I see what you mean." Then he kissed me.

I wiggled off his lap. "Oh, no, you don't! This is the first decent meal I've had in a week and if I let you fuck me one more time, I won't be able to walk for a week."

He stroked my cheek, then winked. "A week with you in my bed, unable to run away. Sounds good to me."

Swoon again.

Damn him.

Changing the subject, I nodded toward the television. "Are you going to watch this or not?"

He sat up. "Oh, yes, I'll like this scene. It has the blond vampire in it."

Spike. Wouldn't it just figure that he would be his favorite character?

* * *

I WOKE up the next morning cuddled in Vaska's arms. I didn't even remember going to bed. I think I must have fallen asleep in his arms on the sofa. I had a vague memory of him carrying me to bed.

It was startling to realize he had stayed. I would

have assumed he'd have snuck off to his own place since I'd said I was too sore to have sex again.

A small part of my heart wondered if he'd stayed despite there not being a promise of more sex because he liked me and wanted to be with me, but my brain told it to shut up.

Before my heart could object, I noticed the time. "Fuck! I'm going to be late for class."

Vaska tightened his arm around my waist as he nuzzled my neck. "Skip class this morning. Stay in bed with me."

I squirmed out of his embrace and reached for my fuzzy pink robe, which was on the floor near the bed. As I shoved my arms into the armholes, I wrapped it around my body before getting out of bed, all the while ignoring Vaska's knowing chuckle.

"You don't understand; it's my Foundation of ESL and Bilingual Education class. I need it to graduate this semester, and the professor is—difficult. I can't be late."

Rushing over to my closet, I pulled out a pair of deep-cuff dark denim jeans, a black-and-white striped off-the-shoulder shirt, and my favorite black biker jacket. I snatched up my pink metallic makeup case and started down the hall for the bathroom.

With a start, I turned and poked my head back into the bedroom. "You can show yourself out, right?"

Vaska raised an eyebrow and just nodded.

"Bye!" I said breezily over my shoulder as I turned back down the hallway.

I raced to the bathroom and slammed the door shut, then leaned against it. I closed my eyes and took a deep breath. I thought I'd pulled that off.

Last night had been so wonderful.

I could feel myself falling in love with this man with each passing minute I spent in his presence.

He was his own gravitational force just pulling me closer and closer against my will.

The problem was I knew I would be torn to pieces by that same energy force if I wasn't careful.

Best to end it now in a *laissez-faire* casual way rather than show him any weakness of the heart.

Besides, a man like Vaska would appreciate a female who wasn't trying to cling to him. He probably got that all the time. I was determined to be different.

I was leaning over the sink drawing a thin black line of eyeliner over my top right lid when I heard the front door close.

He was gone.

My eyes teared up.

I angrily swiped at my cheeks, ruining my makeup. Damn it. And damn him. I grabbed a cotton swab and dipped it in some makeup remover to repair the damage.

Then, plaiting my hair into two soft braids, I tied

them off with pink ribbon and took one last look in the mirror before leaving the bathroom.

I slipped on my pair of jeans and jumped around the bedroom, pulling them over my hips and balancing on one foot as I shoved the other into a pink Converse sneaker. Shoving my other foot into the second sneaker, I put on my leather jacket.

Dumping the contents of my cherry purse onto the bed, I swiped my arm across the coverlet and pushed it all into the open mouth of my Hello Kitty purse.

I glanced at the clock. Fuck.

I hurried into the kitchen and picked up my laptop case off the counter.

As I turned toward the front door, it opened.

Expecting Emma, it stunned me to see Vaska standing there.

He was holding a tray with two coffee cups and a small brown paper bag.

He motioned with his head. "Come on, beautiful. I thought you were late?"

"What … what are you doing back here?"

He winked. "Technically, I never left. I was just getting provisions. Can't go to class on an empty stomach. Come, I'll drive you."

"That's not really necessary."

"And yet I still insist."

It was funny how his Russian accent seemed to

get heavier and sexier when he was giving a command, even a subtle one.

Knowing when I'm beaten, I threw my arms up in defeat and walked out the door.

After he followed me out, I turned to lock it.

"Aren't you going to arm the security system?"

I shrugged. "What's the point? There's nothing in there to steal. Besides, Emma will be here any minute. She has a class at the same time I do."

Vaska shifted his gaze away. "Which would you like, coffee or cappuccino? And by that I mean, choose the cappuccino."

I selected the cappuccino as I narrowed my eyes. "What are you not telling me?"

"What? Nothing."

"Try again. Is Emma okay?"

"I'm sure she's fine."

I raised my eyebrows. "You're sure she's fine? Fine?"

I reached for my phone. "I'm calling her."

He put his hand over my phone. "You won't be able to reach her. She's on a plane with Dimitri. They are on their way to Morocco."

I shook my head. "I'm sorry. Did you just say my best friend was on a plane to Morocco? Why?"

"I guess she's better at skipping class than you are," he said before smacking my ass and motioning toward the door.

I had no choice but to obey and wait for Emma's call and explanation.

I really couldn't be late for this class. I pushed open the outside door and stepped into the sunshine. The first thing I noticed was the Ferrari was gone. I blinked rapidly in case any tears threatened.

It was stupid. I hadn't wanted the stupid, ugly thing anyway. It just sent a very clear message that he wasn't planning on seeing me past shuffling me off this morning.

He opened the passenger door of his car for me and I tried one more time to object. "It's really only a few blocks. If I hustle, I'll make it in plenty of time."

Vaska didn't even respond.

He just gave me that implacable stone-faced stare I was becoming accustomed to.

With a sigh, I got into the car.

As we drove the few blocks to Loyola, he clenched his jaw. He then gestured with his hand to the buildings ahead. "You walk all this way every day?"

"It's really not that far."

He shook his head. "*Net*. No. It is too far for a beautiful woman to walk. This is Chicago. What do you do when it rains or snows?"

I played with the plastic top of my cappuccino. "Um … I get wet?"

He turned his head to flash me a glare. "The only time my woman should be wet is when she is in bed with me."

Fuck. From any other man, that would be a way over-the-top thing to say, but that Russian accent! Damn, it got me every time.

A peevish part of me wanted to fire back that I wasn't his woman, but he had been nice enough to get me breakfast and drive me to class so I just stayed silent. It's not like I would be his problem after this morning, anyway.

To distract him, I picked up the paper bag and opened it. "What's in here?"

"A blueberry muffin."

I smiled. "I love blueberry muffins. Thank you so much."

He winked, then turned his attention back to the road.

I directed him to the building my morning class was in.

I suppressed a groan when I saw Professor Hadley standing near the door. Before the car had even come to a full stop, I was opening the door.

Not giving Vaska a chance to make some excuse about why he was *too busy* or had *other plans* for tonight but would *call me* later this week, I hopped out of the car.

"Thanks for the ride!" I called out and refused to look back.

Professor Hadley blocked my path as I tried to enter the building. The man was easily three times my age and always smelled of garlic and menthol cigarettes.

"You're late, Ms. Fraser," he sneered as he stepped closer.

I averted my face. "I'm sorry, Professor Hadley. It won't happen again."

He stepped closer.

I tried to shift to the left, but another student bumped into me.

I was jostled and found myself with my back to the brick wall of the building a few feet from the entrance.

Class was already starting, so the quad had mostly emptied.

It was just me and Professor Hadley.

He leaned over me and pinched the leather collar of my jacket between his pudgy fingers. "I think you'll have to come to my office today so we can discuss this *privately*."

I swallowed as bile rose in my throat.

His class was a requirement for me to graduate.

I had heard stories of his infamous *chats* with female students.

He usually cornered them for some minor offense and then threatened to flunk them if they didn't submit to his pawing.

Before I could respond, someone violently yanked the professor backwards.

Vaska towered over him.

His feet planted wide, he had the professor by the collar.

Vaska's eyes narrowed as he breathed heavily through his nose. It was like watching a raging bull, and Professor Hadley was the red flag.

"Who the hell are you? Unhand me!" cried an outraged Hadley as he swung his arms about, trying to dislodge Vaska's grip and looking like a hapless puppet hanging by the strings controlled by its master.

"I'm the man who's going to rip out your heart and show it to you before I force it down your miserable throat," growled Vaska.

Oh, my God.

Vaska reached into the man's blazer and snatched his wallet. He tossed it to me. "*Krasotka,* pull out this miserable piece of shit's ID."

My stunned gaze flashed between my professor and Vaska.

Not knowing what else to do, I obeyed and handed it to Vaska.

He looked at it then turned his attention back to Professor Hadley. "Here is what is going to happen. For the rest of the semester, Mary will attend your class only if she feels like it. You will not dare speak to or look at her when she does. And she will get a top grade. Or I will destroy everything and everyone you love."

Vaska patted him on the cheek in that menacing

way mafia guys do in the movies. "Do we understand one another?"

Spittle formed at the corners of Professor Hadley's mouth as he choked on his reply. "Yes … yes … sir. Yes, sir."

Vaska patted his cheek again. "Good. Now run along. Mary will be in when she is ready."

Professor Hadley's beady eyes shifted to me, then back to Vaska. "Of course. Of course. Whenever you're ready, Mary … I mean Miss Fraser … or not. Whatever you like," he stammered before scrambling through the building's door.

Stunned, I asked, "Why did you do that?"

Vaska put a hand against the brick wall, high over my head, caging me in. "No man touches what's mine."

"Yours? You act like we're dating or something."

His brow furrowed. He picked up one of my braids and tugged on it slightly. "And just what do you think this is, *krasotka*?"

Exasperated, I threw my arms up into the air and blurted out, "I don't know! The one-night stand that won't end?"

Vaska tilted his head back as he laughed.

I could see the swirls of tattoo ink peeking through the collar of his shirt as they circled the strong column of his neck.

He then stroked my cheek. I could feel the cold

metal of his signet ring as it grazed my jaw. His dark blue gaze captured mine.

"Trust me, this is no one-night stand, beautiful girl. I have captured myself a pretty butterfly, and I have no intention of letting you go."

He then kissed me on the forehead as if he hadn't just said something earth-shattering and held the door open as I walked into my classroom building in a daze.

What the hell just happened?

Was I somehow now the girlfriend of a Russian mafia badass?

CHAPTER 15

MARY

Vaska was waiting for me when I got out of class.

Leaning against his fancy sports car with his arms crossed, looking like a villain version of Jake from *Sixteen Candles*.

For half a second, I thought about trying to blend into the crowd of students and escaping over the quad. Images of him driving over the curb and chasing me down over the lawn popped into my head and instantly squashed that idea.

Walking up to him, I tilted my head to the side and surveyed him from head to toe. His black hair was still a little wet, so he must have gone home and showered and then returned for me. "I have another class."

He grinned. "That's fine. Is it within walking distance or should I drive you?"

I let out an exaggerated sigh as I narrowed my gaze. "Don't you have a job you need to get to?"

He smirked. "One of the many perks of being an arms dealer is you get to make your own hours."

He then stepped away from the car and opened the passenger door. Making a sweeping gesture with his arm, he said, "Your chariot awaits."

Arms dealer.

He said it so casually, as if he had just said accountant or business owner.

I tapped my foot. "Do I have a choice?"

He shook his head. "Not really."

Then he leaned in to whisper against my lips, "But you would make my day if you tried to resist."

He then kissed the corner of my mouth and leaned back, staring at me with one eyebrow raised.

My thighs clenched as a delicious ripple of pleasure coursed over my body from his sensual threat.

Damn him.

In an effort to wipe the arrogant look off his face, I asked, "What are the tattooed words over your cock?"

He blinked at my abrupt change of subject. His jaw twisted to the right as he looked away briefly.

I knew it.

Very few men got tattooed *there* and didn't live to regret it.

And it wasn't like he trimmed to make it more

visible, which meant it must be something embarrassing.

He inhaled, then slowly exhaled. "It is something I got a long time ago."

I shrugged. "I remember the Cyrillic letters. I can always look it up myself."

"If I tell you, will you get in the car like a good girl?"

I nodded. I figured this would be good, but his answer exceeded my wildest dreams.

He sighed. "It says Mr. Big."

I covered my mouth to stifle a bark of laughter. "What?"

He rubbed his eyes. "I was drunk. *Sex and the City* was new to Russia ... and there was this girl."

I bent over laughing. "Oh, my God, I can't breathe!"

He twisted his fist into my hair and raised me upright.

Pulling my head back, he playfully growled, "That is precisely what you'll be pleading the next time I drive my hard cock deep into your throat."

He then claimed my mouth for a scorching kiss. Several passing students whistled and catcalled, but he refused to relent until he had made his point.

Shaken and out of breath, I got into the car.

Visions from earlier of Mr. Big being forced down my throat as I was on my knees in the shower distracted me for the rest of the day.

* * *

It was the longest, most nerve-racking day of my entire life.

Vaska escorted me to each and every class.

If the professor was a female, he would disappear for an hour.

If the professor was a male, he would sit in the back of the classroom and stare daggers at him.

It got so bad that none of my friends would even approach me, although I got plenty of text messages.

If I received one more text from a girlfriend asking if my hot AF bodyguard was up for grabs, I'd scream.

Vaska was there holding the door open for me when I finished with my last class.

He checked his watch. "Perfect timing."

"For what?" I asked.

He guided me to his car with a possessive hand at my lower back. After I was seated inside, I waited until he took his place behind the wheel.

"For what?" I asked again.

He winked at me. "For dinner, of course."

Halfway through my day, he'd asked if I was going to take time to eat lunch.

"Does the other half of the muffin you gave me earlier count?"

His lips thinned. "No."

Next thing I knew, he was handing me a sandwich, chips, and iced tea from Subway.

I protested, "I don't usually eat between classes."

He placed a finger under my chin and gazed at me with those midnight blue eyes of his. "But you will make an exception today, just for me."

I melted. I couldn't even speak. I just nodded and walked into my next class in a daze.

"Dinner? But I'm still full from the sandwich you gave me earlier."

That wasn't exactly the truth. The real truth was I needed some space and time away from him. In the span of just two short days, Vaska was already taking over all aspects of my life. It was starting to feel like he belonged in my life, and that was beyond dangerous thinking.

Vaska snatched my Hello Kitty purse from my grasp. "Hey!"

He gave me a side-eyed glance before unzipping it and pulling out the clear to-go bag from Subway, still stuffed with more than half a sandwich.

I shrugged. "At least I ate the chips."

Handing me back my purse, he started the car without another word.

I guess I was going to dinner whether or not I liked it.

We returned to my apartment.

Vaska checked his watch. "You have exactly thirty-five minutes to change."

"That is not enough time!" I gestured down my body. *"All of this* just doesn't happen, I'll have you know."

He wrapped an arm around my waist and kissed me hard on the lips. "You now have thirty-four minutes."

With an indignant cry, I squirmed out of his embrace and ran down the hallway.

Diving into my closet, I selected my black halter top dress with the black and white polka dots over the bodice and the red crinoline. Rushing into the bathroom, I stuck several bobby pins between my lips as I pulled out my braids and arranged my hair into several large victory roll curls. I then wrapped a red silk scarf around my hair like a headband. After touching up my eye makeup and lipstick, I shimmied into the dress.

When I opened the bathroom door, Vaska called out from the living room, "Four minutes."

With a frustrated cry, I ran into my bedroom and fell to my knees inside my closet as I dug through all my shoe options. I finally settled on my red velvet pumps. They were a little scuffed at the heel, but no one would notice. I switched to a black patent leather clutch as I pushed my feet into my shoes. With one last look in the mirror, I tightened the saucy little red bow that rested just beneath my cleavage and spritzed Viva La Juicy on my neck and wrists before leaving the bedroom.

As I entered the living room, Vaska handed me a shot of tequila. "For courage."

I drank the shot as he took a sip of that gasoline he called vodka from his flask.

After tucking the flask in his inside suit pocket, he stroked my cheek. *"Ty vyglyadish' prekrasno. Mozhet byt' my ostanemsya doma etot vecher? Ya ne uveren chto khochu delit'sya toboy s mirom."*

"Did I forget to mention I don't speak Russian?"

He chuckled. "I said you look beautiful. Perhaps we should just stay in tonight? I'm not sure I want to share you with the world."

I placed a hand on my hip. "Oh, no, you don't. I got ready. You're taking me out!"

I grabbed him by the hand and marched us both through the front door.

He halted our progress to type the thousand-digit code into the security motherboard. "Humor me by allowing me to actually arm the security system this time," he said with a smirk.

We drove into Lincoln Park along Armitage.

The valet immediately recognized Vaska and started stammering hello and assuring him he would take excellent care of the car.

Vaska handed him a fifty-dollar bill and patted him on the cheek.

Fifty dollars! No wonder the valet recognized him.

We walked down a small flight of stairs.

The Geja's restaurant had a beautiful old European facade with flagstone, wood timbers, and lattice windows.

I had never been, but I knew from Valentine's Day promotions that they considered it one of the most romantic restaurants in Chicago.

The maître d' warmly greeted Vaska as we crossed the threshold. The restaurant was warm and cozy with a low ceiling and lots of candles. Each table was its own private nook, hidden from the view of the other guests by yards and yards of draped fabric in rich jewel tones of gold, ruby, sapphire, and emerald.

They showed us to a secluded table.

I settled myself into the booth on the other side of Vaska as a man quietly strummed a guitar nearby.

When the maître d' tried to hand me a menu, Vaska took it from my hand. "We will both have The Connoisseur and a bottle of your Amarone della Valpolicella, Allegrini."

"Excellent choices, Mr. Rostov, as always." He bowed and left us alone.

I bristled as I snapped the white cloth napkin onto my lap. "As always? So is this where you bring all your women?"

He sat back as he slowly unfolded his napkin. Finally he spoke. "Yes, it is."

Tears pricked the back of my eyes. Well, ask a stupid question …

He reached for my hand.

I pulled it back.

His eyes narrowed. He leaned over the table, snatched my hand, and gripped it within his firm grasp. "You need to understand, *krasotka*. I'll never lie to you. There is no reason for it. This is a restaurant with food I enjoy. I have enjoyed this food with other women before you. End of story."

I looked away, skimming my gaze over the decor and the other slightly hidden patrons to compose myself.

He was right, of course.

Still, it was just one more reminder that I couldn't take any of this seriously. No matter what he'd said earlier, I was still just the woman he was fucking … right now.

Vaska reached into his coat pocket and withdrew a red leather case with the name Cartier in gold embossed script lettering.

He slid it across the table. "For you."

Curious, I opened the lid.

It was a brooch in the shape of a crouching panther. It was in a platinum setting and covered in white and black diamonds with two sparkling emeralds for eyes. There was also a heavy-looking matching clasp bracelet.

I was speechless.

Vaska slid into the seat next to me.

He selected the brooch from its black velvet

cushion and lifted the fabric of my dress to pin it on me. The back of his knuckles gently brushed the top of my breast.

I held my breath.

“According to my research, your unique style favors brooches because of all the dresses and cardigan sweaters. Am I right?”

I nodded yes.

He was right.

Rockabilly outfits looked best with either pearls or a fancy brooch, which were so very much in fashion back in the fifties. That he would research such a thing before buying me jewelry was both shocking and endearingly thoughtful. Damn him.

Next, he picked up the bracelet as he lifted my wrist. The tips of his fingers rested against my skin.

He leaned in. “I can feel your pulse race. Does this mean you like my gift?”

My chest felt tight.

I had to force myself to breathe. “I couldn’t possibly accept these.”

I knew very little about super fancy, high-end jewelry, but I wasn’t an idiot. Cartier plus lots and lots of diamonds meant lots and lots of dollar signs.

He smiled. “Then it is a good thing I’m not giving you a choice.”

Before I could respond, a rather sinister-looking man approached the table. He had a lowered brow and thick lips clamped around the cold stub of a cigar. His hand rested on his protruding stomach, with each finger boasting a gold ring. "Vasili Rostov. It is fortunate we meet this night."

The man's accent was even thicker than Vaska's. He also had an odd way of talking out of one side of his mouth while he kept his teeth clenched down on the cigar stub.

Vaska shook his hand but did not rise. "Olezka, you know I do not conduct business in front of *mixed* company," he said smoothly with a pointed look in my direction.

The man called Olezka gave me a dismissive onceover. "She is just a woman, what does a woman care of men's business? Besides, this cannot wait, Vasili. I promise you. There is a cargo ship docked in the Caspian with thirty cases of IST-12.7 Mubariz sniper rifles meant for the Ministry of Defense of Azerbaijan. There is an opportunity to seize them for ourselves for a tidy profit."

Vaska rose and grabbed the enormous man by the upper arm.

Olezka was so shocked the charred cigar stub dropped from his mouth.

Vaska whispered harshly to him in rapid-fire Russian.

The man paled.

Olezka stepped back to the table and bowed his head in my direction. "Please accept my apologies for offending you. It was disrespectful and wrong."

His beady black eyes gazed intently at me, fear evident in their small depths.

My stomach clenched.

I had the strangest feeling that some harm would come to him if I didn't accept his apology.

I glanced over the man's shoulder at Vaska.

His eyes were narrowed and his jaw tight.

It was obvious he was pissed.

"It's … fine … really," I stammered, alarmed at the possible pending bloodshed.

Olezka immediately breathed a sigh of relief. "Thank you. Enjoy your dinner."

He turned and bowed deeply to Vaska and then left without another word.

Vaska sat back down and casually returned his napkin to his lap.

"Was that just—"

Vaska cut me off. "It was business. Nothing more. It should not have been discussed in front of you."

"But—"

"Mary. No more questions. I mean it."

The uncomfortable reality that I had just witnessed a criminal exchange made me lightheaded. It was one thing to half-jokingly think you are dating a mafia man; it's another to be confronted with the reality of it.

The maître d' approached the table with our wine.

I ran the tip of my finger over the emerald eyes of the panther as I watched the maître d' display the bottle for Vaska's approval before removing the cork and pouring a small taste into a glass.

Vaska swirled the rich red liquid in the glass before he inhaled, then tasted the wine. He nodded his approval.

With a clap of delight, the maître d' poured us each a glass.

A server brought over an orange fondue pot filled with warm Swiss Gruyere cheese followed by another server who situated a small platter of fruits, vegetables, and breads between us.

Finally, we were left alone.

Vaska lifted the lid off the pot and skewered a piece of strawberry. He dipped it into the gooey cheese and held it a few inches from my mouth. "Open your lips," he commanded.

My eyes glanced around the room.

With the dim lighting and heavy drapes, it felt almost as if we were alone. Although I knew he wanted me to taste the strawberry, there was definitely a sexual undercurrent to his demand.

Unable to refuse, I opened my lips and closed them over the sweet and savory bite, slipping my lips suggestively down the skewer before leaning back and slowly chewing.

Vaska growled in response.

I had hit my mark.

Two could play at this game.

I touched the pin, and thought back to that man's

rude interruption, a reminder of the blood-soaked money that had probably bought this jewelry. "I don't care what you say, I'm only going to wear these during dinner, then you are taking them back whether you like it or not."

Vaska skewered a piece of pumpernickel bread and dipped it into the sauce. As he lifted the skewer, he expertly spun it to coat the bread with the drips of warm cheese before raising it to his mouth. "I'm looking forward to seeing you try and make me."

He winked and then snatched at the piece of bread with his sharp white teeth.

Before I could reply, a gorgeous woman approached our table.

The smell of aerosol hairspray and strong rose-scented perfume hung about her like a noxious cloud. Her unnaturally bright red hair was piled high onto the top of her head in a messy twist. Heavy gold hoop earrings weighed down each earlobe as her wrists rattled from all the various gold bangles on them.

She was dressed in a skintight zebra print dress that barely covered her ass and definitely didn't contain her enormous breasts, which were spilling out of the top.

She smiled at Vaska. "Hello, baby, did you miss me?"

CHAPTER 16

VASKA

Admittedly I'd done a great deal in my life to deserve God's vengeance.

I just never thought he'd have a sense of humor about it.

First, Olezka had barreled in practically screaming to Mary that I was a criminal, and now Karina, the paid escort I used to fuck, had turned up.

Karina sidled up to me and tried to stroke my hair. "You're not still angry at your Karina, are you, baby?"

Angry about her trying to cut off my nuts with a knife in a drunken rage?

Yeah, a little.

Ever since meeting Mary, I now knew there was the fun kind of crazy that kept you guessing and always challenged and excited you.

Then there was Karina's type of crazy, which was

crazy wrapped in a psychotic bow with no redeeming benefit.

I snatched her wrists and pulled her off me. "Karina, you are interrupting."

She cast a glance in Mary's direction.

Her upper lip lifted in a sneer. "You can't be serious about wanting to fuck her? Come on, baby. I'm sorry about the whole knife thing. How can I make it up to you?"

She ran her hand up my thigh; I caught it before she could catch hold of my cock.

What the hell had I ever seen in a woman like Karina?

Between her and Mary, I couldn't even imagine the appeal.

Mary was fiery and intelligent.

You never knew what she was going to say or do.

I loved that about her.

She was also beautiful and passionate and warm-hearted.

Karina was all flash and no substance.

Mary tossed her napkin onto the table. "Perhaps I should leave you two alone?"

"No," I ground out.

"Yes," jeered Karina.

Mary rose.

I growled, "Don't even think about it. Sit down now."

Her eyes widened, but she obeyed.

Turning my attention back to the cloying Karina, I said, "And as for you. It's over. It's been over for a while now. Never approach me again without permission, or I'll have you whoring in the slums of Moscow before the end of the day. Do you understand me?"

Karina pouted and stomped her foot. "But baby!"

"Get out of my sight, now."

Turning to Mary, she said, "He'll be back. You are not woman enough to keep a man like Vaska happy. Only I am," before stomping off.

The maître d' hurried over to our table with an apology for the intrusion.

I waved him away without a word, keeping my entire focus on Mary.

I rubbed my jaw, watching her as her gaze settled on anything else in the room but me.

As much as I had tried to deflect, she had a point.

What the fuck was I thinking taking her to the same restaurant I had taken other women to?

I should have anticipated a run-in with someone from my past like Karina. Mary was special and should have been treated that way. She deserved better from me and from this point forward she would get it.

"Mary…."

Her gorgeous eyes filled with tears. "Please, just take me home."

"No."

She crossed her arms over her chest. "I don't want to be here with you."

"Too damn bad," I ground out.

A server arrived to clear away our uneaten tray of fruits, vegetables, and cheese while another set a tray of beef and lobster tail with various dipping sauces in its place.

I picked up a skewer. "We're here to have dinner. Now eat."

"I'm not hungry," she fired back through clenched teeth.

"Eat anyway."

"No!"

"I swear to God, Mary, I don't have the patience for this right now."

"You? You don't have the patience? But it's fine for me to have to sit here and *patiently* watch that … that … *woman* fondle you?"

"She means nothing to me. She's in the past. Now eat your lobster before it gets cold."

"I don't want any fucking lobster!" she shouted before flipping the tray.

The contents flew into the air before landing on the floor with an obnoxious splat. The guitar player stopped playing, and all eyes turned in our direction.

Mary covered her mouth. "Oh, my God. I can't believe I did that!"

Tossing my napkin onto the table, I rose. "Clear the room," I shouted. "Now."

The servers and maître d' scurried from table to table asking the patrons to leave.

Mary and I glared at one another as guests all around us collected their things and left, filling the room with murmured apologies and the squeaks of chairs as they were shoved out from under tables.

Reaching into my wallet, I pulled out a business card and handed it to the maître d'. "Whatever your lost revenue is from this evening, double it, then call this number and the money will be wired into your account. Now leave us and bar the doors."

Mary rose and tried to leave.

"Not you," I commanded. I took a few steps toward her.

She backed away and raised a hand to ward me off. "Don't come any closer. This evening has been a disaster. I'm just going to take a cab home."

"You're not going anywhere," I said through clenched teeth.

If we were going to be together, she was just going to have to accept that I had a past and that my business dealings weren't always on the right side of the law. In other words, she would have to accept me just as I was, just as I accepted her.

I didn't want her to change for me, and I expected the same from her.

And we would be together.

I'd meant what I said earlier.

Mary was gorgeous and smart and unique, and I

had no intention of letting her slip through my fingers.

She snatched a small bowl of clarified butter from a nearby table.

I pointed my finger at her. "Don't you dare…."

"I'll do it! Don't come any closer!" she warned.

I ignored her threat and took two determined steps in her direction.

She threw the bowl.

It hit me on the shoulder, sending a greasy splatter down the front of my suit jacket.

Her eyes widened as her beautiful mouth dropped open.

Keeping my eyes on her, I shrugged out of my ruined jacket and tossed it aside.

I then reached for my belt buckle.

Releasing it, I pulled the belt through the loops, then folded it in half in front of me with an ominous snap. "Here and now, we are going to come to an understanding."

She circled around, putting a few tables between us. "I understand things perfectly. The idea of us as a couple is ludicrous. We need to stop this now before it goes too far."

I palmed the metal buckle and methodically wrapped the leather belt strap around my fist. "See, that is where you're wrong. When I said *we*, I really meant *you*. You need to understand that you're mine now. I decide when this relationship is over and trust me, *krasotka,* I haven't nearly gotten my fill of you yet."

She set her fists on her hips. "I don't know how things work in Russia, but here in America, the woman has a choice in who she dates and I don't choose you!"

I gestured around the empty room that I had cleared out with a single command. "Look about you. You think you are in America right now? *Net, ty v moyem mire, i v moyem mire ya korol'.*"

Her shoulders tensed as her gaze shifted to the door and back to me.

A second later she bolted for the exit.

I was already in motion.

Snatching her around the waist from behind, I wrapped my arm around her middle and clutched at her throat.

I then repeated in English what I'd just said. "No, you are in my world now and in my world I am king."

Mary fought my embrace. "Yeah, well, fuck the monarchy!" she yelled before grinding her heel down on my foot.

I was not expecting that method of attack and released my grip on her in shock at the sudden sharp bite of pain.

She scrambled away, once again placing several tables between us.

With one hand gripping the back of a chair, she

touched the base of her throat with her other hand as she sucked in gulps of air.

I straightened to my full height and looked down at my growing cock.

Her startled gaze followed mine.

My lips lifted in a smirk. "That's right, beautiful girl. You're not the only one who gets turned on by a little pain."

In an unguarded moment, she licked her lips as her indigo eyes lit with desire.

She then shook her head and raised her arm, her hand palm up in a weak attempt to hold me at bay. "No. That's not true. You're twisting things around."

I raised an eyebrow as I stepped closer. "Am I? Are you saying you didn't scream in ecstasy after you felt the kiss of my leather belt on that beautiful ass of yours the last time?"

Her eyes filled with tears as she stumbled backwards, pulling the chair in front of her.

Relentless, I prowled forward, cornering her with both word and deed. "Was it not you who sweetly pleaded that she was a bad girl deserving of punishment?"

"I … no … I …," she stammered.

"Did those gorgeous red lips not plead with me to fuck you rough in the shower last night as you fell to your knees begging to swallow my cock?" I took another step closer.

"Oh, God. Stop."

I rubbed my cock through the fabric of my pants. "Look at it, Mary. Look at my cock. See how hard it is for you? Are you saying you didn't like the feel of me thrusting deep inside of you?"

I reached for the chair between us.

Her only defense.

Grabbing it by the wood seat, I flung it out of the way. It landed hard against a nearby table, sending the delicate wineglasses on top crashing to the floor.

I snagged her around the waist and wrenched her forward, plastering her body to my front, wanting her to feel every hard inch of me. Fisting her hair with the same hand that still had my belt wrapped around my palm, I yanked her head back, exposing her neck.

Leaning down, I licked the soft skin, tasting the bitterness of her perfume. I then sank my teeth into her earlobe, hard enough to make her cry out and drive her nails into my shoulders.

"Say it, Mary. Say you wanted me to thrust into you, over and over again, until you cried out for mercy." I punctuated my demand with a thrust of my hips as my hand clenched her ass, pulling her forward.

"Please, stop. I can't."

"Say it," I ground out. "Say you like the pain of my cock. You like feeling dominated and owned by me. Say you're mine."

I needed her to say it.

Needed to hear it from those lips.

Needed her submission.

This woman was a drug to me, and like a drug, I had become addicted at the first taste.

My need for her was now in my blood. I needed to feel her essence pumping through my veins. Needed to feel her touch on my skin.

Without her, I was certain my heart would stop beating. If she were to walk away now, she would take my last breath with her.

It wasn't rational and it sure as fuck wasn't fair to her, but somehow, this woman had become my salvation. She had filled this empty void inside of me with her passion and energy, and I would be damned if I let her go now.

Her eyes pleaded with me to stop tormenting her, but I was beyond caring. I was more beast than man.

A beast fighting to keep his mate.

Turning, I swiped my hand across the nearest table, sending the glassware, plates, and silverware crashing to the floor. With my grip on her hair, I bent her over the cloth-covered table. I flipped her skirt up, surrounding her prone body with a cloud of blood-red crinoline.

Mary cried out, "Please, Vaska, don't do this."

Gripping the waistband of her black and red polka-dotted panties, I ripped the cheap silk off her body. "I'm sorry, baby. You've left me no choice."

Despite her clenching her thighs to try to keep me

out, I forced my hand between her legs. Giving her no quarter, I speared two fingers deep into her wet cunt.

Viciously thrusting them in and out, I leaned over her and whispered harshly into her ear, "Do you feel that, love? Do you feel how wet your sweet cunt is? Your lips may continue to lie but your body will always show me the truth."

I released my grip on her hair and lowered my arm, allowing the leather belt to slither and uncoil from around my fist.

Mary glanced over her shoulder.

When she saw the belt, she began to cry.

"You asked for this," I said softly before raising my arm.

I whipped the leather strap against both ass cheeks.

Mary's entire body jerked as if shocked by a bolt of electricity.

I struck her with the belt again and again, watching as pale pink slashes marred her creamy flesh.

All the while she cried and begged.

Tossing the belt aside, I stepped behind her.

Rubbing my left hand over her punishment-warmed skin, I lowered my pants zipper with my right. I pulled out my stiff cock and stroked the shaft several times before slipping the head between her legs.

"Put me inside of you." I held my breath and waited, willing her to do as I commanded.

After a moment's hesitation, her small hand reached between her legs and wrapped around my cock.

She slid her feet wider and opened her legs as she guided the head to her tight entrance.

It was all the permission I needed.

I thrust in deep, straight to the base.

Mary's arms rose to flatten her palms on the table surface as her body absorbed the brutal pounding. Caressing her hip, I slipped my fingers between her legs and teased her clit, wanting to feel the sweet ripples of her climax up and down my shaft as I continued to fuck her.

It only took a few swirls from the tip of my finger before

Mary was slapping the table with her palm, crying out, "Oh, God! Yes, harder. Harder! Oh, God, I'm coming!"

Her climax brought on my own.

With abandon, I released a hot stream of come deep inside of her, wanting to brand her both inside and out with my mark.

With Mary still in a daze, I adjusted my pants then lifted her into my arms and carried her back to our booth.

Shoving the table aside with my hip, I sat down and settled her on my lap. Reaching for the wine bottle, I poured a fresh glass and gulped down half the contents before raising it to her lips. "Drink."

She obeyed.

The red wine stained her lips. I couldn't resist leaning in and licking the elixir straight from her mouth. Her head fell onto my shoulder, her body lax and spent. I had literally fucked all thoughts of leaving me from her mind.

Then, in the very next moment, everything changed.

My future happiness with Mary was violently wrenched from my grasp.

CHAPTER 17

VASKA

A shout came from just outside the dining room area. "Boss, *yest' problema.* Mikhail Volkov *pytayetsya svyazat'sya s vami.*"

Mikhail was on loan to us from the Ivanov brothers.

He was supposed to be with Dimitri handling the issue in Morocco.

We thought his sniper skills might come in handy if things became dicey. If he was trying to contact me, then there was a serious problem.

One that was preventing Dimitri from reaching out to me directly. Fortunately, my men knew where to find me at all times.

Checking to make sure Mary was covered, I called out for them to enter.

Two of my men crossed the dining room, not even sparing a glance at the destruction Mary and I had wrought. They knew better. One of them handed me the bulky satellite phone we used for secure, international calls.

"Vaska?" asked Mikhail.

"*Da*," I answered.

"*U nas problema. Oni pokhitili zhenshchinu Dimitriya.*"

"Fuck, Emma?" I blurted out without thinking.

Mary's startled gaze swung to mine.

She might not understand our Russian conversation, but she clearly heard the name of her friend.

I wrapped my hand around the side of her neck and gave her a slight squeeze as my eyes bored into hers.

She didn't have to say a word; I could see the terror in her eyes.

"*Chto my znayem?*" I asked Mikhail.

"*My dumayem, chto master porta zameshan. Eta poteryannaya partiya AR-15 byla na nem, a ne na Amir*," responded Mikhail.

So the fucking port master double-crossed us. He was the one who'd stolen the shipment of AR-15s that forced Dimitri to fly to Morocco to investigate. Goddamn it. We never even suspected him, and now my best friend and business partner had walked straight into a trap.

No, worse, his girl was now in danger.

His girl and my girl's best friend.

I stared at Mary's anxious face. *Fuck.*

I tightened my grip on the phone as I snarled, *"Ubey ikh. Ubit' ikh vsekh. Sozhgi yego dotla, no naydi devushku."*

After instructing Mikhail to kill them all and burn it to the ground, but not before he found the girl, he told me to consider it done. *"Schitay, chto delo sdelano."*

I hung up the phone and handed it back to my man. "Get the car."

He nodded. "Yes, boss."

Mary clutched at the fabric of my shirt. "What's wrong? What's happened to Emma?"

I wrapped my arm around her shoulders. "I need to get you out of here."

Her lower lip trembled as her eyes filled with tears. "Tell me."

I stood and put Mary on her feet, then cupped her cheek. "I will, *krasotka,* just not here."

Her knees buckled.

Sweeping her back up into my arms, I carried her out of the restaurant and climbed into the back seat of my car. I held her close as one of my men drove us back home in my car while the other followed us in theirs.

The moment I entered the penthouse, I placed a still-dazed Mary on the sofa. Running to the bedroom, I snatched the thick down blanket off the bed and returned to the living room to wrap it about her.

I tightened my hold on her while I explained what I knew about the situation in Morocco.

While this was happening several of my men were setting up a command post on the kitchen island. There were several laptops, satellite phones, and tracing equipment.

I cupped both sides of her face with my hands. Swiping at the tears on her cheeks, I said, "Baby, I need to get to work but I'll be right over there in the kitchen, okay?"

She only nodded, her tearstained gaze unfocused.

"Would you rather go into the bedroom?"

She reached past the blanket and clutched at my upper arm. "No! Please, let me stay."

I nodded. "Okay. Do you need anything?"

She shook her head.

I rose and motioned to one of my men. "Do me a favor."

"Anything, boss."

"Call your wife, Anna. Get her here. I think Mary should have another woman nearby … just in case."

He nodded. "On it."

I clapped him on the shoulder before glancing back at Mary.

Her silence both worried and terrified me.

I hadn't known her for long, but I knew that this was not natural for my little spitfire. She was a fighter.

Now she looked beaten and scared.

I clenched my fists.

I had never wanted to kill someone with my bare hands as badly as I did now.

My only regret was I would not be the one to do it.

For the rest of the night, we monitored the situation from afar, getting constant updates from Mikhail and the other men on the ground there. Dimitri was too focused on finding Emma and getting her to safety.

I couldn't blame him.

I looked over at Mary, who had finally fallen into an exhausted sleep.

She was wrapped in the blanket and curled up in a ball at one end of the sofa. She looked so small and vulnerable it made my chest ache, but at least she was here safe with me under my protection.

I couldn't even imagine what my friend was feeling right now, knowing his woman was in the hands of his enemy. I wouldn't blame him if he burned the entire city to the ground trying to find her.

Finally, in the early morning hours, we learned Emma was safe.

The three of them—Dimitri, Mikhail, and Emma—were all on a plane on their way back to Chicago.

I knelt before Mary and stroked her soft black hair.

In the early morning sunlight, it looked sleek and

smooth, like a raven's wing. "Baby, wake up." Her eyes fluttered open.

I rubbed her cheek with the back of my knuckles. "It's over. She's safe."

She blinked a few times. I wasn't sure if she understood, so I nuzzled her hair away from her face and cupped her cheek.

"She's safe," I repeated.

Mary burst into tears.

I grabbed her and held her close, hoping to absorb all her pain and fear. Rising, I sat on the sofa and pulled her onto my lap. I rocked her in my arms and whispered calming nothings against her forehead in Russian.

I have no idea how long we stayed like that, but finally she stirred.

She pushed against my chest and sat up straighter.

I could feel the growing distance between us.

An icy chill swept over my body.

She refused to meet my gaze.

As she stared down at her twisting fingers, she said softly, "I want to go home."

I wanted to rage that she *was* home.

That her home was here, with me.

I kept silent with a nod, though, transferring her to the sofa and rising to make the arrangements. I called for the car to be brought around and went into the bedroom to change. I emerged with the hockey jersey she had worn the last time she was here.

I held it out before her. "Here, put this on."

I knew she would probably be uncomfortable in the morning chill wearing her halter top dress that exposed her shoulders. Without an argument, she took the jersey from my hand and pulled it over her head.

I wish she'd argue with me.

We drove back to her apartment in silence.

I escorted her to the door and punched in the security code when we entered.

Mary dropped her purse on the counter and turned to me. Her face looked drawn and tired.

"Vaska…."

"Don't."

She sighed. She took off the jersey and tried to hand it back to me.

I refused to take it.

With another sigh she draped it over the back of the sofa. She then reached for the brooch I had pinned to her dress.

My eyes narrowed.

"Don't even think about it," I ground out through tight lips as my hand fisted at my side.

"But…."

"I mean it, Mary. Don't."

I was holding on to my rage by a thin thread as it was.

If she tried to return the jewelry I had so carefully chosen for her, I would howl.

She lowered her head. "I'm sorry."

My control snapped.

I closed the distance between us and pulled her into my arms.

My mouth crashed down on hers, my tongue sweeping in to take possession. As I cupped her jaw, I angled her head back and claimed her for my own.

I needed her to know, to understand, that it was not over between us.

Her lips molded to mine as I swallowed her moan.

I growled deep in my throat as her hands reached up to cling to my shoulders. I deepened the kiss, knowing I was bruising her lips, but I didn't care.

I poured my dark, imperfect soul into the kiss.

After we broke apart, I held her close, pressing my forehead to hers.

Mary started to speak.

"Don't say it," I pleaded.

"I'm sorry," she repeated.

I closed my eyes as the pain made it hard to breathe. I stepped back.

Her face was pale as tears flowed over her cheeks. "Goodbye, Vaska."

I clenched my jaw.

No, I would not let this happen.

I understood her emotions were raw in this moment. Her friend had been put in mortal danger because of her association with Dimitri and our business. I had barreled into her life and turned everything upside down with my demands and my rules. I had never given her the chance to acclimate to her new reality.

I had essentially thrown her into the deep end and commanded her to swim. It was no wonder she was now closing in on herself and rejecting me and us.

I understood, but understanding did not mean acceptance.

I didn't know the how's or why's of it but I knew that Mary and I belonged together. I had never been so sure of anything in my life. I knew it with a deep-seated, unshakeable confidence.

She was the woman I had been searching for my whole life without even realizing it. She filled the void.

I had meant every word of what I'd said earlier; I would never let her go.

But I could give her time.

Time I hadn't allowed her earlier.

That had been my mistake, and I would own it now.

I pulled off my family's signet ring.

Reaching for her hand, I raised it and laid the ring in the center, then closed her fingers around it.

Hoping she would feel the warmth of the metal from my skin as it pressed into her palm. "This is not goodbye."

Her face crumpled. "Vaska...."

"No, Mary. I mean it. This isn't goodbye."

I knew from conversations with Dimitri that both Emma and Mary graduated in two months.

Two months.

It would feel like a lifetime, but I could give her that if it would secure a lifetime with her.

I continued, "You have two months."

Her brow furrowed. "What?"

"Two months, that's all I can give you. Then I'm coming back for that ring … and you."

She sighed as she swiped at a tear. "That's not how this works."

I gave her a sad smile before leaning in to kiss her on the cheek. "Haven't you learned by now, *krasotka,* we are playing by my rules, not anyone else's. Two months. Then I'm coming for you."

I turned and left the apartment.

As I closed the door, I could hear her burst into tears.

I reached for the doorknob and stopped.

I was nothing if not a man of my word.

I'd told her I would never lie to her, and I would not start now. I had said I would give her two months to grow accustomed to the idea that she was now mine and I would stand by it.

Forcing myself to step away from the door, I took out my cellphone. I had countless arrangements to oversee.

For starters, I would place her under twenty-four-hour surveillance.

I would need to bribe someone at her college registrar's office to get her complete schedule and the names and addresses of all her professors. I would also need to pay a visit to the bar she used to work at to make sure the owner understood that under no circumstances was she to be allowed to return to work or it would mean his very painful death.

Which reminded me, I would have to see about getting her tuition paid off and gain access to her bank accounts so I could place a generous allowance in them.

She would have her two months, but that didn't mean I wouldn't be watching over her.

She was mine, and I protected what was mine.

CHAPTER 18

MARY

Two months later

WORST. Mistake. Of. My. Life.

I turned onto my side on my bed and lifted my knees up high, curling up in a ball.

I grasped the collar of the hockey jersey I was wearing and brought it to my nose, inhaling deeply.

I bit my lip as tears formed. It no longer smelled like him.

That was to be expected. It had been two months.

Two full months.

Two months of obsessively checking my phone for a text message or phone call that never came.

Two months of my heart skipping a beat every time I heard someone at my apartment door.

Two months of looking over my shoulder, wondering if he was somewhere nearby, watching.

I pulled up the thick silver chain I kept around my neck, exposing Vaska's heavy silver signet ring that dangled from it.

During a sentimental moment, I had strung it on a chain around my neck and had not taken it off once since that terrible day I'd told him goodbye. I wore it close to my heart and often touched it just to feel its warmth.

Two full months—and nothing from him.

No contact whatsoever. Damn him.

The first week had been brutal.

Emma returned home, and we clung to each other and cried for a week straight.

I was a fraud.

She thought I was crying for her and her broken heart over Dimitri, who had broken up with her shortly after they returned to Chicago, but that wasn't entirely true. Of course I had been scared to death for my friend, and beyond happy when she returned safely, but I cried as much for Vaska as I did for her.

I'd never told her about my brief … I'm not even sure what you would call it? A fling seemed too light-hearted. An affair seemed too seedy and yet it was too short of a time to truly call it a relationship. Whatever you called my intense time with Vaska, I had kept it to myself.

Emma was hurting and the last thing I'd wanted to do was pile on my pain as well.

After a week of crying together, I remember sitting on her bed and trying to coax her out of her funk, hoping it would coax me out of mine. "Look, I know it doesn't feel like it right now, but you'll get over him."

Maybe I could take my own advice.

Her eyes had teared up. "No, I won't."

I'd stroked her back. "Everyone feels that way about the first guy they've loved, but eventually you move on."

Again, fingers crossed.

She objected, "I don't want to move on. I know you think it's crazy and will probably say I just met the guy and barely know him but ..."

A few weeks ago, yes, I'd have thought she was crazy.

I would have lectured her about confusing a silly crush with long-lasting love.

I would have been relentless in trying to convince her that what she was feeling was nothing more than an infatuation.

But now I knew it was possible to fall in love at first sight.

To know, deep down inside, that you'd met the person you wanted to be with for the rest of your life.

I knew what it felt like to be confused and excited and scared all at the same time.

I knew precisely how she was thinking and feeling.

How she was now questioning her own reasoning, doubting her own heart.

Wondering if it had all been real or just a product of her overactive imagination.

"Actually, I think I'd focus more on the whole he's-a-dangerous-Russian-mobster angle more than the you-two-crazy-kids-just-met trope," I quipped as I opened a bag of Doritos, trying to hide the truth of my own emotions behind humor, hoping she wouldn't see through it.

She snatched a chip out of the bag. "So he has his faults. No guy is perfect."

"Emma. The man is a fucking mobster! A criminal. I'd say that is a pretty big fault."

Who was I trying to convince, her or me?

"It's not like he's out there robbing banks or shooting up restaurants! Besides, from what I've seen, he's mostly a businessman. If you think about it, half of corporate America are criminals in one way or another." She grabbed a handful of Doritos.

"Emma, if you are going to accept the man for what he is, then you can't justify it or paint it a color it isn't. You have to look at this in black and white terms."

"Does it make me a bad person if I say I don't care if he's a criminal?"

I adjusted the red kerchief in my hair to give

myself time to think. "A few days ago, I would have said yes. That you couldn't possibly consider being with a man like that … Now, I don't know."

She looked at me slyly. "This wouldn't have anything to do with Dimitri's friend, Vaska?"

Fuck.

I should have known I wouldn't be able to completely hide my feelings from Emma.

I let out a frustrated sigh. "That man is the most insufferable, brutish, stubborn, obstinate, mule-headed person I've ever met."

"You do realize all those words are technically synonyms?"

Not wanting to reveal any more than I already had, I sprang off the bed. "Fuck this iced tea. I'm getting the tequila."

I returned with a bottle of Cuervo and my favorite Rhett Butler shot glasses that said *I Don't Give a Damn* in black scroll.

After I poured us both a shot, Emma raised her glass and toasted, "To bad choices!"

We drank.

I looked down at my glass and voiced my own fears. "What if he gets you killed?"

She snatched the bottle and poured us another shot. "That's not a fair question. I could get hit by a bus tomorrow. Life is random."

"It most certainly is a fair question! You were

kidnapped by a lunatic who held a gun to your head because of him."

"It wasn't his fault."

"He may not be directly responsible, but you have to face facts. If you'd been there with a boring accountant, the likelihood of something like that happening dramatically decreases."

We both drank, not bothering to toast.

"Why did Buffy love Angel … or fuck Spike?"

I poured us a third shot. "I get it. He's your Angel and Spike all rolled into one." *That is precisely how I feel about Vaska.* I raised my arm high. "To bad boys!"

"To bad boys!" Emma shouted.

We both drank.

"Well, okay. You love him and damn the consequences … so what are you going to do about it?"

Emma huffed, "Hello! He broke up with me!"

"So what? You think Elizabeth or Beatrice or Catherine or Jane or Bathsheba would take that lying down? You think *they'd* be curled up in bed in their pajamas feeling sorry for themselves? Ask yourself, WWBD?"

What Would Buffy Do? Maybe I should be asking myself the same thing.

Emma sat up straighter. "No! No, they wouldn't!"

"You're damn straight they wouldn't!"

"Mary, I have an idea, but I'm going to need your help."

"Hell, yeah! Let's go get that criminal demon vampire bad boy of yours!"

That day Emma had gotten her beloved Dimitri back … and now, weeks later, I was still curled up in my bed like a sap, pining after Vaska, while wearing his old hockey jersey.

This was so fucked up.

At the time, I'd had no idea if I was giving Emma terrible or good advice.

On the one hand, I believed what I said to her, but on the other I wasn't following my own damn advice.

I was telling her to trust in her heart and go get Dimitri back while at the same time I was desperately trying to forget and move on from Vaska.

The problem was with each passing day I'd missed him more and more.

I'd missed the arrogant, infuriating way he would know what I wanted despite my protests to the contrary.

I missed the way he would call me his beautiful girl in Russian.

I even missed the high-handed way he would take care of me.

Fuck, I had it bad.

Despite all rational thought and reasoning and despite all my attempts not to … I had fallen in love with the man.

No, I hadn't just fallen in love.

I had gone straight off the cliff, fallen deeply, irrevocably, *he's the one for me,* in love.

And then I just let him walk out of my life. Worse, I'd practically shoved him out of it.

After they got back together, I heard that Vaska was the one who had given Dimitri the kick in the ass he'd needed.

Apparently, Vaska had lectured him about not letting the woman he loved get away from him. For days after learning that I kept expecting Vaska to show up at any moment, snatch me into his arms, and kiss me senseless while he demanded that we get back together.

It never happened.

True to his word, he had stayed away.

Far away.

He had actually stayed away longer than two months.

Technically, it had been two months, three days and fourteen hours—but who was counting, right?

When we passed the two-month anniversary and I still hadn't heard from him, I knew it was truly over and my heart broke all over again.

The hope and anticipation of a second chance died that day.

But that was then, and I had to set that all aside, because today wasn't about me.

There would be plenty of time to wallow in self-pity later.

I looked at the alarm clock and groaned, knowing I had to get up soon.

The day had finally arrived, the day of reckoning.

The day I would have to steel my spine and not show the slightest emotion.

Today I will see Vaska for the first time in two months, three days and fourteen plus hours.

Because today was….

Emma burst through my bedroom door and pounced on my bed.

"I'm getting married today!" she shouted with glee.

CHAPTER 19

VASKA

I turned to Dimitri and brushed a piece of lint off his tuxedo.

He straightened my tie.

I patted him on the shoulder. "So, old friend, are you ready to become a husband?"

Dimitri smiled as he shook his head. "I never thought I'd find a woman I'd actually want to spend the rest of my life with, but I have to be honest, I cannot wait to make that beautiful woman truly mine."

I slapped him on the back. "You are a lucky man, my friend."

Dimitri nodded toward the girls' closed apartment door. "Jump in, the water's fine."

Once the dust had settled between him and Emma, I'd told him more about my relationship with Mary.

It was a new and still strange dynamic to our friendship.

We had never really talked about women before.

Well, at least not in these terms. Talking about which escort was worth the money hardly counted, but something had shifted in both of our lives after meeting these two quirky and fiery females.

It was a seismic shift in our lives.

Everything had changed, from how we viewed our business endeavors to our very purpose in life. Now, instead of life being about the blood money and danger, it was about love and making our women happy.

Fuck, we were both even talking about children.

Soon, instead of discussing which barrel length, the 24" or 26", was more accurate at a distance on the Remington Model 700 Tactical Chassis with the .338 Lapua Mag, we'd be comparing SUV model safety standards.

The thought should have terrified me.

Instead, I couldn't wait to join him, and I planned to start today.

Mary's two months were up.

It was time to finally claim her as my own.

No more watching over her from the shadows.

No more seeing her face turn pensive and sad and knowing I was the cause but not allowing myself to comfort her.

Being with me was not an easy decision, and I

needed to be sure she was making it with a clear head.

I knew if I had persisted soon after her friend had been kidnapped she would have hardened her heart to me and that would have been it.

I knew giving her these months would provide her a chance to think about our relationship in different terms and to come to grips with her feelings about me outside of the chaos, danger, and fights.

Or at least I hoped it would. I would find out in a few moments.

I held up my bottle of Moskovskaya vodka. "Are you ready to go ransom your bride?"

We were about to introduce Mary and Emma to one of the most hallowed of all Russian wedding traditions, the ransoming.

Where the groom essentially searches the bride's home looking for his intended all the while 'bribing' her friends and family to let him carry her off to the church.

Since it would just be us four, it would be less of a riotous affair but I still intended to send my friend off in true Russian style.

We both took a few steps back and eyed the door.

Dimitri laughed. "That asshole landlord is going to be so pissed."

"That's one of the best parts of today," I agreed.

We were finally getting the girls out of this stupid first-floor apartment. From day one we had both hated that they lived in a building so lacking in security. Their piece of shit slumlord of a landlord didn't help.

We'd tried to upgrade the girls' security with the insanely high-tech system we'd had installed, which monitored the doors and windows.

The problem was neither of the girls bothered to learn the code or how to operate it, so it often was left unarmed. We finally just relented and put their apartment on twenty-four/seven surveillance.

They had no idea, but we had actually taken over the apartment above them to the left and stationed several men there.

But after today, it was over.

Emma was moving out to live with Dimitri. She had mostly been living with him full time on the weekends the last two months, but she still stayed here to keep Mary company during the week because it was close to her school.

Mary was also moving out—just not to where she supposed.

She thought she was moving to a small basement apartment in Lincoln Square close to her new teaching job.

Let's just say I had other plans. She was making it easy for me by already having most of her belongings boxed up and ready to go.

I nodded to Dimitri.

He stormed to the door and gave it a solid kick.

The ancient wood door splintered and swung open, dangling from only one hinge.

"Where is she?" bellowed Dimitri as he entered the apartment.

I followed quickly behind him and came to a dead stop.

Mary stood there in the center of the living room, looking breathtakingly beautiful … and vulnerable.

In that unguarded moment, as her gaze swung to mine, her lower lip trembled as those gorgeous indigo eyes.

I had missed so much filled with tears.

Her hair was upswept in an elaborate hairstyle of curls and twists. She was dressed in a black halter dress. A red crinoline peeked out below the hem, reminding me of the dress she'd worn the last time I had seen her.

At her waist was a red belt that matched the red rose bouquet she was holding. Even her feet looked gorgeous with her black peep-toe high heels, which gave me a glimpse of her red pedicure.

I really loved this quirky style of hers. It was so feminine and sassy.

I looked at the bodice of her dress but didn't see the Cartier panther brooch. My gaze then flicked to her wrist, and the bracelet was missing too.

Well, I would soon rectify that. I planned to buy my girl lots of jewelry and perfumes and all the dresses and heels she wanted, to her heart's content.

After today, never again would I not see some sign of my ownership on her body … or more important, her ring finger.

As I looked closer, I did see a silver chain around her neck.

I couldn't prevent my lips from lifting in an arrogant smirk.

I knew what that chain meant.

Breaking her reverie, Mary seemed to give herself a mental shake, and got into the spirit of the day.

She yelled back, "You can't have her!"

"Tell me where she is now!" roared Dimitri with a wink at her.

Mary pointed to Emma's bedroom door and mouthed *in the closet.*

It was part of the custom that the bride hid from the groom, forcing him to find her.

We then motioned for her to step aside.

With each of us taking a side, we upended the sofa, allowing it to fall back with a crash.

Mary picked up a glass and looked at us both.

We nodded enthusiastically.

She raised her arm high and threw the glass to the floor, shattering it.

I called out loudly for Emma's benefit, "Not until you pay! Hand over the ransom."

"There's your payment. Now where's my bride?"

Dimitri crossed over the threshold into Emma's bedroom.

We were left alone.

I took a few steps toward her.

She held up her hand in a defensive gesture. "Don't. Just don't. Today should be about Dimitri and Emma."

She was right, of course.

I had no intention of causing drama at my best friend's wedding, but that wouldn't stop me from taking advantage of the day.

Ignoring her plea, I pressed close to her, inhaling the sweet scent of her perfume as I brushed her hair off her shoulder, exposing her neck.

Fuck, I'd missed her.

It had been two months, three days, fourteen hours, and thirteen minutes since the last time I'd been this close to her and I had ached to touch her every second of it.

I skimmed my lips up the soft column of her neck.

I could feel her body tremble. Glancing down at the exposed curve of her breasts, I wished the corset-like top of her dress didn't prevent me from seeing if her nipples were hard.

Flicking the tip of my tongue over the shell of her ear, I whispered, "Time's up, *krasotka*. I've returned to claim what is mine."

Her head turned sharply in my direction, her eyes wide as she searched my face. A spark of fire replaced the temporary sadness as her gaze narrowed.

Her full crimson lips formed a pout. "You're assuming I waited ... or still want you."

God, I fucking missed this.

I could already feel the warm blood pumping again in my veins, giving me renewed energy.

I had to rein in my lust as I felt my cock stirring back to life. Never since puberty had I gone two months without sex, but after Mary no other woman held the slightest appeal to me.

She was the one.

The only one I desired and wanted in my bed.

Placing a fingertip under the silver chain, I lifted it slowly.

She closed her fist around it in a feeble attempt to stop me. I raised an eyebrow and met her challenging look.

Realizing she had no choice, she relented.

I pulled on the chain, revealing the heavy signet ring I had given her two months earlier, nestled between her breasts.

We both knew what it meant. I gave her a knowing wink. "There is no turning back now, beautiful girl."

As Dimitri and Emma emerged from the bedroom, Mary snatched the chain out of my grasp and pushed the ring back between her breasts.

I smiled. "I'll be thinking about where that ring is all day."

Mary flashed me a glare before she stepped away

to pick up a bottle of tequila and shot glasses on the counter, then greeted the happy couple.

I followed close behind.

Emma put her hands on her hips and teased, "Is that all I'm worth? Two cheap bottles of liquor?"

I teased her back. "Actually, just one bottle of cheap tequila, I brought my own."

"I refuse to buy that swill," quipped Dimitri.

"A toast to the bride and groom before we head to the church," called out Mary as she held up four shot glasses.

Dimitri and I righted a small table we had turned over.

I stood close as she placed the four shot glasses in the center. I was pleased to see her hand shake slightly as she poured out two shots of tequila. I knew my presence affected her as much as hers did me.

Unscrewing the cap to the bottle I held, I poured out two shots of vodka.

I held my shot aloft. "*Za zhenikha i nevestu!* To the bride and groom!"

"To the bride and groom!" repeated Mary.

I leaned over to whisper in her ear, "Now we chant *Gor'ko*. It means bitter. It encourages the bride and groom," I stroked her bare arm with the backs of two fingers, "to kiss passionately to sweeten the day."

Mary inhaled sharply as goosebumps appeared on her arm.

Oh, yes, I had a feeling this was going to be the most fun I'd ever had at a wedding.

Stepping slightly away from me, she chanted, "*Gor'ko! Gor'ko! Gor'ko!*" I joined her.

Dimitri pulled Emma close and told her he loved her. "*Ya tebya lyublyu, moya kroshka.*"

"*Ya tozhje tebya lyublyu,*" Emma answered. *I love you too.*

A tightness seized my chest with a harsh, deep yearning.

I longed to hear Mary say she loved me in my native tongue.

I captured her gaze and held it.

And that day would come very soon.

The moment this wedding was over, I would put my plan into motion.

CHAPTER 20

MARY

This was torture.

Pure torture.

There should be a law against being paired up at a wedding with ex-one-night-stand pseudo boyfriends.

I thought I was prepared to see Vaska again.

It was stupid to even think that.

Nothing could have prepared me for the impact of finally seeing him standing in the middle of my apartment after weeks apart.

At first it reminded me of the first time we met, him just arrogantly standing there as if he owned the place. Except this time something was different.

It was hard to put my finger on it, but he didn't look quite as put together as the last time.

He still looked devastatingly handsome in his tuxedo, but there was a roughness to him.

His jaw not as smooth-shaven. His hair a little

longer and less kept. And those intense blue eyes of his looked slightly tired.

Could it be he'd suffered from our separation as much as me?

Was it possible he truly meant it when he said he wanted us to be together?

All this time I'd been forcing myself not to hope. Reminding myself he was a player and not the relationship kind. Trying to convince myself that at the end of two months he would have forgotten all about me.

And when the two months were up and I hadn't heard from him, I thought it was true.

Now he was standing near me, devouring me with his gaze. Unnerving me with slight brushes of his hand or whispers in my ear. Always standing just a little too close.

It was torture, pure and simple.

We were standing in the center of the Holy Trinity Orthodox Cathedral. We were about to start the crowning part of the Russian wedding ceremony. I took a deep breath as I took my place behind Emma.

I could feel Vaska standing close.

This was so weird.

Standing here this close to the altar and priest, it almost felt as if we were the ones getting married.

I took a deep breath and looked up, trying to

focus on the elaborate gilt decor of the cathedral rather than the man standing by my side.

All I could think about was how the sapphire blue robes on the angels surrounding the top dome of the church matched Vaska's eyes.

I was going to hell.

The priest handed me a heavy gold crown, then turned and handed a similar one to Vaska. It was now my duty to suspend it over Emma's head. Apparently, this was the moment similar to the exchange of rings in the American marriage ceremony, the moment when my best friend would truly be married.

The priest spoke. "The servants of God, Dimitri and Emma, are crowned in the name of the Father, and of the Son, and of the Holy Spirit."

The crown was heavier than I thought it would be.

My arm shook as panic gripped me.

Oh, my God. What if I dropped it?

Would that be an unforgivable sin in the Russian Orthodox Church?

Would they take it as a bad omen of their marriage?

Just as I could feel my palms sweat and the crown slipping from my grasp, a warm hand enclosed mine.

Vaska took possession of my crown and, along with his, held them aloft over the heads of Dimitri and Emma.

Instead of just taking my crown, he had stepped

behind me to reach for it with his left hand.

I now had no choice but to stand within his embrace.

I could feel the warmth of his body against my back. Smell the spicy bergamot of his cologne.

I was sure if I tilted my head to the side and back, I could rub my cheek against the soft stubble of his jaw.

I had that feeling like when I finally slipped between the cool sheets of my bed after a long day and felt the weight of the blanket cover me as a wave of contentment and a sense of being safe and secure would wash over me.

It was like that standing within the span of Vaska's arms. Like I was finally home and safely tucked into bed where nothing could harm me.

With a sigh, I leaned back.

Vaska pressed his cheek against my hair. He whispered for my ears only, "I've missed you, beautiful."

I blinked away tears as I bit my lip.

Damn him.

He always knew just what to say to strike right at my heart.

Before I could respond, it was time for the couple to process around the center of the church to signify taking their first steps with God as a married couple. Vaska lowered his arms and stepped back.

He placed both crowns on the table to the side.

As we watched Dimitri stare down lovingly at

Emma, Vaska reached for my hand and held it securely within his.

In that moment, I thought anything was possible.

Maybe, just maybe, we could make it work.

Maybe it was possible I could have my own happily ever after with Vaska.

The rest of the day was a blur of champagne, caviar, dancing, and endless toasts. We'd headed to Maple & Ash, the restaurant where Dimitri had taken Emma on their first real date.

We got a private room and with the feast of lobster, filet, oysters, and caviar on display on large pewter platters set between massive candelabras down a long, polished table, you would have thought a small army was coming to celebrate their nuptials instead of just the four of us.

Dimitri had asked Emma if she wanted a large wedding, but she'd said no. She wasn't close to her parents and the two of us didn't have many close friends. Besides, larger weddings took time to plan and they were both eager to start their life together.

Throughout the evening, Dimitri and Vaska competed to see who could take the top off a champagne bottle with a saber better.

It really was a sight to see, watching these two large men chant in Russian as they brandished sharp swords. With each strike of the saber, foamy champagne would coat the table and all of us. Emma and I held up our champagne flutes, hoping to catch a few drops as we laughed and took bets on who would do it best.

They each opened several thousand-dollar bottles of champagne, way more than we could possibly drink, but we all certainly tried.

As a small quartet of musicians arrived, we pushed the table aside to make a small dance floor.

It was heavenly being taken up in Vaska's strong arms as he twirled me about the room while singing the words to each song in his deep baritone. It was so lighthearted and fun.

It felt right and wrong at the same time.

We weren't this type of couple.

We were the type who threw things during fights and had lots of angry make-up sex.

Still, this was a glimpse of the type of couple we could be if perhaps I just stopped fighting our attraction.

If I gave in to the force of nature that was Vaska Rostov.

At the end of the night, I was surprised when Vaska gave me a chaste kiss on the cheek before ushering me into a waiting car … alone.

He had arranged for one of his men to drive me home.

I wrapped my arms tightly around my chest.

The thought of what was waiting for me when I got there sent a chill through my body.

The apartment would be cold and empty without

Emma there.

I had already packed most of our belongings in preparation for our moves: Emma to Dimitri's home and me to a rather dull basement apartment in Lincoln Square.

It was all I could afford on a new teacher's salary without a roommate.

At least I was nicely buzzed.

Hopefully, after such an eventful day, I would just fall into bed and go right to sleep.

Of course, I knew that wouldn't be true.

I was probably going to stay up and analyze to death every single interaction I'd had with Vaska today, right down to the slightest brush of his hand.

Starting with why he'd sent me home alone and hadn't even tried to seduce me.

As I walked down the hallway, I could see a large piece of plywood where our door used to be.

One of Dimitri's men had repaired the damage while we were at the wedding. They had cut a hole in the plywood and reinstalled the old doorknob, so my key still worked.

With a resigned sigh, I slipped the key into the lock and turned it.

The moment the door opened, the motherboard beeped.

I turned and punched in the code Dimitri had forced us both to finally memorize a few weeks ago.

I then flicked on the lights and screamed.

Everything was gone.

Everything.

The furniture.

The boxes.

Everything!

Oh, my God, we had been robbed!

Someone had actually taken the trouble to rob us of all our crappy, worthless stuff. My high heels echoed in the stark and empty apartment as I took a few steps inside.

With my mouth open in astonishment, I stepped in a circle, staring in amazement as I tried to wrap my mind around what was happening, when a piece of white paper on the kitchen counter caught my eye.

Picking up the paper, I read the heavily slanted, very masculine scrawl.

Hello, beautiful,

Your stuff is at my home, where it now belongs.

The driver is still outside waiting to take you there.

See you soon,

Vaska

Of all the insufferable, brutish, stubborn, obstinate, mule-headed, arrogant, high-handed things to do!

I was going to murder him.

CHAPTER 21

VASKA

The moment the elevator door opened, she was already in mid-rant.

"—insufferable, brutish, stubborn, obstinate, mule-headed, arrogant, high-handed—"

The way she was rattling off those characteristics made me think this was a practiced litany of hers when referring to me.

I shrugged.

At least I'd made an impression.

I had ditched the tuxedo for a pair of loose jeans.

She was still in her bridesmaid dress.

Probably because all of her clothes and belongings were here.

I tilted my head as I surveyed her from head to toe.

God, I'd missed her.

These last two months had been torture, watching

her from afar but not allowing myself to talk to or touch her.

She needed space, and I needed time to settle certain matters from my past.

Never again would Mary be disrespected by having another woman approach me.

I also knew both she and Emma would need time to process their new realities.

Whether or not they liked it, their lives would change through their relationships with us. There were strict rules for their safety that would need to be followed.

Emma had experienced the dangers of loving Dimitri firsthand in Morocco. I would do everything in my power to make sure Mary never learned that same lesson.

Everything except give her up.

These last two months weren't just for Mary, they were for me as well. I hadn't just thrown away my proverbial little black book. I had torn it to pieces and set it on fire.

My past and any other women in it had been laid to rest. I had also done my best to place safeguards and buffers between my personal life and the dangers of my business.

I may be a selfish bastard, but I wasn't a cold-hearted one.

I knew the chaos and upheaval I would bring into Mary's life. It wouldn't be fair to do that and just walk away after I had my fill.

She was practically a sister to my best friend's now wife. She deserved better. So I needed to make damn sure that I was in it for the long haul.

After two months apart, I was certain. There was no one in this world I wanted in my bed and in my life more than her.

I grinned. "Hello, beautiful."

She tossed her purse onto the hallway table and placed her fists on her hips. "Don't you fucking dare *hello, beautiful* me! You broke into my apartment!"

We had both been on our best behavior during Dimitri and Emma's wedding, but it felt good to get back to our true nature as a couple. The type who loved to fight and then fuck.

"I had a key—and the security code."

"You stole all my stuff."

"Not true, I simply arranged to have it relocated. It's all right here, present and accounted for."

She crossed her arms over her chest, which only served to push up her breasts. I, of course, wasn't going to apprise her of that. Why deprive myself of such a glorious view?

Her eyes flashed.

In this light they looked even more purple than usual.

Fuck, she was beautiful, especially when she was royally pissed off at me.

I would have to make her angry more often,

which judging by our relationship so far, shouldn't be a problem.

She pushed her chin out. "I'm not moving in with you."

"Technically, you already have."

She threw her arms up in the air and paced. "Do you have any idea how insane this is? You moved my stuff without my permission. Who does something like that?"

I smirked. "Off the top of my head, I would say a very powerful man with lots of money, low morals, and a loose definition of what is and is not considered legal."

Her head swiveled sharply from side to side.

My brow furrowed. "What are you doing?"

"Looking for something to throw at you to wipe that arrogant smirk off your face."

As she stepped toward the massive floral arrangement in the center of the entryway table, I blocked her path.

Her lips opened on a gasp as her gaze scanned my chest.

I moved closer. I grasped one silky curl and ran it over my palm, tugging gently on the end. "How long are you going to keep this up?"

She stared at my mouth, then her cute pink tongue slipped out to lick her own lips. "Keep what up?" she asked, slightly breathless.

Leaning down, I stopped only a few inches from

her mouth. I felt as well as heard her sharp inhale as I watched her pupils dilate. I knew if I reached for her wrist, I would feel her elevated pulse. "This pretense that you're angry with me."

She swallowed.

I watched the gentle movement of her throat. "I … I am angry with you."

I pulled her against me and claimed her mouth.

The need to taste her was like a physical pain deep in my chest. I stepped forward, forcing her backwards until her body slammed against the wall.

Releasing my grip on her face, I reached for her arms. Caressing their soft length, I snatched each of her wrists and pulled them high over her head. I transferred both wrists into my left hand and lowered my right to cup one full breast as my tongue swirled and played with hers.

Twisting her head to the side, she broke our kiss and pulled her hands free. "Wait. This is a mistake."

With my gaze locked on hers, I again reached for the silver chain around her neck.

She huffed. "It means nothing."

We both knew that wasn't true.

A woman didn't wear a man's ring close to her heart unless he meant something to her. The tip of my tongue traced her full lower lip.

My lips skimmed hers as I rasped, "Liar."

I captured her mouth again and rubbed my hips

against her stomach, needing to feel some contact to ease the ache in my already hard cock.

She pulled on my grasp around her wrists as she struggled in my embrace. "Vaska, I can't."

I reached up to wrap my other hand around her throat under her jaw.

I slipped the tip of my tongue along the delicate whorl of her ear before threatening, "Don't make me force you, Mary. Give in to me."

Her body stilled.

It was enough of an answer for me and I dropped my shoulder against her stomach.

Slinging her over my shoulder, I lifted her high and carried her to the bedroom.

She renewed her protests, but by now it was way too late.

I spanked her ass to quiet her struggles as I kicked open the bedroom double doors and strolled inside. I dropped her in the center of the bed.

She bounced a few times, then sprang up onto her knees. Her eyes were bright and alert as she scanned the room, familiarizing herself with the layout no doubt, and searching for exits.

There were none.

Her only way out was through me, and I wasn't budging.

I nodded toward her dress. "Is that sentimental?"

She covered her bodice protectively with her hands. "Why?"

"Because in about two seconds, I'm tearing it off your body."

Her eyes widened. "I love this dress."

"I'll buy you a new one. Hell, I'll buy you a hundred new ones. Now take it off."

"But … wait … I am not having sex with you. We need to talk about this … about us … about what you did."

"We'll talk later."

"Vaska…."

I unbuttoned the top button of my jeans. "One second."

She huffed. "You are the most insufferable, brutish, stubb—"

Ignoring her practiced rant, I smirked. "Time's up."

CHAPTER 22

MARY

There are no words in the English language to describe what it feels like to have a six-foot-plus, heavily muscled and tattooed man suddenly pounce on you.

I screamed and tried to scurry off the bed.

He was too quick.

His hands wrapped around my waist and forced me onto my back. He straddled my hips as he reached up to untie the knot in the halter around my neck.

I clawed at his wrists.

With a growl, he instead tore the halter straps at the seams where they attached to the bodice. As he whipped the strip of fabric from around my neck, he held it up between his hands.

He quirked one eyebrow as he looked at the knot in the center of the long strip of black fabric. He then looked down at my mouth. "I think I know how to put this to good use."

My mouth fell open before I snapped it shut. I seethed through clenched teeth, "You wouldn't dare."

He placed a hand on either side of my head and leaned down. The movement pushed his hard cock against my stomach. "Haven't you learned by now I will dare whatever the fuck I please?"

He kissed me hard on the lips before leaning back. He once again held up the fabric. "Are you going to be a good girl?"

My eyes narrowed as I bucked my hips, trying to dislodge him. "Fuck you."

He smiled. "Gagged it is."

Despite my squirming and protests, he gripped my jaw and pressed his fingertips into my cheeks.

My teeth cut the inside of them. I had no choice but to open my mouth.

He slipped the fabric knot between my teeth before flipping me onto my stomach. He tied the halter strap around the back of my head, anchoring it in place.

I reached up with my arms to untie it, but he effortlessly clasped my small wrists in his firm hand, pinning my arms behind my back.

With his free hand, he flipped off my high heels. He then ran his palm up the back of my leg. "I love you in these stockings."

I was wearing a pair of retro back-seam black

stockings to match the fifties vibe of my dress. I held my breath. It was only a matter of seconds before he discovered—

Vaska chuckled, "Why, you naughty minx."

He pulled on the elastic band of one of my garters and snapped it against the sensitive skin on the back of my thigh.

I jumped from the sharp bite of pain.

He leaned his body over mine, caging me in. He ran his finger along the garter strap. "Did you wear these just for me?"

No.

Yes.

Maybe.

Damn him.

I struggled against his restraining hand, which still had my arms pinned, as I cursed him out through my gag. "Fuff ooo. Uf ie ee!"

He released my arms, but only to gain access to the back zipper of my dress.

As I tried to shimmy away, he gripped the zipper and pulled it down.

My movements only helped him strip the dress from my body. He tossed it and the red crinoline onto the floor. I flipped onto my back and scrambled up against the headboard of the bed.

He'd left me only in a black corset, panties, and my garter belt and stockings.

If his sapphire gaze were a blue flame, it would

have scorched every inch of my body. "*Ya nikogda ne vypushchu tebya iz etoy krovati.*"

My brow furrowed.

He repeated in English, "I'm never letting you leave this bed."

A shiver went up my spine at the sexual threat and the image of being tied to the bedpost, forever at his mercy, as he relentlessly fucked me over and over again.

Oh, my God.

Helplessly mesmerized, I stared as his large, tattooed hand slowly lowered the zipper on his jeans.

It was impossible not to notice the hard length of his cock as it pressed against the denim along the inside of his thigh. He pushed his jeans off his hips, dropping them to the floor. His cock bobbed several times, the heavy head enlarged and almost purple.

My thighs clenched at the memory of his thick length pushing its way into my tight body.

Belatedly, I realized my arms were now free. I reached up and untied the gag from around my head.

Vaska's upper lip lifted in a smirk. "Good, I prefer hearing you scream my name as I fuck you."

Keeping his gaze on me, he shifted to the left and opened the drawer of the nearby nightstand—and pulled out a knife.

I cried out and jumped off the bed, running for the door. He blocked my path. As he prowled forward, I was backed against a wall. "What … what are you doing, Vaska?"

My heart was beating so fast, I feared I might pass out.

"Shhh …. *krasotka*. Stay very still."

I bit my lip enough to taste blood, as he lifted the knife and tilted the point at my stomach.

Oh, God.

Fear paralyzed me. I couldn't move my arms to defend myself.

The cold metal pressed against the skin of my lower abdomen. In the silence of the room, I heard the soft rending of fabric.

My panties fell off my left hip. He shifted the knife to my other side. Slipping it beneath the fabric, the sharp blade easily sliced through the fabric until my ruined panties fell to the floor.

He smiled as he tossed the knife aside, then slipped his hand between my legs. "It needed to be done. It's the only way I can taste this sweet pussy of yours while keeping your sexy garter belt and stockings on."

I blinked.

It took a moment for his words to register.

All the blood rushed back into my body, making me dizzy with confused emotions of fear, anger, and desire. Recovering, I raised my arm, my hand curled into a fist. "Why, you—"

He grabbed my wrist and turned me, pinning my

arm against my lower back. Pushing my body forward, he lowered me onto my knees on the bed. His hand released my arm and fisted into my hair, holding me in place. He knelt behind me, the warm skin of his stomach brushing my now-bare ass.

He pushed a knee between mine and forced my legs open.

He growled, "Are you going to be a good girl?"

I stubbornly refused to answer.

He slapped my ass with his open palm. *"Ty sobirayesh'sya byt' khoroshey devochkoy?"*

"Yes!" I cried out as hot needles of pleasurable pain raced over my skin.

He released my hair and set his strong, warm hands on my hips before slipping them over my ass. Pressing his thumbs into the seam, he pried open my cheeks.

I could feel his breath against my hidden flesh. Humiliated, I buried my face into the bedcovers as I felt the heat of his gaze.

"Tilt your hips back," he commanded in his dark, gravelly voice.

"Please," I begged.

He offered me no quarter. "Don't make me repeat myself, *krasotka*. You don't want me to get my belt."

My body jerked in alarm as if his threat had carried the literal weight of a strike from the leather strap.

Submitting to his demands, I pushed my hips out, further exposing myself to him.

"Good girl." The low 'r' rolled off his tongue like the purr of a panther.

Without warning, the tip of his tongue licked the length of my pussy.

I fisted the bedcovers as my back arched. It may damn me to hell with him, but I missed this.

His tongue flicked my clit. "I've missed the taste of this sweet pussy of yours. That's it, baby, show me how much you missed the feel of my mouth."

A low moan escaped my lips.

His hands gripped my ass as his tongue swirled and circled my clit, applying gentle pressure.

I pushed my hips out further, wantonly pushing myself onto his tongue. His right hand shifted before I felt his thumb swipe over my dark hole.

I inhaled sharply as I tensed.

He swiped a second time before applying the slightest pressure with the pad of his thumb. He pushed inside.

My mouth fell open on a gasp as memories of the time he'd fucked my ass in the shower crashed over me in deep, dark waves.

He thrust his thumb in and out of my ass as he continued to tongue my clit.

My hips rocked back and forth as I moaned, "Faster, faster."

He increased the rhythm of both his tongue and thumb.

"Oh, God, Vaska. I'm coming!" I screamed.

In that moment, he twisted his thumb deep inside of me as he shifted his hand to push two fingers into my cunt.

The sudden thrust of his fingers sent me over the edge.

I saw stars behind my eyelids and shocks of pleasure raced up my spine. Before I had come down from my spiraling orgasm, he lifted me off my knees and centered me in the bed on my back.

Kneeling between my open legs, he fisted his shaft. Running his hand up and down the length, he ordered, "Push your corset down. I want to see your breasts."

I obeyed. Hooking my thumbs into the sides, I pushed until the corset shifted lower on my torso, exposing my breasts.

He licked his lips. The erotic sight damn near gave me a second orgasm. With his free hand, he ran his palm up my inner thigh before grasping the thin silky elastic of my garter. He pulled it taut and snapped it against my skin.

"Ow!" I objected even as the sting only heightened my pleasure.

He winked and snapped the other garter. Then his body dipped low as he placed his left forearm near my head and pressed his hips between my legs.

He nuzzled my neck. "I dreamed of sinking my cock into your tight heat every night we were apart."

He reached between our bodies and lodged the head of his shaft at my entrance.

I held my breath as I braced for the painful pleasure I knew was coming. He thrust in deep, tearing me apart and filling me all at once.

My fingernails dug into his shoulders.

He shifted his hips and thrust again and again.

I raised my legs to wrap them around his hips, pulling him closer, asking for the pain as my body adjusted to his hard, thick intrusion.

He cupped my right breast as he leaned down to take my left nipple between his teeth, alternating between biting and licking the sensitive bud. He increased his pace, pounding into me with the same rhythm as my rapid heartbeat.

He leaned up to gaze down into my eyes. He was slightly breathless when he said, "I'm never letting you go, *krasotka*."

Two months ago my heart and mind would have dismissed his heated declaration as just the type of lie a man like him knew a woman wanted to hear.

I now knew better.

He wasn't lying. He really wanted to be with me. Hell, he'd literally moved me into his home.

What further proof did I need of his intentions?

Curling his hands into fists, he rested them just above my shoulders and straightened his arms, leaning back. His thrusts stilled with him deep inside of me.

His eyes narrowed as he breathed heavily through clenched teeth. A fine sheen of sweat glistened over his chest. His arms shook as he restrained himself from thrusting. "Tell me you love me," he growled.

My mouth opened in shock. "What?"

He ground his hips against my core but didn't thrust. "Tell me you love me," he repeated.

There was a big difference between finally accepting you love someone you know could potentially shatter your heart into a million pieces and actually saying it out loud.

Saying it out loud made it real.

Saying it out loud would force me to accept the truth of it.

Worse, saying it out loud would forever seal my submission to his dominance.

"Vaska—" I pleaded, not ready for what he was asking of me.

"Now, Mary," he roared.

Shocked, I blurted out, "I love you."

He closed his eyes as if savoring the sound. When he opened them, his sapphire gaze pinned me to the bed with a dark intent that seared my soul.

With a growl, he pulled his cock almost free.

The wide head pushed at my entrance from the inside before he surged forward. He pounded into my body with such violence I was certain we would break the bed.

My legs ached from straining to stay open for the repeated thrust of his hips.

I could feel every inch of his thick cock as he speared into me. Reaching between us, I swirled the tips of my fingers over my still-sensitive clit, feeling another climax build.

Just as my pleasure crested, Vaska's body stiffened.

He threw his head back as his back bowed. With a guttural roar, he filled me with his seed. After a few heavy breaths, his body jerked, then he fell forward. His heavy weight pressed me into the mattress for a moment before he rolled onto his back, taking me with him. He pressed me against his side as he kissed the top of my head.

Both of us were out of breath and dazed from the intense experience.

After several minutes, Vaska shifted the covers out from beneath us and tucked me under the blanket, but not before he unfastened my corset and pulled it off my body.

I was now left in only my garters and stockings. I thought I should probably take them off, but I didn't want to move. He spooned me from behind.

Eventually his breathing became steady and even. "You're staying with me."

I didn't have the energy to argue. Snuggling closer against his warmth, I said, "We'll talk about it later."

His grasp on my breast tightened. "There is nothing to discuss, Mary. My decision is final."

Icy fingers of dread gripped my heart.

Perhaps I was overreacting.

It had been a long, emotional day.

I would try to reason with him later when we weren't lying naked in bed.

His hand shifted to cover my stomach. "And I want you off birth control starting now."

I swallowed as fear closed my throat.

Before my eyes, I had a vision of gleaming gold bars slamming into place.

One by one they surrounded me, caging me in … for life.

CHAPTER 23

MARY

I awoke to the smell of bacon.

I crawled out of bed and snatched up the robe that Vaska had left slung over a nearby chair.

Wrapping myself in its cozy warmth, I inhaled his spicy cologne scent, which still clung to the fabric. Tightening the belt, I padded barefoot down the hallway toward the kitchen and the scent of breakfast.

Vaska was standing over the stovetop dressed in only a pair of jeans.

His entire back was covered in colorful tattoos.

I tried not to focus on the specific images, but just the splashes of color. If I focused on the images, I would remember what I'd learned from Emma's Russian prison tattoo book. I had enough on my plate without dealing with a Pictionary story of Vaska's violent past.

Past? Probably present as well. What the hell had I gotten myself into?

Without turning around, he said, "There's coffee."

My gaze scanned the kitchen counter until I saw the expensive-looking espresso/coffee machine with the fresh pot. Picking up an empty mug, I poured myself a cup and dumped in several spoonfuls of sugar.

Again, without even turning around, Vaska offered, "There's chocolate sauce in the fridge."

I scrunched up my face. I hated the fact that he knew me so well after so short of an acquaintance.

Out of spite, I stuck my tongue out at his turned back.

"I saw that," he chuckled, still without turning around.

No wonder he didn't like *Buffy the Vampire Slayer*.

It was clear the man was part demon with eyes in the back of his head, so obviously he wouldn't like seeing his kind die in a hail of dirty dust episode after episode.

With an annoyed huff, I pulled the heavy stainless steel refrigerator door open and found the Hershey's syrup. I had to remove the clear plastic wrap.

My heart lurched.

He had bought this just for me. Dammit. Why did

he have to be so thoughtful and considerate and yet such an arrogant bully at the same time?

I poured a generous amount of syrup into my mug and stirred as I grabbed one of the leather-topped stools positioned around the white marble kitchen island.

Out of curiosity, I looked at the stack of magazines casually tossed in the center.

Vaska didn't really strike me as the magazine type, except for maybe *Guns and Ammo*.

Casting a quick glance at his back, I pulled the stack toward me. Sliding one magazine after another off the top, I saw they were all decor magazines.

He turned to face me, placing a plate of scrambled eggs, bacon, and toast in front of me.

"I thought you might like to look those over before the decorator gets here later today," he offered as he turned away to grab utensils.

"Decorator?"

He placed a fork and knife in front of me. "Eat."

I picked up a slice of bacon—because bacon—but I wrinkled my nose at the rest. "I don't usually eat breakfast."

"I know. It's one of the things that is going to change about your life. From now on, no more vending machine crap for my girl."

"Really, I'm not—"

"Eat."

"Fine!" I pushed the tines of the fork through the

scrambled eggs. "Why are you hiring a decorator?" I braced for his response, already knowing the answer.

"I wouldn't expect you to live in a home you don't like. I know you don't like all the white, so we'll change it."

My stomach twisted as the bite of egg turned to dust in my mouth. "Vaska, we need to talk."

His eyes narrowed. "No. We don't. I've already told you. My decision is final. You live here with me now."

"We barely know one another."

He shrugged. "I know enough."

"Enough for what?"

"Enough to know I want you by my side."

"Yes, but for how long? You expect me to uproot my entire life for some fling?"

With an angry growl, he rounded the island and spun my stool to face him, pinning me against the marble edge.

He leaned his palms on the island countertop, caging me in. "I'm losing patience with you, Mary. If you continue to deny me, and deny what we have, I'm going to get angry. Trust me, you don't want to see me angry."

My body froze as all the blood drained from my veins. I swallowed but could think of nothing to say.

He ran his knuckles down my cheek, before trailing his fingertips over the rapid pulse at the base of my throat. “This isn’t a fling, Mary. I’ve made my intentions clear.”

I licked my lips. “Are you saying you want to marry me?”

He smiled. “I’m saying I *am* marrying you.”

It was a sharp left turn that left me dizzy.

To go from assuming this man was a one-night stand player who would love me and leave me to hear him talking not just a long-term relationship but marriage.

Turns out he was no different than his friend, Dimitri.

I wonder if all Russian men were as stubborn and decisive when it came to the women they wanted?

Despite the chaotic emotions his nearness was causing, I pressed on. “Do I get a say in any of this?”

He pushed a lock of hair behind my ear. “Of course. You get to pick out your dress and the flowers.”

“That’s not what I meant.”

“I know.” His lips thinned. “But answering the question you really asked would only anger me.” He kissed me hard on the lips and walked away as he tossed over his shoulder, “I have a meeting. Eat your breakfast. Your clothes are already in the closet. A driver is waiting to take you wherever you want to go.”

I hopped off the stool and followed him into the

bedroom. "What about the apartment I already rented in Lincoln Square?"

"I've taken care of it."

My fists went to my hips. "What is that supposed to mean?"

He opened the double doors to a massive walk-in closet. It was so big that each side contained a bureau and two floor-to-ceiling mirrors. To the right were rack after rack of black and gray suits.

To the left, hanging just as neatly, were all of my clothes.

He pulled a cable-knit charcoal gray sweater from a hanger and tossed it on.

I was pissed at my momentary disappointment as he covered his muscles and tattoos.

He opened a drawer and chose a pair of socks. "It means your landlord and I have come to an understanding. You no longer have a lease with him. Your security deposit is back in your account."

"You canceled my lease?"

"You cannot think I would let you live in that fucking tiny, moldy basement apartment?"

I huffed as I crossed my arms over my chest. "I'm sorry! Not all of us are blessed with endless riches. People like me have student loans and bills to pay. We can't afford high-rise penthouses."

After tying on a pair of boots, he lifted the lid on a beautiful mahogany watch case and selected one of the uber-expensive-looking watches, which were slowly rotating like spinning dials. "That is not true."

"What is not true?"

He turned to me as he latched the watch around his wrist. There was just something so sexy about seeing a man's strong hand and thick wrist with a watch on it. It was just so old-school gentleman in a good way.

Like he was the type of man who opened doors and ordered for you at restaurants, which, of course, described Vaska perfectly.

He responded matter-of-factly, "You are not one of those people, because you no longer have any student loans or bills to pay. I have taken care of all of it."

His heavy Russian accent made his statement sound even more ominous.

He had paid off all my student loans?

Just like that?

It was close to a hundred thousand dollars between college and graduate school.

More gold bars slammed down around me.

"Do you expect me to be okay with being your kept mistress, earning my keep on my—"

The movie *Pretty Woman* had definitely steered an entire generation of women wrong. That movie made it seem like it was sexy and fun to have a handsome crazy-rich man shower you with money and gifts in exchange for some companionship.

It wasn't.

Not even the tiniest bit.

It was terrifying.

My entire life was now in the palm of his hand.

At any moment he could clench his fist and destroy me.

Vaska stepped toward me.

He wrapped his hand around my neck and pulled me close. His voice was soft and low, but no less threatening.

"Do not finish that sentence. I expect to treat you like my future wife."

I squeezed my eyes shut, hating that several tears fell onto my cheeks. "Vaska, this is all too much. I can't deal with all—"

He swiped at the tears with his thumb before kissing me on the forehead. "Shhh, *krasotka.* Don't cry. You must understand, I'm doing this for your own safety as well as for us. It is better if you are fully under my protection."

"Yes, but—"

He leaned down to gaze into my eyes. "The money is no matter to me. Let me spoil you."

I wrapped my hands around his wrists as he continued to caress my cheeks. "This is moving too fast. I can't think."

"I know. Take this first step. Stay with me. *Be with me.* We'll talk about marrying later, when you're ready."

I stared into his dark sapphire eyes. “Do you really mean that?”

One side of his mouth quirked up. “I *want* to mean it. Does that count?”

It would have to.

Like everything else, I didn’t see how I had a choice in the matter.

CHAPTER 24

VASKA

The man's pleading drowned out Dimitri's greeting.

He had postponed his honeymoon with Emma until the winter.

He wanted to take her home to Russia, but she was insisting on seeing the *Anna Karenina* version from her imagination, which meant furs, snow-covered cathedrals, and sleigh rides.

He was in love with her enough to make it happen.

I was fairly certain if there was no snow when they arrived, he would make that happen too. I could see him paying to carpet half of St. Petersburg in fake snow just to please her.

He was that much in love with her.

I knew the feeling.

Nodding, I accepted the to-go cup of coffee he offered.

We leaned against a stack of crates as one of our men punched the midsection of a former employee who currently dangled by his wrists from a heavy chain suspended from a steel girder.

The thief had been caught trying to steal a shipment of Stechkin select-fire machine pistols from us.

He had told us the crates had been confiscated by customs. A common enough occurrence in our business if a shipment arrived unexpectedly early or late and one of the customs officers we kept on the payroll with bribes was not on duty. He was then caught trying to sell them to various street gangs.

That was when he'd truly crossed the line.

You never shit where you eat.

We supplied guns to governments and paramilitary operations, but never to gangs and definitely never to a gang in Chicago. While there was no guarantee of preventing an innocent life being spilt by a government or paramilitary organization, at least it was usually avoided.

That wasn't the case with gangs.

Innocent victims were a foregone conclusion.

Dimitri and I were already rich men.

We didn't need that much blood money.

Dimitri ripped the foil off a fresh pack of Sobranie cigarettes and offered me one. I selected one of the black paper-wrapped and gold foil-tipped cigarettes. Digging into my pocket, I pulled out a lighter.

After lighting my own, I held out the flame for him.

He took a long drag. "I received an odd phone call from Emma on the way over here. Is it true you are holding her best friend prisoner?"

I scoffed as I blew out a cloud of smoke. "My penthouse is hardly a prison. When I left Mary was unpacking the countless boxes of Fifi Chachnil lingerie I had ordered her from Paris while sipping hot chocolate. Trust me, she is not suffering under my care."

Dimitri took a sip of his coffee. "So it's true. What exactly is your endgame, Vaska?"

I turned to face him. "I don't interfere with Emma. You don't interfere with Mary."

He raised an eyebrow. "You know I can't stand by and let you hurt her. If you upset Mary, you upset Emma and I won't allow anyone, even you, my friend, to upset my wife."

I took a long drag off my cigarette before responding.

Dimitri was my best and oldest friend but I would be damned if I'd let him interfere in any way with my relationship with Mary, regardless of his intentions.

"I have warned you before, Mary is my concern, not yours."

He flicked ash onto the filthy cement floor.

"Should I be congratulating you?"

I smiled. "As soon as I can arrange it."

Dimitri laughed.

Tossing the remains of his cigarette aside, he pulled me into a bear hug. Clapping me on the back, he said, "I am happy for you. Although I think you will have your hands full."

I winked. "That's half the fun."

He quickly sobered. "You may have to act fast."

I was already having a custom-made engagement ring created for her as we spoke.

I wasn't a patient man, but I planned to give Mary at least until the end of the summer to come to terms with her new life as my wife.

My brow furrowed. "What's going on?"

"I saw Gregor last night at that art museum event. He was with Samara."

I tossed my cigarette onto the cement and crushed it with my toe. "Really? So he finally found his runaway bride?"

The most powerful Russian families kept tabs on one another.

It was no secret Gregor Ivanov had arranged to marry Samara Federov over three years ago by giving her father a tidy sum to handle his debts.

The girl ran off in the middle of the night the moment she learned of the arrangement.

He refused to let her go, chasing her and her friend clear across the United States and back these last three years. They'd had several close calls but the two girls always managed to slip their grasp.

He nodded. "Hiding out here in Chicago, no less. Gregor wants to meet with us in an hour. Trouble is coming."

The man pleaded for mercy again.

I looked over my shoulder to watch as his limp body swung back and forth, propelled by the punches to his gut. *"Dovol'no. Ubey yego."*

Obeying my sharp command, they put a bullet in the thief's head and prepared to dump the body. "What kind of trouble?"

Dimitri finished his coffee and crushed the cup in his fist. "Novikoffs are trying to claim Gregor's woman. Apparently they made a second deal with her shifty as fuck father. We have intelligence they might already be in our territory. It could interfere with … business."

The Novikoffs were a pain in everyone's ass.

Stupidity and violence were always a bad combination, and the Novikoff father and sons had both in spades, especially if they were in our territory without our permission. That kind of transgression could start a war no one wanted.

Territory wars attracted the attention of the authorities, which was bad for business.

Two of our men dragged the thief's dead body past us, as a third mopped up the bloody trail with a rag he pulled beneath his boots in their wake.

I looked on with dispassionate interest. "Well, we know how we treat those who interfere with our business."

"I'm having the safehouse prepared in case I need to protect Emma."

"Good, I'll be prepared to bring Mary there if necessary, as well."

Dimitri chuckled.

I frowned. "What?"

He shook his head. "Better bring handcuffs … and maybe a small army."

My friend probably wasn't far off the mark.

I knew Mary started her new job as a summer school teacher tomorrow.

I doubt she would take lightly to me informing her she had to quit and hide out in a safehouse for a week or more until we determined the trouble had passed.

It was a hard reality of being with me, one she would have to learn to accept. There would be times where her safety was more important than her career. Besides, I could always pay off any supervisors who tried to make trouble for her.

Still, that didn't mean Mary would be okay with the arrangement.

Maybe Dimitri was right, having a pair of handcuffs handy might be a good idea.

Just in case.

CHAPTER 25

MARY

One week later

THIS LAST WEEK had been surreal.

It was like I was living in a fifty's sitcom, but with a Godfather mafia twist.

Vaska had taken over my life and my thoughts.

I sat behind my desk, opened my lesson planner, and tried to focus.

"All right, class, who can tell me the function of the gravediggers in Act Five of *Hamlet*?"

No one raised their hand.

It was okay.

I enjoyed a challenge, and there were few things more challenging than a classroom of high school juniors forced into summer school. If I did well during this trial period, I hoped to secure a permanent position on the teaching staff.

"Open your copies of *Hamlet* and review," I raised my voice over their groans, "Act Five, now. You have fifteen minutes then I expect an answer."

I pretended to work, but really I was thinking of Vaska.

Again.

Every morning he made me breakfast.

We would eat it at an actual table, not over the sink or out of a paper bag, while he asked questions about my new job, and not half-ass boyfriend, I'm-only-asking-so-you-won't-bitch-later questions that just feigned interest.

Real questions.

I made the mistake of reciprocating by asking him about his work and got treated to a blunt response about taking care of some guy who tried to steal from them and having to monitor an incoming shipment of super scary-sounding sniper rifles being smuggled in on a cargo ship from Africa.

It gave a whole new definition to TMI.

It was strange.

It was hard to be bothered by the criminal aspects of Vaska and Dimitri's business when they were both so candid about it.

You'd think they were just a couple of businessmen making widgets with how they talked about gun shipments and the street market price of the latest smuggled surface-to-air missile launcher.

It was easy to fall into this false sense of complacency that what they did wasn't that bad.

And in reality, it wasn't.

They truly weren't any worse than the average American CEO trying to make a buck.

At least they weren't taking advantage of cheap labor or stealing from pension funds or trying to get half of America addicted to opioids. All I was saying was there were probably worse things in this world than being an arms dealer.

A sentence I never thought I would ever utter in my entire life.

Every day he had a driver take me to work.

I made the driver drop me off a block away from the school, just in case. There was no point in having the other teachers see me roll up in a top-of-the-line Mercedes, complete with a uniformed driver.

Every afternoon, precisely at my lunch break, a catered lunch would arrive from some high-end restaurant or other from around the city, followed by a text from Vaska demanding I eat *real food.*

When I complained he was making me look bad to my coworkers who had to sit there with their sad ham and cheese sandwiches with wilted lettuce and watch while I ate sushi or steak or lobster, he responded by sending a catered lunch for the whole teaching staff every day.

Needless to say, I was the most popular teacher on staff.

At night we played house—or at least Vaska's version of house.

My cheeks burned as I remembered last night.

First, he'd cooked us an amazing dinner of roasted quail with baked apples in a red bilberry sauce, a specialty dish from the Bolshoi, one of his favorite restaurants in Moscow.

I swore I could almost forgive that man anything while he cooked.

Often after returning home, he would change out of his expensive suit into a pair of jeans, or even better, a pair of gray sweatpants, and pad around barefoot and bare-chested as he cooked dinner.

He quickly picked up on how sexy I thought his collection of watches was, so he often left the watch on. *Swoon.* Not to mention, the man had missed his calling. If he hadn't turned to a life of crime, he certainly could have been a master chef.

I found myself enjoying sipping wine as I sat on a stool around the island each night watching him cook, while he encouraged me to chat about my day.

It was all just so *normal.*

You'd never guess I was practically there against my will.

Well, almost against my will.

Certainly at first against my will—but that was becoming less and less so with every passing day.

He would often turn and hold a spoon or fork up to my mouth for me to taste a sauce or a juicy bite of meat. Whenever he did that, the heat and promise in his gaze as I trailed my lips seductively along the tines of the fork made me want to melt straight into the floor.

Last night he turned decorating decisions into a game of strip tease, as we went through his decorator's ideas to add more color and incorporate some of my belongings and style.

I'd walked slowly around the living room before stating emphatically, "The white sofa has to go."

Vaska smirked as his gaze caressed my body from head to toe. "What's it worth to you?"

I crossed my arms and smiled. "Nothing since you already ruined it with that big ass red wine stain."

He shrugged and sent me a challenging look. "I can live with it."

I narrowed my eyes. He knew damn well that stain was already driving me crazy. "What's your offer?"

"Your shirt and bra."

That would leave me in only my panties and socks since I had already bid away my slacks to get rid of the glass coffee table with the ostentatious thick gold trim.

"No way! For a stained sofa? One sock."

He shook his head. "Your shirt. Final offer."

"Throw in this terrible white shag throw rug."

"Deal."

I peeled off my form-fitting black sweater with the sugar skull on the front. Just to tease him I adjusted the cups of my black satin bra with the pink polka dots.

Vaska crossed the room to me, but I quickly put the sofa between us.

I pointed at the white canvas with the minuscule purple dot he was calling art, which hung in pride of place over the sofa, dominating the room. "This."

I made a slashing motion across my throat.

"Fine, but that framed poster of the weird blond vampire cannot go up in its place."

I feigned shock. "You can't expect me to give up my Spike poster."

I actually had no intention of hanging that on the wall, anyway.

There was a difference between your school apartment and your adulting one. The primary difference being getting art that doesn't come rolled up in a piece of cellophane.

But Vaska didn't need to know that.

He raised an eyebrow. "No photos or posters of other men, especially weird vampire ones."

"Fine, but I'm going to need something in return."

He smirked. "Name it."

"Your jeans." It was pretty much the only thing I could ask for since he didn't have a shirt or socks on.

Without hesitation, his hands reached for the zipper of his jeans.

After unfastening them, he pulled them off his hips and dropped the denim to the floor.

I covered my mouth as I laughed. "Oh, my God! You're naked! Where are your boxers?"

He wriggled his eyebrows and stalked me around the sofa.

I laughed as I tried to outmaneuver him. "No fair. You're cheating."

His eyes widened as he tried to look innocent. "How is this cheating? You started with more clothes than me."

I rounded the bamboo and white upholstery chair as I playfully taunted him over my shoulder. "Not my fault you don't know how to play the game."

Vaska lunged and caught me around the waist.

I screamed and kicked out.

He tossed me onto the sofa.

The weight of his body followed, pinning me against the cushions. His hips pressed between my legs as his hard cock was wedged between our bodies.

He sank his teeth into the fabric of my bra and pretended to try to tear it before saying in a low, sinister voice, "You are under my control. Beg me for mercy."

Loving the feel of his hard muscled body on top of mine, I played along with this change in the game.

Thrusting my chin out, I declared emphatically, "Never!"

Vaska grinned as his fingers slipped into the waistband of my panties. "Then accept your punishment."

He shifted his body until his face was between my legs. I shrieked and squirmed out of his embrace.

I shimmied backwards and then flipped onto my stomach, preparing to launch myself off the sofa, but Vaska was too quick for me.

He grabbed my panties and pulled them off my ass and down my thighs before tangling them around my ankles.

I tried to kick out, but he flipped me onto my back and placed his enormous chest between my thighs.

He tore the panties off me. Twirling them around his index finger, he winked. "I win. Now for my prize."

"That's not how you wi—" All protest died on my lips as his mouth fell on my pussy like a man starved. "Oh, my God!"

My fingers delved into his hair as I lifted my hips off the sofa, pressing my body against his tongue.

"Ms. Fraser. Is the answer comic relief?"

I blinked. "What?"

One of my students from the back called out again, "Is the answer comic relief?"

I swallowed as I pressed my palms to my cheeks,

trying to cool them down as I came crashing back to reality. Resisting the urge to fan myself, I nodded as I rose from my seat.

Clearing my throat, I responded, "Yes, Matthew, partly. What other function could they serve in the scene in relation to Hamlet?"

Before anyone could respond, my classroom door was pushed violently open, crashing against the wall.

Vaska appeared in the doorway.

There was an audible gasp from the students.

I couldn't blame them.

While still in one of his customary expensive suits, he had no tie on and several top buttons of his shirt were undone, exposing some of his more salacious tattoos. With his suit jacket unbuttoned, you could clearly see his shoulder harness with the butt of a handgun tucked under his arm.

As if all that wasn't enough to cause alarm, there was Vaska's thunderous expression as he commanded in Russian, *"Nam nuzhno uyti seychas zhe."*

I stepped forward in a pathetic and fruitless attempt to block my students' view of him. "What?"

He waved his hand in the air, motioning for me to step forward.

His brow furrowed as he growled in frustration when he realized he'd spoken in Russian, not English. "We have to leave. Now. No questions. Come."

My mouth dropped open.

I cringed when I heard the unmistakable sound of fabric rustling behind me. In other words, the sound of each and every student reaching for their cellphones.

Vaska stepped forward, his legs spread wide and his hands going to his hips. Which pushed back the sides of his suit coat, unabashedly exposing his sidearm. “Put the phones down.”

Hazarding a peek over my shoulder, I saw each wide-eyed student immediately obey as they slammed their phones face down onto their desks.

At least I wasn’t the only one who was terrified of Vaska in this state.

I shook my head. “What is going on? I can’t leave my students.”

He turned his powerful gaze on me. “I’m not asking, *krasotka,* I’m telling. We need to leave now.”

I crossed my arms over my chest. “No.” I then leaned in and whispered harshly, “Now you better get out of here before one of these students calls the police or sounds the alarm.”

A frustrated sigh escaped through his clenched teeth. “Have it your way.”

He fisted the fabric of my white striped sailor shirt and yanked me against his chest. The class hooted and called out as he landed a fierce kiss on my closed lips.

Their shouts blocked out the distinctive metal click until it was too late.

When Vaska pulled away, I realized he had handcuffed us together. "What the fu—"

He pulled me against his side and dragged me out of the classroom as my uncaring students continued to holler and egg him on.

I was being kidnapped … by my own boyfriend.

CHAPTER 26

VASKA

There was no hope for it.

I'd gotten the call from Dimitri less than an hour ago.

Gregor's Samara had been attacked in his home in the early morning hours.

We confirmed the Novikoffs were involved.

There was also increased chatter on the street about the Los Infieles gang asking questions about the whereabouts of a blonde Russian female who matched the description of Samara's friend, Yelena Nikitina.

The woman Damien was tracking down.

Two separate factions were striking at us where we were most vulnerable, our women.

Everything and everyone needed to be locked down.

Dimitri already had Emma at the safehouse.

I needed to pick up my Barret M82 sniper rifle, which was in Dimitri's gun safe, and then Mary and I were headed straight there.

I was also going to meet up with Damien Ivanov, who had secured Yelena and was using our helicopter to get her out of the city and to safety fast.

We had offered the use of our safehouse, but he wanted to return to Washington, D.C. as soon as possible.

I couldn't blame him. D.C. was Ivanov territory. He would be in a better position to protect her there, rather than relying on our resources here in Chicago. Home base advantage was always better.

After parking in Dimitri's garage, I circled around and opened the back passenger door, which I had of course child locked when I'd tossed her back there. There was also a thick glass privacy divider I used on the rare occasion I had a driver, which helped keep her contained.

I leaned in and asked, "Are you going to be a good girl, or do I have to put the cuffs back on?"

Her foot hit me square in the chest as she kicked out.

Fortunately for me, she was wearing a pair of those cute leather ballet slippers she favored for work and not her usual five-inch heels.

I smirked as I grabbed her ankle. "That answers that."

I dragged her out of the car and hooked the dangling cuff from my right wrist to her left.

Mary's eyes narrowed as she pulled on her arm and threw her weight back, resisting my efforts to walk forward. "Do you have any idea what you have done? You have ruined my career. I'll be fired for sure."

I cupped her face, swiping my thumbs under her eyes to clean up the slight smudges from her mascara caused by her tears.

I hated that I'd made her cry, and that I didn't have time to fully explain, but I would make this up to her.

For now, I could at least ease her fears about her job. "Baby, the principal of your school is a degenerate gambler who owes over seventeen grand to the Italians. One call from me and they call in the debt. Trust me, your job is safe."

"But what about my students?"

"The moment we left, I had an … associate of mine … take over the class. They think she's their substitute teacher and you're involved in some high-level terrorism drill."

Her lips thinned. "An associate? You have an escort watching those kids right now, don't you?"

I shrugged. "I needed someone with a kind-looking face who could role play. Kandy fit the bill. She's into the whole teacher/bad schoolgirl thing. Don't worry. I never slept with Kandy. You've been the only woman for me since the first moment I laid eyes on you."

"Is that supposed to make this all somehow okay?"

I gave her a quick, hard kiss on the lips. "It should. Come on. I need to pick up a few things, then I'm taking you to Emma."

I entered the house in time to open the front door for Damien who had just arrived with who, I assumed judging by her blonde hair, was Yelena.

Despite her wrinkled clothes, she was obviously a very beautiful woman—and I couldn't care less. Her looks were nothing compared to the glossy black hair and flashing indigo blue eyes of the woman I loved.

Nothing reassured a man he had found his forever mate than having no interest in any other woman, no matter how beautiful.

I turned to say as much to Mary, but judging from her tight-lipped glare, I decided it would be best to share my revelation with her later.

Damien slapped me on the shoulder in greeting then turned to the blonde. "Yelena, this is my friend, Vasili Lukovich Rostov."

"Please, call me Vaska, and this is Mary."

Mary raised her arm to give a small, reluctant wave. "Hello."

Yelena's eyes widened when she saw the handcuffs. Damien ignored her reaction and asked, "You heard Gregor is already back in D.C.?"

I nodded. "Dimitri has taken Emma to a secure location just to be on the safe side until things calm down. I've already called for the helicopter to take you to Midway. It should be arriving any minute now."

"Thank you, my friend. I'm sorry we have caused so much trouble in your city this visit."

I laughed. "Things were getting boring with only the Petrov brothers to kick around. Besides, we owed you for your help with that Morocco mess."

Mary shifted.

I knew Emma getting kidnapped in Morocco was still an open wound for her. It was also a big hurdle in our relationship.

Being with me put her in danger. There was no way to get around that. Today's events certainly weren't helping.

Yelena interrupted. "I'm sorry, but …."

Damien cut her off by pulling her closer to his side and giving her a warning look.

Knowing what she was going to say, I pulled on my arm, jerking Mary forward slightly.

She pulled right back. "Mary has decided to stubbornly refuse my protection."

"Because *Mary* can take care of herself and doesn't need an overbearing Russian barging into her life barking orders," responded Mary curtly.

Yelena cast Damien a sour look. "Mary, if you

need any tips on how to easily pick a handcuff lock, let me know."

Damien laughed. "Just make sure you don't need to do it quietly or quickly, or you're fucked."

Mary asked Yelena, "You don't—by any chance—have a gun on you, do you?" Before turning to innocently bat her long black eyelashes at me.

The *thwap, thwap, thwap* of the helicopter interrupted our conversation, reminding us this wasn't the time for pleasantries.

As Damien climbed the stairs with Yelena to the helipad, I took Mary into my arms. "Keep misbehaving, baby girl. I'm keeping a tally and trust me, you are going to feel the sting of my belt on that cute ass of yours when this is all over."

Her brow furrowed. "You can't honestly think you'll still be my boyfriend after all this mess?"

I drove the fingers of my free hand into her sleek hair and pulled her face close. "Absolutely not, I'll be your husband."

I swallowed her gasp with a kiss, forcing my tongue between her lips, tasting her surprise.

She may have thought I had forgotten about marriage after first mentioning it a week ago then quickly dropping the subject, but I hadn't.

I was now more determined than ever to have her as my own.

In my world, a girlfriend or mistress was fair game for intimidation, but you stayed away from a man's wife unless you wanted your entire existence burnt to the ground.

The shrill ring of my cellphone cut her retort off.

I checked the screen and frowned.

It was John, our helicopter pilot.

I answered and cursed. "Baby, I need you to run. Now!"

With no time to unlock our handcuffs, I vaulted up the stairs after Damien and Yelena, calling out over my shoulder to Mary, "The pilot of the helicopter is not my man. Damien and Yelena are in danger."

She kept pace with me as we ran up the stairs, down the hallway, and through the doors to the rooftop terrace.

We screamed in unison and waved our free arms, raising the alarm.

Responding to our frantic shouts and motions, Damien turned and clung to the helicopter landing skids as gunfire from inside the helicopter rang out.

They were trying to kill Damien so they could make their escape with Yelena who was trapped inside, but the glass was bulletproof.

They only succeeded in causing large cracks in the glass.

The helicopter pitched and wobbled in the air until Damien lost his grip.

Reaching for my gun, I called out to him as we ran across the rooftop.

The moment he turned, I tossed the handgun to him.

He caught it and turned, intending to fire and disable the helicopter, but it was too late.

It was too high in the air.

To fire at it now would only endanger Yelena.

Mary cried out as we all watched helplessly as the helicopter rose higher and higher, taking Yelena with it.

"Oh, my God!"

The enormity of what I was trying to avoid finally hit her.

The danger she was in was real.

We walked toward Damien.

I placed a hand on his shoulder.

He turned on me, fists raised.

I stepped in front of Mary to protect her but was too late.

In his grief-induced rage, he attacked me, the force of which knocked Mary to the ground.

Her pained cry brought out my own rage.

After lifting her to her feet, I swung my free arm and clipped Damien on the jaw with my fist.

The strike brought us both back to our senses.

Pulling Mary close, I cupped her chin and lifted her gaze to mine. "Are you okay, baby?"

She nodded. "Yes, I just fell on my shoulder, but I'm fine. He didn't mean it, Vaska."

I reached into my back pocket for the keys to the

handcuffs, knowing they were no longer needed. "I know."

I unlocked the handcuffs and pulled her close again.

Looking over the top of her head, I said to Damien, "I need to secure Mary. Then we'll go."

He protested, "I can't wait that long."

"You don't know what you're walking into there. We haven't even confirmed who's involved. They could still have a team of men on the premises."

"It's them. I know it. They have her, Vaska, and it's my fucking fault. Do what you have to do to protect your girl, but I'm not waiting one fucking second to go after mine."

Cradling her arm against her middle, Mary protested, "I'm not his girl, and I'm fine. Go with him."

Giving her a glare to quell her protest, I said, "I'll text you the address. I'm taking Mary to where Dimitri has Emma. After you learn all you can, meet us at the usual place. We'll gear up with some firepower and go after the bastards."

Mary's eyes filled with tears. I could tell the stress of the last hour was wearing on her. "Vaska, I'm scared. I didn't mean what I just said, please, I don't want you to go, stay with me."

I cursed under my breath.

There was nothing I wanted more than to keep her by my side and reassure her that everything was going to be okay, that I would keep her safe, but I couldn't.

When you attacked one of us, you attacked all of us.

Damien's girl was in danger.

He needed our help.

I kissed her gently on the forehead. "I promise. We have ... ways ... of convincing people to talk. We will learn where they have taken Yelena and get her back quickly. No one—no one—does something like this to us and gets away with it. You have nothing to fear. You and Emma will be safe and I swear to God, so will Yelena."

"Let's just call the police," she begged.

I smiled. "That's not how we handle things, *krasotka*."

That was the best answer I could give her.

To tell her we planned on hunting down the men who took Yelena and making them die slow and agonizing deaths would only traumatize her further.

And possibly convince her once and for all what a monster I truly was ... I couldn't let that happen.

CHAPTER 27

MARY

My heart pounded in my chest at a sickening pace as we careened through the city.

Ditching his fancy sports car in the garage, we drove off in a less flashy black Range Rover.

Apparently the safehouse was in a quiet neighborhood, and Vaska didn't want to attract attention by rolling up in a hundred-thousand-dollar Mercedes.

Neither of us spoke the entire ride out of downtown Chicago to one of the northern neighborhoods.

We turned onto a street lined with small two-story brick houses common throughout Chicago.

Knowing what I did about safehouses only from the movies, I guess it was perfect.

Each house looked identical and nondescript.

In other words, none screamed super scary mafia

shit happening in this house, which I guess was the point.

We circled around to the alley and parked in a free-standing garage.

Vaska cautioned me to walk slowly and not to look around or appear anxious.

Taking a deep breath, I slid my hand through his arm and did my best to appear calm and nonchalant as we navigated the old cement walkway, which was riddled with cracks and weeds, to the back door of the house.

Vaska rapped on the door with his knuckles.

I was a little disappointed that it was an ordinary knock and not some kind of secret code double then single then double knock sort of thing.

Within seconds, a large man who stayed out of sight in the shadows of the small mud room opened the door.

Vaska placed his hand on my lower back and ushered me inside.

The house was cold and silent.

Heavy room-darkening curtains were pulled tight over all the windows. Several men dressed in all black holding semi-automatic weapons greeted Vaska with a nod but said nothing.

I rubbed my arms as a chill raced up my spine.

"Where is Emma?" I asked.

"In a minute, first you and I need to talk," responded Vaska.

"I'd rather see Emma."

Vaska gave me a sad smile. "Then once again I'm forced to disappoint you, *krasotka*."

Wrapping his strong fingers around my upper arm, he half escorted, half dragged me past the kitchen and into the living room, then up the stairway. He chose the first bedroom on the right.

He pushed me over the threshold before barking an order in Russian to the man guarding the hallway as he slammed the door shut. He then leaned against the door and crossed his arms over his chest.

I paced deeper into the room, feeling the tension like a thick smoke that was slowly encircling me, cutting off my air.

Vaska pierced me with that dark stare I always found so terrifying yet mesmerizing.

He inhaled a deep breath, which he seemed to let out through clenched teeth. When he spoke, his voice was deep and calm, as if he were measuring each word carefully. "The time for playing games is over, Mary. First thing tomorrow morning, I'm taking you to the courthouse and we are getting married."

No proposal.

No down on one knee.

No declaration of love.

No ring.

Just an ultimatum.

No, not an ultimatum.

An ultimatum would imply I at least had a choice to make.

I reached for his signet ring, which I still wore on a chain around my neck. The warmth of the silver offered little of its usual comfort. “So this past week, when I thought we were making a genuine effort to get to know one another to see if this relationship could work and whether or not I was going to live with you—to you it was just a game?”

He straightened to his full height.

Out of instinct, I shifted further into the room, placing the king bed between us.

Like the rest of the house, heavy curtains blocked out all the sunshine. Only a small lamp on a bedside table illuminated the room.

Its weak rays cast Vaska’s harsh, angular face into deep shadow, giving him an almost sinister appearance.

He nodded. “Yes, I was just humoring you. There was never a chance of me letting you go.”

Hysterical laughter bubbled up inside my chest and threatened to choke me. “Well, at least you’re honest.”

“That makes one of us,” snapped Vaska.

“What is that supposed to mean?” I fired back.

He stormed across the room, cornering me.

As my back pressed against the wall, he raised his arms and his palms went to either side of my head, caging me in.

"Yes, *honest*," he bit out the word like a curse. "From the very first moment I met you, I've been nothing but honest with you—about my profession, my intentions, my feelings for you."

I scoffed as I rolled my eyes. "Yes, that you wanted to fuck me."

His gaze traveled to my mouth, then back to my eyes. "Yes, I wanted to fuck you. You were by far the most beautiful creature I'd ever laid eyes on and when you opened that sweet mouth of yours and nothing but fiery sass came pouring out, I wanted to fuck you even more."

He shifted his hand to my throat, pressing his fingers against my jaw, forcing my head back as far as the wall would allow. "And the moment I fucked you, the very moment my cock sank deep into that tight pussy of yours, I knew you were mine. Not for a night or a weekend or a few months of fun. Mine. Forever mine."

He rubbed his thumb across my lower lip, smearing my matte blood-red lipstick. "This mouth opened on a sweet gasp and all I could think was how I wanted to be the one to breathe oxygen back into your lungs. I wanted the clothes I bought to be the only ones that touched your skin. I wanted the food you ate to only come from my fingertips. I wanted, no, I selfishly craved, to be your everything. I have never hidden that fact from you. You've known my intentions from the start. I love you, Mary. I never thought

I was capable of that emotion until you and I know you love me too. You're just too scared to admit it. To admit you fell in love with the wrong kind of man."

I inhaled deeply through my nose, trying to calm my hammering heart.

It didn't work.

I could smell the sexy spicy scent of his cologne and feel the warmth of his body as it pressed against my hips.

I closed my eyes, trying to block him out. "This can't be love. It's too much. My whole life has been turned upside down because of you."

He slammed his fist against the wall over my head before wrapping his hands around my shoulders and pulling me close to him. "Goddamn it. Open your eyes. Look at me."

I obeyed, meeting his intense sapphire gaze.

He squeezed my shoulders tighter, pressing me closer as he loomed tall and powerful over me. "Yes, Mary. *This is love*. It's messy and inconvenient. I'm not the knight in shining armor you imagined as a little girl. But I am the man who would fight the devil himself to keep you by his side. Who would give his last living breath to protect you. I swear to God there will never be a moment in your life you won't feel wanted and cherished and loved by me. Just say it, please, Mary, say what I want to hear. Say what I know you feel, but have refused to admit."

I slipped my arms between his and swiped at the tears on my cheeks.

I could feel myself falling but still resisted the final fall. "All we do is fight."

"That's not true. We fight and we fuck, and we laugh and we eat good food and drink good wine. We're both passionate, stubborn people determined to suck the marrow out of life. You can fight me all you want, but stop fighting us."

Before I could respond, there was a soft knock on the door.

Someone called out something in Russian.

Vaska lowered his head before releasing me with a resigned sigh.

Bitter cold rushed in where there had been warmth.

He opened the door.

The same guard spoke to him in rapid, hushed tones.

Vaska nodded.

He looked over his shoulder at me.

I hadn't moved.

As strange as it sounded, I wasn't sure I could stand let alone walk on my own without Vaska by my side, holding me up.

My stomach clenched.

The cruel reality of what might be happening crashed down on me.

I opened my mouth to tell him I loved him, but I couldn't form the words.

He left without saying another word.

I fell to my knees and cried.

* * *

I DID NOT KNOW whether it was hours or minutes later that I became aware of Emma's arms around my shoulders.

She spoke in soothing tones, but I didn't hear a word.

I allowed myself to be led out of the room and downstairs.

She sat me in the center of the sofa and wrapped a blanket around me. I stared blankly ahead as she spoke to one guard. She was using broken English so

I could only assume the four or five guards I had seen so far mostly spoke Russian, but I heard the words tequila and Doritos before the guard turned and headed out the back door.

The sofa dipped as she sat next to me.

She wrapped her arm back around me and lowered her head to my shoulder. "Reinforcements are coming."

"Am I making a mistake?"

She answered without hesitation. "Yes."

I huffed, then cast her an exasperated glare. "Don't sugarcoat it, just give it to me straight."

She smiled. "Don't worry. I will, because I know you'd do the same for me. Look, Vaska is a good man. Did you know he's the one who convinced Dimitri to get back together with me after we broke up?"

I turned to face her as I fisted the blanket in front of me. "Really?"

She nodded. "He marched straight over to Dimitri's and told him what a damn fool he was being. Gave some big dramatic speech about love and not letting the woman you want slip through your fingers."

My vision clouded with tears. I sniffed as I snatched a throw pillow up and clutched it to my chest. "That sounds like him. For being a scary mafia dude, he's surprisingly poetic when it comes to love."

Emma laughed. "They would howl if they heard us say it, but really they're both just a couple of big growly teddy bears."

I sighed. This time I put my head on her shoulder. "What's wrong with me?"

Vaska was the whole package. Tall, dark, handsome, sexy, and rich, but he was even more than that. He was also fun to be with. I loved our time spent at home cooking or cuddling on the couch as I forced him to watch *Buffy*.

Home.

It struck me.

In just a few short days, it had become home to me.

Vaska had made a home for us.

It was warm and safe and filled with laughter and fun. Here I was determined to focus on all the bad when there was also a great deal of good.

She stroked my hair. "Nothing. You're in love. There are few things more terrifying than that. And let's be honest, it certainly doesn't help things that we both fell in love with two good men who happen to have bad men jobs. Relationships are hard enough without having to worry about bullets flying over your head."

"Or getting dragged away in a freaking helicopter," I chimed in.

"You know he's only reacting this way because he's scared to death the same thing that happened to me will happen to you. He's controlling because he loves you and wants to protect you."

I nodded. "True. It doesn't help that he can be so insufferable, brutish, stubborn, obstinate, mule-headed, arrogant, and high-handed."

"One of these days I'm going to cross-stitch that onto a pillow for you."

I hugged her. "It's way too long of a phrase. Just stitch Vaska and I'll know what you meant."

There was a knock on the back door.

The three guards who had been sitting nearby, staying a discreet distance from us, all stood, hands on their weapons.

Emma said, "That must be our reinforcements."

I let out the tense breath I hadn't realized I had been holding. I had forgotten she had sent one of the guards out for tequila and chips.

The guard nearest to the back opened the door.

The fifth guard took a single stiff step inside.

Alarm bells went off in my head.

Something felt wrong.

His body language was off.

There was a loud *thwap* sound, like a bullet being shot into a mattress.

The guard dropped the bag of groceries he was holding.

His knees crumpled as he toppled to the floor.

Emma and I screamed as a large group of men rushed into the house with guns raised.

Our guards tried to exchange gunfire, but they were outmanned.

One guard shielded Emma and me as he yelled in Russian, "*Ubegat'! Ubegat'!*"

I didn't have to speak Russian to know that meant run.

I pushed Emma in front of me and we raced toward the front door as the intruders poured in through the back.

There was no guarantee they weren't also covering the front, but we had to take that chance.

Emma unlocked the door and swung it open.

There was another volley of oddly muffled shots over our heads.

They must be using silencers.

The gunshots were muted but just as deadly.

Plaster chips rained down on us as the bullets hit the surrounding walls. Without the actual sound of gunfire, there was little chance the neighbors would hear and call the police.

Our only chance was to reach the outside and scream for help.

I looked over my shoulder and saw the wide-eyed, slack-mouthed face of the guard a second before he collapsed.

Behind him stood a stocky Latino man in black fatigues.

Turning, I shoved Emma over the threshold and slammed the door shut, hoping it would buy her a few precious seconds to escape.

The man raised his arm and pointed a handgun only a few inches away from my face.

My last thought was of Vaska and how I should have told him I loved him when I'd had the chance.

Then everything went black.

CHAPTER 28

VASKA

We had been successful in rescuing Yelena from the Colombian gang, the Los Infieles.

Their leader, Santiago Garcia, had kidnapped her and paid the ultimate price. Damien was already on his way back to D.C. with her.

It had been our plan to let things calm down and learn more about the Los Infieles before we wiped them off the planet for daring to fuck with us.

They were a well-armed gang with connections.

It would take careful strategizing to ruin them without starting a war with any of their other gang affiliates.

We also needed to learn how politically connected they were and who we'd need to bribe or blackmail to look the other way. Dimitri and I didn't gain a reputation for coldblooded ruthlessness by striking in the heat of anger. We preferred calculated, targeted attacks over a sloppy scorched-earth approach.

Of course, that was before we got word of the attack on the safehouse.

That was the moment everything changed.

I drove like the hounds of hell were at my heels, not giving a damn for any traffic lights or other cars on the road.

An entire fleet of police cars could have been in my wake and I wouldn't have taken my foot off the gas.

We walked into a scene of absolute carnage.

Five guards dead on the floor.

There was blood everywhere and both Emma and Mary were missing. Dimitri and I stood in the center of the room, absorbing each other's blistering rage and pain.

The crunch of shattered glass under a foot had us both turning, Glocks drawn.

Emma stood in the doorway, shaking and pale.

Dimitri crushed her in his embrace, falling to his knees amongst the debris, overcome with relief.

My gaze trained on the door, willing Mary to step over the threshold.

I lunged for the door and stepped outside, searching for her.

There was no sign of her.

I turned back and looked at Emma.

Her eyes filled with tears. "I'm so sorry, Vaska. They took her."

My whole world shattered into a million blood-soaked pieces.

I didn't hear anything after that—a beastly howl of rage filled my ears, blocking out all sound and reason.

* * *

IT WASN'T long after Emma appeared that I received a secure, coded text with nothing but an address.

I showed my phone to Dimitri.

Keeping one arm around Emma, he took out his own phone and searched the location.

He held his phone up for me to see. "It's a boarded-up restaurant."

Before I could respond, a second text message arrived.

Bile rose in the back of my throat.

I gripped my phone so hard, I heard the screen crack.

Dimitri laid a calming hand on my shoulder as he wrestled the phone from my grasp.

He looked at the screen and cursed.

Before he could shield her, Emma looked at the screen as well and shrieked. She would have collapsed had Dimitri not caught her.

On my phone was a photo of Mary.

She had a black eye and her mascara was smeared and running over her cheeks. Her glossy black hair was wrapped in the fist of a man we knew was named Alejandro as he wrenched her head back at an awkward angle.

Another text came through.

It was a time to meet, thirty minutes from now.

A final text came through with only one sentence.

Alone or she dies.

After getting word of his brother Santiago's death, Alejandro of the Los Infieles hadn't wasted any time in striking at us again. We were certain it was part revenge for his brother's death but done mostly out of self-preservation.

He knew we'd come after him, so he decided to hit first.

It was a mistake he wouldn't live long enough to regret.

Thirty minutes later, I was standing alone in the parking lot of the abandoned restaurant.

I closed my eyes and took a deep breath.

The crisp air did nothing to cool my rage.

I clenched my fists at my sides and marshaled every ounce of discipline I possessed.

Throughout my career, I had sat across the table from the most notorious, soulless piece of shit excuses for human beings the world had ever seen.

Each time I kept calm and professional; there was no place for emotion in a negotiation.

That's all this was, a negotiation, a business transaction.

Except it wasn't.

Far from it.

Mary's life and our future happiness depended on the outcome.

I would be damned if I let her down.

Just outside the grimy glass double doors, I raised my arms and let two of Alejandro's men pat me down before I entered.

Thin brown paper was taped over the restaurant windows, blocking out the last of the fading sunlight. The tables scattered about the dining room were in varying states of disarray. Some were bare, others had red and white checkered tablecloths with place settings, still others had the last remains of some forgotten diner's meal. There were also several tables and chairs turned over. A thin layer of dust covered the scuffed linoleum floor and surfaces.

The restaurant had obviously been abandoned under some extreme circumstance.

Sitting at a table in the center of this frozen chaos was Alejandro.

Mary sat next to him—with a revolver to her head.

Her lower lip trembled but otherwise she remained still.

I didn't need her to speak.

Her wide frightened eyes told me all I needed to know.

I vowed then and there I would spend the rest of my life erasing that look of terror from her gaze.

"Vasili Rostov, so nice of you to come. Join us," said Alejandro with misplaced mirth as he gestured to the seat opposite him.

I surveyed the room, taking note of the three men standing guard.

A fourth approached the table with a bottle of Devil's Springs vodka and two shot glasses. He placed the items in the center of the table and, with a nod to Alejandro, backed away.

Alejandro gestured to the vodka. "You see what a gracious host I am being? This is what you Russians drink, right?"

I glanced at the vodka label, one-hundred sixty proof, perfect for my plan.

I then picked up the shot glass and raised an eyebrow. "Will there be children joining us? Or can I have a man's glass?"

The smile left Alejandro's face.

I forced myself to breathe as I kept my features passive and calm.

The hardest part was not looking straight at Mary.

I couldn't risk having any emotion, especially not fear, cross my face.

Never show your cards to your enemy.

After another tense moment, Alejandro laughed.

He gestured to his guard and called out something in Spanish. The guard returned with two double old-fashioned glasses. He took the shot glasses with him as he stepped back.

Alejandro wagged a finger at me as he laughed again. "I like you, Vaska. I'm sure you and I can come to an arrangement."

I leaned in and picked up the bottle. "May I?"

"Please do."

I nodded then poured us both a glass.

Alejandro noticed the generous pour in my own glass, but said nothing, probably assuming all Russians were drunks who drank their vodka half a glass at a time.

We raised our glasses. I then said, "To a satisfactory arrangement."

We both drank.

I took that moment to glance quickly at Mary.

She kept her gaze steady on me.

I gave her a wink as my lips lifted in a small smile.

She took a deep breath, a small assurance my gesture calmed her.

Alejandro grimaced. "I don't know what your people see in this crap. It tastes like water."

I shrugged. "It's an acquired taste."

"You and I need to come to an understanding."

I twisted the glass in my hand. "First, lower your gun."

Alejandro sneered as he pressed the gun harder against Mary's temple. "Does it upset you to see a gun to the head of the woman you love? Maybe we should play a game of Russian roulette?"

I wasn't taking the bait. "It upsets me to see a gun to the head of any beautiful woman. Surely, any real man could keep a woman in line without needing a firearm."

Alejandro took the bait.

He lowered the gun.

I kept my breathing shallow, knowing a deep breath of relief would reveal more than I intended.

Alejandro spoke. "You killed my brother Santiago."

"Your brother took something of ours."

Alejandro nodded. "Yes, yes, the blonde. He was rash. We did not know she was under the protection of the Russians."

"Well, now you do."

"Taking the girl was a miscalculation on my brother's part," offered Alejandro.

I flicked my gaze to Mary and back to him. "One you have repeated."

Alejandro held up a placating hand. "It was the only way to get you face to face. A man needs to look into another man's eyes to know his true intentions and I wanted to make sure I had your full attention."

I rubbed a hand over my jaw before responding. Inhaling through my teeth, I said, "Well, you have it."

"I don't want a war with the Russians. You have killed several of my men. I have killed several of yours. Let it end here."

"And the girl?"

Alejandro raised his gun back to Mary's head. "The Russians killed my brother. That must be avenged if I am to save face among my family and men. I'm afraid the girl must die. Blood for blood. Then all will be settled between us."

Mary gasped as fresh tears flowed over her cheeks.

I reached for the inside pocket of my suit jacket. Every guard in the room stepped forward, guns raised. I lifted my open palms. "Just reaching for my cigarettes, boys."

Alejandro nodded and they backed off.

I pulled out a packet of Sobranie cigarettes and a Zippo lighter. Selecting one black-and gold-tipped cigarette, I turned my attention to Mary.

Her lips trembled.

For the first time she spoke. Her voice was rough from crying. "I love you, Vaska."

I smiled. "I love you too, *krasotka*."

Even with a bruised eye, smeared makeup and a tearstained face, she was still the most beautiful woman I had ever laid eyes on. "Mary, do you remember that episode of *Buffy* you made me watch where the librarian guy used the crossbow? I think it was called 'Passion.'"

I stared at her intently, praying she wasn't too distraught to catch on to my warning.

I knew I wouldn't be able to communicate directly with her, so I had to come up with a plan she would understand without being told.

I waited.

Her eyes widened with understanding. She tilted her head forward slightly.

Good girl.

Alejandro sneered. "I was told you were a ruthless man, Vaska, but I was misinformed. Only a stupid man tells another the rock he's holding is actually a jewel. Since she means so much to you, maybe I won't kill her. Maybe I will keep her. As my insurance against any further retaliation by you or Dimitri."

I flicked the Zippo open.

I had already turned the flame up as high as the lighter would allow. "You weren't misinformed, Alejandro."

I then shouted to Mary, "Now!"

It all happened at once.

Mary dove for the floor as I flung my entire glass of vodka onto Alejandro.

He reeled back.

Shock turned to horror as he looked at the alcohol splattering his front and then the trail splashing across the table leading right back to me.

Staring the dead man straight in the eyes, I dropped the Zippo.

A flash of blue flame rose the moment the lighter touched the vodka.

With a whoosh it raced across the table, leaving a fiery path before igniting Alejandro's clothes.

The man was engulfed in flames before his guards even knew what was happening.

It was just the distraction we needed.

I threw my body onto Mary, protecting her as my own men crashed through the doors and windows, taking out Alejandro's guards as he screamed in agony.

He stumbled around the room, igniting the thin tablecloths and wooden tables.

I picked Mary up into my arms and bolted for the exit.

Racing with her to the safety of my car, I set her as gently as I could in the passenger seat before getting behind the wheel and peeling out of the parking lot.

After I had put several miles between us and the crime scene, I pulled over onto a quiet street.

I got out of the car and circled around.

Yanking open the passenger door, I caught Mary as she flung herself into my arms. I held her close as I ran my hands over her body, searching for any sign of injury or broken bones.

I cupped her face and gazed at her intently. "Did

that bastard hurt you?"

She shook her head, then pointed to her eye. "His man hit me with a gun, knocking me out, but they didn't ... they didn't ... touch me. I'm not hurt, just shaken up."

I closed my eyes as a wave of relief almost drove me to my knees.

"Emma?"

I swallowed as tears threatened to fall. My voice was hoarse with emotion. "She's fine. You saved her. My God, Mary. I'm so sorry. We had no idea the safe-house had been compromised."

She placed a cool palm on my jaw. "I know, Vaska. I know."

I could feel every cell in my body recoil from what I was about to do.

A primal scream welled up in my chest in defiance, but I knew it was the right thing to do.

I had been too selfish assuming I could hold on to her. That I could live in hell but keep my taste of heaven. Tonight's events had proven that to me. I would have to let her go.

I opened my mouth to speak, but Mary cut me off. "The answer is yes."

My brow furrowed. "What?"

"The answer is yes. I will marry you."

I stood there stunned.

She continued, "I mean technically you didn't officially ask me, it was more of a demand, but—"

My mouth cut her off as I kissed her with all the fierce love I felt for her.

I pulled back slightly, rasping against her lips, "Are you sure, Mary? Because this is it. There will be no turning back."

She gave me a watery smile. "You rescued me by referencing the *Buffy* episode where Angel goes all vampire nuts and Giles attacks his lair by lighting a table on fire with a flaming arrow. That was fucking brilliant! If I wasn't in love with you before, I sure as hell would be now."

God, I fucking loved this woman.

Taking her hand, I knelt down on the side of the road.

"Vaska, what are you doing?"

"Giving you a proper proposal. Mary Katherine Fraser, will you do me the honor of becoming my wife?"

Mary's mouth twisted into a smirk. "Hmmm … I'm thinking."

I rose and snatched her back into my arms.

I said with a playful growl, "You better say yes, *krasotka,* or I'm going to take off my belt."

She shimmied her hips against mine. "Promise?"

I gave her cute ass a smack.

She cried out, "Yes! Yes! I will marry you. You insufferable, brutish, stubborn, obstinate, mule-headed, arrogant, high-handed—"

I cut off her tirade with another kiss.

EPILOGUE

MARY

L*as Vegas, NV—One month later*

"How in the world did you talk Vaska into this?" asked Emma as she watched the makeup artist finish pinning the final victory curl in my hair.

We were in a side room of the chapel getting ready.

Putting the finishing touches on my red matte lipstick, I surveyed my reflection in the mirror. "I shamelessly guilted him into it."

I rose and smoothed the cream satin of my mermaid-cut wedding dress over my hips and adjusted the Cartier panther brooch.

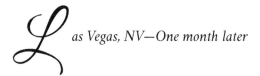

"Still, I thought he'd want a church wedding," persisted Emma as she also rose and fluffed the black crinoline under her red rockabilly-style bridesmaid dress.

I reached for the open bottle of Jose Cuervo tequila and poured us each a shot and held one out to her. "We are having a church wedding … sort of."

She laughed. "Oh, boy, you have that man wrapped around your little finger."

I winked, a habit I'd picked up from Vaska as I raised my glass. "To the schoolteacher and librarian and the bad boys who love them!"

Emma toasted, "To our bad boys!"

We both drank.

Emma handed me my rose bouquet as we headed for the door.

I took a deep breath.

Emma took my free hand and squeezed it. "Ready?"

I nodded.

The moment the door swung open, the pianist started playing 'Can't Help Falling in Love.'

If ever there was a theme song to my relationship with Vaska, that was it.

I looked down the short aisle.

Vaska looked so handsome standing there in his tuxedo, with Dimitri to his left.

Against my better intentions and good sense, I had fallen head over heels in love with the man, and I knew deep in my heart I would never regret my decision to become his.

As I walked down the aisle, my gaze shifted to the man standing to Vaska's right, then back to Vaska.

He followed my gaze then looked back to me and shook his head as he let out a resigned sigh.

I burst out laughing.

As I took his arm, he leaned down and whispered, "Hello, beautiful girl."

I rested my head on Vaska's shoulder as the Elvis impersonator said in his best Elvis accent, "Dearly beloved …."

***

Continue the steamy, enemies to lovers drama of the Ruthless Obsession series with Ivan & Dylan's Story.

Get a Sneak Peek of Chapter One on the Next Page.

Sweet Savagery
Ruthless Obsession Series, Book Three

SWEET SAVAGERY

CHAPTER ONE

Dylan

Chicago, Illinois

I sat on the floor of my tiny studio apartment staring at the piles of cash around me.

The boxes arrived a few days ago from Russia, sent by my uncle Harry. Despite receiving a stern email from him warning me not to open the boxes, I didn't waste any time tearing into them.

I was the *weird* one in my family.

The only one who had chosen not to pursue a life of crime.

I rarely spoke to anyone related to me and hadn't seen my uncle Harry since my father's last parole hearing over ten years ago, when I was still a teenager.

So when I received the boxes and a cryptic email from my uncle addressed to his *favorite niece*, I was, of course, suspicious.

And judging from the stacks of cash taking up half my apartment floor, I had every right to be.

Five hundred thousand dollars.

Five hundred thousand dollars!

My uncle had sent me five hundred thousand dollars through the freaking mail.

What was strange was each box only weighed about six pounds.

I totally would have thought thousands of hundred-dollar bills would have weighed more.

Although, to be honest, that wasn't the truly strange part.

The truly strange part was that I had freaking *five hundred thousand dollars* strewn about on a ten-dollar, slightly stained throw rug I had purchased from the Salvation Army last month.

Once again, I picked up my cell phone and tried to call my uncle Harry.

I had no idea what time it was in Russia, or even why he was there, and I didn't care.

I wanted an explanation.

When he didn't answer, I tried calling my other uncle, Uncle Frank.

If anyone else was involved in this mess along with Uncle Harry, it would be my uncle Frank. They were two petty criminal peas in a pod.

Uncle Frank's cell number was disconnected. Typical.

Tossing the phone aside, I sighed as I surveyed the money.

There wasn't a doubt in my mind this money was dirty, *like really, really dirty.*

Anything anyone in my family touched was always filthy.

They wouldn't know how to make an honest dollar if it slapped them in the face.

What the hell was I going to do?

I glanced at the alarm clock and cried out.

Damn, I was late for work.

Work, another concept my family was completely unfamiliar with.

I was the first in our family to attend community college.

Now I was scraping money together for a real estate broker license.

Four thousand three hundred and sixty dollars, that's how much I was in the hole right now.

Between the pre-licensing courses, licensing exam, my basic real estate agent license, and now the desk fees at the brokerage where I worked to become a licensed broker, I was in serious credit card debt. It had taken me three years of saving some of my server tips just to scrape enough together to cover costs while I took a huge pay hit launching my new career.

I lifted the edge of my Murphy bed and tucked it

back into the wall cabinet so I could open the bathroom door, and turned the knob for my shower.

The old pipes rattled and clanked. Rusty water spurted from the faucet. I turned the knob to cold so I wouldn't be wasting hot water and money as I waited for the water to run clear. I turned on the coffeepot and reached for my toothbrush.

One thing about being poor and living in a tiny studio apartment, everything I needed was literally within arm's reach, especially when the kitchen and bathroom shared the same sink. Swishing the mint foam around my mouth as I brushed, I glanced over my shoulder at the money still lying on the floor.

Forty hundred-dollar bills.

Forty out of five thousand hundred-dollar bills.

That's all I would need.

Forty thin pieces of rectangular paper and most of my problems would be gone.

Disgusted at my thoughts, I spit in the sink and shrugged out of my T-shirt before stepping in the shower. My breath seized in my lungs as the icy water hit my chest. I had forgotten to turn the hot water knob. Sidestepping out of the freezing stream, I frantically turned the knob to add warm water, but it broke off in my hand.

With a resigned sigh, I inhaled a deep breath and braced myself for the arctic chill as I flipped my long hair over my head and reached for the shampoo.

As I closed my eyes to avoid the suds, all I could

see were the neat stacks of cash lying only a few feet away.

Wouldn't I be doing a good thing by using just a tiny portion of the money for honest purposes?

I wanted to have my own brokerage firm one day.

A firm where female real estate agents could safely work without having to worry about getting their asses pinched or being told to fetch coffee. It may be the twenty-first century, but in many ways the real estate industry was still living in the 1950s.

In order to do that, I needed money, way more money than I was currently making.

It would be at least ten years before I could afford to start my own business, unless—I peeked around the shower curtain at the money.

With a frustrated huff, I finished scrubbing the suds out of my hair and got out of the shower.

Wrapping a slightly scratchy towel around my middle, I poured coffee into my favorite chipped mug and added sugar and powdered cream. No daily Starbucks on the way to work for me.

I couldn't afford such tiny luxuries.

I unplugged the coffeemaker and plugged in the hair dryer. As I combed through the tangles in my hair with my fingers, I looked in the mirror and once again saw the cash.

It wasn't like I would use it all, maybe just fifty thousand dollars' worth.

That would be enough to cover rent for a year,

office furniture, equipment, and some splashy colorful marketing brochures.

If I borrowed just a few thousand more, I could even get a professional website done instead of a basic do-it-yourself WordPress one.

The appearance of wealth in this business was essential in getting the higher-end clients.

Money attracted money.

It was why I spent my rent money on nice dress suits and real-looking pearl necklaces. I would get nowhere in this business showing up in an ill-fitting thrift store outfit.

I leaned over the sink to apply mascara.

My gaze traveled again to the cash.

Okay, sixty thousand dollars and not a penny more.

I would buy myself a decent wardrobe and maybe lease a nice Lincoln Town Car to shuttle my clients around Chicago to different properties for sale.

Sixty thousand dollars wasn't that much, only six hundred bills out of five thousand.

It probably wouldn't even be missed.

I would then donate the rest to charity or maybe play Santa Claus to the other hard-up residents in my building.

Or perhaps I could leave little envelopes of cash for each of them to help cover rent and food.

Seriously, I couldn't go to hell for using dirty money if I used most of it for good, right?

Going to the police was out of the question.

I may have distanced myself from my criminal family, but I still shared their aversion to authority.

Besides, with my juvenile record, there was no way they would take me at my word that the cash had just arrived on my doorstep and that I had nothing to do with it.

And of course there was the bonus that it had arrived in boxes from Russia.

Sure, nothing shady about that.

My eyes rolled so hard I gave myself a headache.

Crossing the room, I tiptoed between the piles of cash to my bedroom/hall/linen/pantry closet.

After selecting a deep cranberry red A-line skirt with white flowers and matching white silk blouse that I had gotten a few weeks ago at the Anne Taylor factory outlet, I got dressed. A pair of black ballet flats and my favorite fake-but-real-looking pearl necklace completed the outfit.

I would rather wear four-inch platform heels to make up for my five-foot six-inch frame, but I had an open house today and would be on my feet for hours.

It was smarter to wear the flats. It was a shame. My life was a little easier when I was taller than the men around me. Especially when one of those men was Larry, my boss. Middle-aged, balding, and with a pooch of a belly, he somehow thought he was God's gift to women.

I stared down at the cash at my feet.

It was nice to dream, but there was no way I was going to touch one lousy bill of it for myself.

That's how it would start.

Compromising my principles once would make it that much easier to compromise them again, then again.

I had turned away from that life when I was a teenager.

It had taken years to clean up my act and break free of my criminal family's binds, and I wouldn't turn back now.

Even if abandoning those principles now made my dream of owning my own brokerage firm a reality, I would always know I had purchased it with tainted money. It wouldn't be truly mine. It wouldn't be something I had earned through hard work and determination.

With a sigh, I bent down to pick up several piles of crisp hundred-dollar bills. I turned and surveyed my apartment.

Where the hell could I hide all this money until I figured out what to do with it?

I had precious few options in my studio apartment.

There were no cabinets under the sink, and I'd already stuffed my closet full of clothes and ramen noodles.

I surveyed the Murphy bed. It would have to do.

I pulled the bed back down to the floor, piled the

cash on top and then quickly raised the bed frame back into its upright position. I snatched several wayward bills as they floated in the air and shoved them between the mattress and wall.

With one last sip of my now lukewarm coffee, I raced out the door.

I would figure out what to do about the dirty money later, after I got ahold of one of my uncles.

For now the money, and I, were safe enough.

Although we weren't close, there was no way my uncle Harry would have shipped the cash to me if he thought someone was actively looking for it, or if it would put my life in danger.

Family was still family.

So it wasn't like I had to worry about some big Russian thug breaking down my door for it.

***

Sweet Savagery

Ruthless Obsession Series, Book Three

Ivan & Dylan's Story

ABOUT ZOE BLAKE

Zoe Blake is the USA Today Bestselling Author of the romantic suspense saga The Cavalieri Billionaire Legacy inspired by her own heritage as well as her obsession with jewelry, travel, and the salacious gossip of history's most infamous families.

She delights in writing Dark Romance books filled with overly possessive billionaires, taboo scenes, and unexpected twists. She usually spends her ill-gotten gains on martinis, vacations, and red lipstick. Since she can barely boil water, she's lucky enough to be married to a sexy Chef.

ALSO BY ZOE BLAKE

RUTHLESS OBSESSION SERIES

A Dark Mafia Romance

Sweet Cruelty

Ruthless Obsession Series, Book One

Dimitri & Emma's story

It was an innocent mistake.

She knocked on the wrong door.

Mine.

If I were a better man, I would've just let her go.

But I'm not.

I'm a cruel bastard.

I ruthlessly claimed her virtue for my own.

It should have been enough.

But it wasn't.

I needed more.

Craved it.

She became my obsession.

Her sweetness and purity taunted my dark soul.

The need to possess her nearly drove me mad.

A Russian arms dealer had no business pursuing a naive

librarian student.

She didn't belong in my world.

I would bring her only pain.

But it was too late…

She was mine and I was keeping her.

Sweet Depravity

Ruthless Obsession Series, Book Two

Vaska & Mary's story

The moment she opened those gorgeous red lips to tell me no, she was mine.

I was a powerful Russian arms dealer and she was an innocent schoolteacher.

If she had a choice, she'd run as far away from me as possible.

Unfortunately for her, I wasn't giving her one.

I wasn't just going to take her; I was going to take over her entire world.

Where she lived.

What she ate.

Where she worked.

All would be under my control.

Call it obsession.

Call it depravity.

I don't give a damn… as long as you call her mine.

Sweet Savagery

Ruthless Obsession Series, Book Three

Ivan & Dylan's Story

I was a savage bent on claiming her as punishment for her family's mistakes.

As a powerful Russian Arms dealer, no one steals from me and gets away with it.

She was an innocent pawn in a dangerous game.

She had no idea the package her uncle sent her from Russia contained my stolen money.

If I were a good man, I would let her return the money and leave.

If I were a gentleman, I might even let her keep some of it just for frightening her.

As I stared down at the beautiful living doll stretched out before me like a virgin sacrifice,

I thanked God for every sin and misdeed that had blackened my cold heart.

I was not a good man.

I sure as hell wasn't a gentleman… and I had no intention of letting her go.

She was mine now.

And no one takes what's mine.

Sweet Brutality

Ruthless Obsession Series, Book Four

Maxim & Carinna's story

The more she fights me, the more I want her.

It's that beautiful, sassy mouth of hers.

It makes me want to push her to her knees and dominate her, like the brutal savage I am.

As a Russian Arms dealer, I should not be ruthlessly pursuing an innocent college student like her, but that would not stop me.

A twist of fate may have brought us together, but it is my twisted obsession that will hold her captive as my own treasured possession.

She is mine now.

I dare you to try and take her from me.

Sweet Ferocity

Ruthless Obsession Series, Book Five

Luka & Katie's Story

I was a mafia mercenary only hired to find her, but now I'm going to keep her.

She is a Russian mafia princess, kidnapped to be used as a pawn in a dangerous territory war.

Saving her was my job. Keeping her safe had become my obsession.

Every move she makes, I am in the shadows, watching.

I was like a feral animal: cruel, violent, and selfishly out for my own needs. Until her.

Now, I will make her mine by any means necessary.

I am her protector, but no one is going to protect her from me.

Sweet Intensity

Ruthless Obsession Series, Book Six

Antonius & Brynn's Story

She couldn't have known the danger she faced when she dared to steal from me.

She was too young for a man my age, barely in her twenties.

Far too pure and untouched.

Unfortunately for her, that wasn't going to stop me.

The moment I laid eyes on her, I claimed her.

Determined to make her mine…by any means necessary.

I owned Chicago's most elite gambling club, a front for my role as a Russian Mafia crime boss.

And she was a fragile little bird, who had just flown straight into my open jaws.

Naïve and sweet, she was a temptation I couldn't resist biting.

My intense drive to dominate and control her had become an obsession.

I would ruthlessly use my superior strength and wealth to take over her life.

The harder she resisted, the more feral and savage I would become.

She needed to understand… she was mine now.

Mine.

Sweet Severity

Ruthless Obsession Series, Book Seven

Macarius & Phoebe's Story

Had she crashed into any other man's car, she could have walked away—but she hit mine.

Upon seeing the bruises on her wrist, I struggled to contain my rage.

Despite her objections, I refused to allow her to leave.

Whoever hurt this innocent beauty would pay dearly.

As a Russian Mafia crime boss who owns Chicago's most elite gambling club, I have very creative and painful methods of exacting revenge.

She seems too young and naive to be out on her own in such a dangerous world.

Needing a nanny, I decided to claim her for the role.

She might resist my severe, domineering discipline, but I won't give her a choice in the matter.

She needs a protector, and I'd be damned if it were anyone but me.

Resisting the urge to claim her will test all my restraint.

It's a battle I'm bound to lose.

With each day, my obsession and jealousy intensify.

It's only a matter of time before my control snaps…and I make her mine.

Mine.

Sweet Animosity

Ruthless Obsession, Book Eight

Varlaam & Amber's Story

I never asked for an assistant, and if I had, I sure as hell wouldn't have chosen her.

With her sharp tongue and lack of discipline, what she needs is a firm hand, not a job.

The more she tests my limits, the more tempted I am to bend her over my knee.

As a Russian Mafia boss and owner of Chicago's most elite gambling club, I can't afford distractions from her antics.

Or her secrets.

For I suspect, my innocent new assistant is hiding something.

And I know just how to get to the truth.

It's high time she understands who holds the power in our relationship.

To ensure I get what I desire, I'll keep her close, controlling her every move.

Except I am no longer after information—I want her mind, body and soul.

She underestimated the stakes of our dangerous game and

now owes a heavy price.

As payment I will take her freedom.

She's mine now.

Mine.

Sweet Jealousy

A Ruthless Obsession Vella

Serg & Maya's Story

Every day I watch her. She has no idea who I am or the power I wield.

To her I'm just the man who likes his coffee black and tips well.

She has no clue, I'm one of the most ruthless and dangerous Russian mafia crime bosses in the city.

That I'm the man who will dominate her, demanding her complete submission.

For soon, she will be mine.

For her own protection, I must keep to the shadows.

My enemies can never know of my obsession for her.

Of how I crave to possess her sweet innocence.

They cannot know how I jealousy guard over her, using my money and influence to control her life.

She can never know that the man who sits quietly at the end of her lunch counter each day…

is also the man who sneaks into her bedroom each night, ties her to the bed and makes her scream with pleasure.

She can quit her job, move apartments, even try to change her name.

It won't matter.

Come nightfall, when the shadows deepen.

I will find her and once again make her…

Mine.

-

IVANOV CRIME FAMILY TRILOGY

A Dark Mafia Romance

Savage Vow

Ivanov Crime Family, Book One

Gregor & Samara's story

I took her innocence as payment.

She was far too young and naïve to be betrothed to a monster like me.

I would bring only pain and darkness into her sheltered world.

That's why she ran.

I should've just let her go…

She never asked to marry into a powerful Russian mafia family.

None of this was her choice.

Unfortunately for her, I don't care.

I own her… and after three years of searching… I've found her.

My runaway bride was about to learn disobedience has consequences… punishing ones.

Having her in my arms and under my control had become an obsession.

Nothing was going to keep me from claiming her before the eyes of God and man.

She's finally mine… and I'm never letting her go.

Vicious Oath

Ivanov Crime Family, Book One

Damien & Yelena's story

When I give an order, I expect it to be obeyed.

She's too smart for her own good, and it's going to get her killed.

Against my better judgement, I put her under the protection of my powerful Russian mafia family.

So imagine my anger when the little minx ran.

For three long years I've been on her trail, always one step behind.

Finding and claiming her had become an obsession.

It was getting harder to rein in my driving need to possess her… to own her.

But now the chase is over.

I've found her.

Soon she will be mine.

And I plan to make it official, even if I have to drag her

kicking and screaming to the altar.

This time... there will be no escape from me.

Betrayed Honor

Ivanov Crime Family, Book One

Mikhail & Nadia's story

Her innocence was going to get her killed.

That was if I didn't get to her first.

She's the protected little sister of the powerful Ivanov Russian mafia family - the very definition of forbidden.

It's always been my job, as their Head of Security, to watch over her but never to touch.

That ends today.

She disobeyed me and put herself in danger.

It was time to take her in hand.

I'm the only one who can save her and I will fight anyone who tries to stop me, including her brothers.

Honor and loyalty be damned.

She's mine now.

CAVALIERI BILLIONAIRE LEGACY

A Dark Enemies to Lovers Romance

Scandals of the Father

Cavalieri Billionaire Legacy, Book One

Being attracted to her wasn't wrong... but acting on it would be.

As the patriarch of the powerful and wealthy Cavalieri family, my choices came with consequences for everyone around me.

The roots of my ancestral, billionaire-dollar winery stretch deep into the rich, Italian soil, as does our legacy for ruthlessness and scandal.

It wasn't the fact she was half my age that made her off limits.

Nothing was off limits for me.

A wounded bird, caught in a trap not of her own making, she posed no risk to me.

My obsessive desire to possess her was the real problem.

For both of us.

But now that I've seen her, tasted her lips, I can't let her go.

Whether she likes it or not, she needs my protection.

I'm doing this for her own good, yet she fights me at every turn.

Refusing the luxury I offer, desperately trying to escape my grasp.

I need to teach her to obey before the dark rumors of my past reach her.

Ruin her.

She cannot find out what I've done, not before I make her mine.

Sins of the Son

Cavalieri Billionaire Legacy, Book Two

She's hated me for years... now it's past time to give her a reason to.

When you are a son, and one of the heirs, to the legacy of the Cavalieri name, you need to be more vicious than your enemies.

And sometimes, the lines get blurred.

Years ago, they tried to use her as a pawn in a revenge scheme against me.

Even though I cared about her, I let them treat her as if she were nothing.

I was too arrogant and self-involved to protect her then.

But I'm here now. Ready to risk my life tracking down every single one of them.

They'll pay for what they've done as surely as I'll pay for my sins against her.

Too bad it won't be enough for her to let go of her hatred of me,

To get her to stop fighting me.

Because whether she likes it or not, I have the power, wealth, and connections to keep her by my side.

And every intention of ruthlessly using all three to make her mine.

Secrets of the Brother

Cavalieri Billionaire Legacy, Book Three

We were not meant to be together… then a dark twist of fate stepped in, and we're the ones who will pay for it.

As the eldest son and heir of the Cavalieri name, I inherit a great deal more than a billion-dollar empire.

I receive a legacy of secrets, lies, and scandal.

After enduring a childhood filled with malicious rumors about my father, I have fallen prey to his very same sin.

I married a woman I didn't love out of a false sense of family honor.

Now she has died under mysterious circumstances.

And I am left to play the widowed groom.

For no one can know the truth about my wife…

Especially her sister.

The only way to protect her from danger is to keep her close, and yet, her very nearness tortures me.

She is my sister in name only, but I have no right to desire her.

Not after what I have done.

It's too much to hope she would understand that it was all for her.

It's always been about her.

Only her.

I am, after all, my father's son.

And there is nothing on this earth more ruthless than a Cavalieri man in love.

Seduction of the Patriarch

Cavalieri Billionaire Legacy, Book Four

With a single gunshot, she brings the violent secrets of my buried past into the present.

She may not have pulled the trigger, but she still has blood on her hands.

And I know some very creative ways to make her pay for it.

Being as ruthless as my Cavalieri ancestors has earned me a reputation as a dangerous man to cross, but that hasn't stopped me from making enemies along the way. No fortune is built without spilling blood.

But while I may be brutal, I don't play loose with my family, which means staying in the shadows to protect them.

I find myself forced to hand over the mantle of patriarch to my brother and move to northern Italy…

…or risk the lives of those I love.

Until a vindictive mafia syndicate attacks my family.

Now all bets are off, and nothing will prevent me from seeking vengeance on those responsible.

I'm done protecting the innocent.

Now, I don't give a damn who I hurt in the process…

…including her.

Through seduction and the power of punishment, I shall bend her to my will.

She will be my rebellious accomplice, a vital pawn in my

quest for revenge.

And the more my defiant little vixen bares her sharp claws, the more she tempts me to tame her until she purrs with submission.

Scorn of the Betrothed

Cavalieri Billionaire Legacy, Book Five

A union forged in vengeance, bound by hate, and... beneath it all...a twisted game of power.

The true legacy of the Cavalieri family, my birthright, ties me to a woman I despise:

the daughter of the mafia boss who nearly ended my family.

Making her both my enemy...and my future wife.

The hatred is mutual; she has no desire for me to be her groom.

A prisoner to her families' ambitions, she's desperate for a way out.

My duty is to guard her, to ensure she doesn't escape her gilded cage.

But every moment spent with her, every spark of anger, adds fuel to the growing fire of desire between us.

We're trapped in a volatile duel of passion and fury.

Yet, the more I try to tame her, the more she fights me,

Our impending marriage becomes a dangerous game.

Now, as the wedding draws near, my suspicions grow.

My bride is not who she claims.

DARK OBSESSION SERIES

A Dark Romantic Suspense

Wicked Games: A Dark Romance

Dark Obsession Series, Book One

She's caught in my game… she just doesn't know it.

For weeks, I've been watching her. Stalking her.

Now it's time to start playing with my beautiful little pawn.

From the moment I first saw her from afar, I knew she would become my prized possession.

I will gaslight her into thinking she is my obedient ward, trapped in the Victorian era.

She is my unwilling captive, forced to play my sadistic game for her own survival.

She will have no choice but to bow to my rules and discipline.

In time, her memories of a modern life will fade.

If not, she will pay a painful price.

Her pretty mind is so caught up in my nightmare, she will never escape me.

The most wicked deception of all?

This isn't the first time we're playing this game.

Sinister Games: A Dark Romance

Dark Obsession Series, Book Two

She's trapped inside my twisted game.

And I am never letting her go.

I've started a new game. This one more sinister than the last.

Every time she tries to fight what we have, I just pull her deeper into my deception.

The slightest disobedience to my rules brings swift punishment.

I've pushed her to the edge.

She wants to kill me.

The only problem is… she loves me.

Against her will, she loves every punishing, controlling thing I've done to her mind and body.

She's caught in my web; the harder she struggles, the more entangled she becomes.

My beautiful girl will have no choice but to accept that I am her new reality.

She is just a pawn in my game.

Savage Games: A Dark Romance

Dark Obsession Series, Book Three

She broke the rules of our game… she ran.

Now she will pay.

When will my pretty pawn learn that I am the master of

this game?

And only I will be the victor.

She thinks she can hide from me.

She thinks she can escape my wrath.

She’s wrong.

This time when I catch her, there will be no escape.

I no longer want her as just my beautiful captive.

She will now become my wife, even if I have to drag her down the aisle.

I want her under my complete control.

I want her every breath, her every movement, her every thought to be only of me.

This is no longer a game.

She changed the rules, but I will still win.

Cruel Games: A Dark Romance

Dark Obsession Series, Book Four

I'm not interested in love, it's the chase which intrigues me.

I saw her in the park, my pretty little prey.

I intend to make her mine, and the closer I get the more she will lose.

Her friends.

Her family.

Her freedom.

Each move will bring her more under my control until she

has nothing left... but me.

Am I playing a cruel game? Of course.

But I warned you: It's not love that I want.

Vicious Games: A Dark Romance

Dark Obsession Series, Book Five

I have taken everything from her.

She has no friends.

No money.

No one to turn to for help.

She's finally under my complete control, and yet, it's not enough.

I hold her body captive, but not her heart.

She knows I destroyed her life to possess her, so she fights me at every turn.

But she hasn't guessed the true purpose of my game.

She needs to understand that I will do anything to win. Anything.

She is my possession. Nothing, and no one, not even her, will keep us apart.

If she denies me much longer, she will learn just how vicious I can become when I don't get what I want.

And I want her... all of her.

THANK YOU

Stormy Night Publications would like to thank you for your interest in our books.

If you liked this book (or even if you didn't), we would really appreciate you leaving a review on the site where you purchased it. Reviews provide useful feedback for us and our authors, and this feedback (both positive comments and constructive criticism) allows us to work even harder to make sure we provide the content our customers want to read.